Everything and Nothing

Book 1

The Everything Series

Karina Morrell

Everything & NOTHING

The Everything Series

Book 1

Karina Morrell

Print Edition ISBN: 9798218285371

Digital Edition ASIN: B0CJ699RPJ

Cover design by Karina Morrell, Kirsten Morrell and Kevin Edgley

Library of Congress control number 2018675309

Printed in the United States of America

This book is dedicated to my husband, Lorin, for his never-wavering support of me and my crazy dreams. Here's to weird.

Chapter One

"Oh hey, Sean. Are you all done for today too?" Elle asked, spotting the older gentleman near the front entrance of the gym. She had just finished her workout and was headed out to run some errands. She needed to restock the fridge in her rented Airbnb. It was in sad shape.

At ninety-one, Sean was the oldest gym regular. A small group of locals came faithfully and chatted regularly, mostly griping about the heat or the snowbirds, depending on the time of year. Sean was there seven days a week, flirting with all the ladies. Elle smiled. Old guy had more game than dudes half his age.

"Sean? Are you feeling okay?" Elle asked as she caught up to him. He was pale and trembling.

"Oh hey, hon," Sean replied, his arm shooting out to reach for her hand. "Not feeling"—he gasped for air—"so good,"—another gasp—"all of a sudden."

"Here, let me help. Come sit down for a minute and catch your breath," Elle instructed. She set down her gym bag, held his arm, and led him gently toward a chair by the gym entrance.

Sean nodded as he leaned against her, breathing shallowly and walking slowly beside her.

Elle caught the eye of the young employee behind the counter. She couldn't remember his name. Kyle, maybe? She waved him over.

Suddenly, Sean slipped out of her grasp, collapsing. He hit his right shoulder on the side of the counter next to the chair and then the side of his head, letting out a low moan as he landed.

"Oh, Sean!" Elle cried, just barely able to slow his fall and keep him from hitting the floor too hard. She frantically called over her shoulder to Kyle. "Call 911. Now!"

Her friend Ryan hurried over. "Hey, let me help." He and Elle gently laid Sean on the floor together. He put his jacket under Sean's head, cushioning it from the hard concrete floor.

"Sean, listen to me. You're going to be fine," Elle said, hoping she sounded calmer than she felt. "Just breathe, okay? We're getting you some help."

Elle looked up to see her friends Nate and Sarah hurrying over.

"Elle, what happened?" Sarah asked, her brow furrowed. "Is Sean okay?"

"I'm not sure. He just collapsed and then he hit his head. An ambulance is on its way," Elle replied as her heart pounded, taking deep breaths to fight off the panic.

Ryan reached out and put a hand on Sean's chest. "Hold on, buddy," he said calmly, leaning down. He looked up at Elle. "I don't think he's breathing. Do you know CPR?"

"I do. Let me in there," Kyle said. "And I called 911. An ambulance is on its way."

Elle and Ryan moved back but she continued to hold Sean's ice-cold hand. *No, this can't be happening,* she thought. Tears formed in her eyes as Kyle performed CPR.

"I think I hear the ambulance," Sarah said, resting her hand on Elle's shoulder. "Thank God."

It was another full minute before the EMT and paramedic came rushing through the front door, dragging a gurney.

"Let us in there. Move please," the paramedic commanded, bending down to assess Sean.

Elle, Ryan, Nate, and Sarah quickly moved back. Kyle stopped CPR, letting the EMT take over.

"I've got a faint heartbeat. How long has he been unresponsive?" the EMT asked the group.

"Maybe four minutes, five at the most," Elle volunteered, though it was all kind of a blur.

The EMT turned back to his partner. "Let's get him onto the gurney and ready for transport."

The small group watched as Sean was lifted onto the gurney and hooked up to a cardiac monitor.

"Okay, let's go," the paramedic said as they hurried Sean out to the ambulance. Once he was loaded in, the doors closed and the ambulance sped away.

Sarah grabbed Nate's arm, her eyes wide. "Did that just happen? Not Sean! Is he going to be okay?"

Ryan and Elle shared a look, both at a loss for words.

"The ambulance got here fast, and the hospital is only a few minutes away. He'll get good care there," Nate said. He and Sarah went over to talk to a group standing nearby with matching expressions of shock and disbelief. Sean was beloved by everyone at the gym.

"You okay?" Ryan asked Elle, concern in his dark eyes.

Elle nodded. "Yeah–well, no, not really," she replied, shaking her head with a frown. "I just feel so helpless. I'm still kind of in shock. Just praying that he will be alright."

"You did everything you could. Everyone did. Sean is a tough old fucker. I'm sure he'll be okay," Ryan replied, reaching down first to pick up his gym bag, then rescuing his jacket from where it lay abandoned on the floor.

Nate approached the two again. "Sarah knows Sean's daughter. She went to call her to let her know what happened and that we can meet her at the hospital, if she wants us to."

Elle nodded again. "Okay, good. Thank you for that. Please keep us posted."

Nate gave Elle a quick hug. He patted Ryan on the shoulder and then went to find Sarah. Elle picked up her gym bag. She and Ryan walked through the nearly empty gym to the entrance. Most people had left after the shock of Sean being taken away in an ambulance. It was suddenly quiet, the atmosphere subdued.

Elle followed Ryan out of the building to the parking lot. She had parked her Jaguar next to his GMC. Ryan threw his bag in the back of his truck and turned around to lean against the door.

"Man, I can't believe that just happened," he said, letting out a deep breath and crossing his arms in front of his chest with a sigh. "I was just talking to him like twenty minutes ago and he seemed fine."

"I know," Elle replied, choking back a sob. "Sorry. I guess I feel a little shaky. Hell, I think I need a drink after that." She rubbed her hands up and down her arms, feeling a sudden chill even though it was easily eighty degrees out. Fall in Arizona. Ha.

"It's understandable. It's the adrenaline wearing off. Kind of felt like I was having a heart attack myself. Shit. I think I could actually use a drink, too. I know a good place," he said, opening the passenger door of his truck and motioning for her to climb in. "Hop in. We'll come back for your car later."

Elle paused. Maybe grabbing a drink with Ryan was a bad idea. Todd, her soon-to-be ex-husband–at least, she hoped it would be soon–was always lurking around. Always popping up when she least expected it and causing trouble, though she did her best to avoid him. She never wanted to be alone with him again.

She looked up at Ryan. Surprisingly, she felt safe with him. He had a calm, thoughtful presence about him.

Remembering Sean unresponsive on the floor, his hands ice cold and the ambulance racing away from the gym, Elle nodded. "Okay, yeah, a drink sounds pretty damn good right about now."

Ryan opened the passenger door and she climbed into the cab of his lifted white pickup with blacked-out windows. A sexy truck for a sexy man. Elle watched as he got in the driver's seat. Ryan Daley, late thirties, dark-brown eyes, dark hair under his ball cap. He had it on backward, giving him a rakish look. His beard had just a little gray in it, only making him more handsome. He was around six feet five and two hundred thirty-ish pounds, all of it rock-hard muscle. She knew–she'd watched him lift.

She blushed. *Stop it. What are you even thinking about right now? Sean was just rushed to the hospital and you're sitting here thinking about how hot Ryan is. Seriously, what is wrong with you?* Elle sighed, looking out the passenger side window as he drove out of the gym parking lot.

"To SEAN?" Ryan asked, holding up a shot glass.

"Yes. To Sean. Hopefully, he's doing better." Elle clinked her shot against Ryan's before tossing back the tequila. She winced as it burned the back of her throat.

Elle looked around the bar, a small hole-in-the-wall dive in downtown Scottsdale. She'd never even known this place was here. Lord knows Todd would never be caught dead in a place like this. There were autographed dollar bills stapled to the ceiling, cracked plastic bar stools and obvious years of wear on the bar. But she liked the place and its atmosphere, even the ancient jukebox playing an old Hank Williams song. She thought Sean would approve also.

"It's been here over forty years," Ryan offered when he saw her looking around. "Old Jack over there"–he pointed toward the bartender, who looked about as ancient as the jukebox–"opened this place in the late seventies and still runs it."

"Hey, it's Handsome Jack, son," Jack called from the other end of the bar. He grinned at them with crooked, tobacco-stained teeth. "Get it right."

Ryan rolled his eyes. "He's had a bunch of offers to buy this place, some pretty damn good ones actually, but he refuses to sell. Says his retirement plan is to die behind the bar."

Just not today please, Elle thought. She'd had enough excitement for one afternoon.

It was almost empty in the bar, probably because it was a Tuesday, way past lunchtime but a little too early for happy hour. The only other patrons were two middle-aged guys drinking beer and chatting quietly with Jack at the other end of the bar.

"So, why choose tequila?" Ryan asked, setting down his empty glass on the bar and signaling Jack for another round.

Elle smiled. "I remember Sean telling a story once about a bar fight he got into. He had been drinking tequila and started flirting with this hot blonde." She grinned. "His words. Anyway, it turned out that the hot blonde had a date who was not impressed with their flirting and took offense. Sean said he ended up with a broken nose, but he got the girl. They were married fifty-eight years. He told me that she passed about ten years ago, but he still talks to her every day."

"Wow, what a great story. Fifty-eight years. Damn. My last relationship lasted eight months," Ryan said, shaking his head and frowning.

Elle looked him over again. Ryan was the whole package. Hot–again using Sean's word–definitely hot. Even when he frowned. Handsome, smart, sexy, hot– wait, she'd already said that. She smiled.

"What?" Ryan asked.

"Eight months, huh? I feel like there's a story there," Elle pressed, raising an eyebrow.

Ryan looked down, clearing his throat. "Yeah. There's definitely a story," he answered dismissively as Jack brought over a second set of shots.

"Never seen Ryan bring a woman in here before," Jack said with a wink at Elle, setting the glasses down in front of them. "And a pretty one, at that."

"Shut up, Jack. You talk too much," Ryan said, turning back to Elle and holding up his glass. "To ...?"

"How about to crazy?" Elle smiled a little. "Crazy days. I've had a few lately," she added vaguely before tossing back the shot.

Ryan nodded in agreement. "Okay. To crazy."

They set their empty glasses down. "Do you want something to eat?" Ryan asked. "The food here is surprisingly good, for bar food."

Elle shook her head, grimacing. "No, the thought of food right now sounds kind of terrible."

Ryan nodded, looking up at the TV over the bar playing a recap of last night's football game. The Dallas Cowboys had beaten the Arizona Cardinals.

"I think one of my favorite things about Sean is the colorful outfits he always wears to the gym," Elle said with a smile. Sean always matched his tennis shoes to his shirt. She shook her head. He must own over twenty pairs.

"Right? Especially the tie-dye shoes. Doesn't he even have a matching ball cap for that outfit?" Ryan turned back to her, rolling his eyes good-naturedly.

"I don't know anyone else who could rock that look," Elle replied.

Ryan nodded again, his attention back on the TV.

"So, give me the sixty-second rundown on Ryan Daley," Elle said, giving him an inquisitive look. They chatted often enough at the gym about superficial things, but she realized she didn't know much about him.

"It won't take sixty seconds." Ryan shrugged, eyes still on the TV.

"Okay," Elle said slowly. Jeez, getting this man to open up was like pulling teeth. "Then the thirty-second version."

"Well, I'm an A&P, that's an airframe and powerplant mechanic, for Daley Charters," Ryan explained, finally looking back at her.

"Wait, Daley–is that your company?"

"No–yes–well, kind of, I guess. Mine and my sister's, though Lisa runs it now. My folks started the company about thirty years ago but were killed in a car accident around six years ago."

"Oh, wow. I'm so sorry," Elle replied softly.

"It was a long time ago now," Ryan replied. "It's smaller now than it was. Lisa sold off several jets–it was just too much and she had two toddlers at the time. So we have four jets now–two Gulfstreams, a Citation Bravo, and a Beechcraft King. And we also have a single-engine Piper Saratoga. And yeah, that's what I do, keep the planes running and fix whatever needs fixing."

"And that's it?" Elle teased. "You eat, sleep, work out, and fix planes?"

"Yep." Ryan shrugged. "That's it. Told you it wouldn't take me sixty seconds."

Elle frowned. Tall, dark, handsome, and moody as shit. She sighed. "What do you do for fun?"

"Well, I've been remodeling my house over the last few years. I guess it's fun. It keeps me busy, and it is nice to see a completed project," Ryan replied.

"I totally get that." Elle nodded enthusiastically. "I've been doing design work in my dad's architecture firm for, well, since I graduated college ten years ago. He and his team do the architecture side, and now I head up the interior design department. I was always rearranging my bedroom when I was growing up, wanting to change the paint color every six months. Made my mother crazy." She smiled at the memory of how mad Ava would get coming home to find her covered in paint again. That was about as rebellious as she had ever gotten. "So I guess I'm lucky–I get to do my dream job every day."

"That's cool," he said, looking back at the TV.

Elle sighed again, biting her lower lip. Ryan was definitely the strong-and-silent type. *And Lord knows I'm terrible at small talk*, she thought. She was curious why his last relationship had only lasted eight months, but he obviously didn't want to talk about it.

They sat in silence, each lost in thought. After a few minutes, Jack approached again. "Another? You two look like you could use it. Rough day?"

Elle looked at Ryan, smiling weakly. "Yeah, you could say that.

Why not?" The tequila had warmed her earlier chill and relaxed her. "I think Sean would approve."

Ryan's hand brushed against hers on the bar as he pushed the empty glasses toward Jack. At the quick contact, Elle felt warm from something other than the tequila. She looked up at Ryan again, finding his dark eyes watching her intently. *God he is sexy,* she thought.

"What?" Elle asked, suddenly nervous. His expression was unreadable. Flustered, she looked away. Maybe another shot was a bad idea. The tequila already had her fantasizing about what it would be like to kiss him, to have his strong arms around her.

They had never been this close to each other at the gym. He smelled good, she noticed, leaning toward him a little. Masculine and heady. The white compression tee shirt he'd worn to the gym emphasized his chest. She wanted to reach out and feel those muscles, run her hand up his arm to his chest. *Good grief, knock it off.* She swallowed hard.

Too late to turn back now, Elle thought as Jack set two more shots in front of them.

"To crazy. And Sean," Ryan said, holding up his glass.

"To crazy. And Sean," Elle seconded. And they tipped back shot number three.

Chapter Two

The third shot hit Ryan harder than it should have. Suddenly, he wasn't worrying about Sean anymore. Instead, he was thinking about Elle and wondering how tequila would taste on her lips. *Must be the lack of food,* he thought, the omelet he'd had for breakfast long gone. The thought of pulling her into his arms and kissing her couldn't be making him feel warmer. No, it had to be the tequila.

You've sworn off relationships, he reminded himself. His last couple dips in the dating pool had been disastrous. He'd yet to find a woman who could handle his past. But whatever, he'd accepted it. It was what it was. He was just meant to be alone.

Ryan glanced at her left hand. Nope, no ring. Funny, he'd been certain she wore one in the past. Regardless, there was no way he was getting involved with Elle, or anyone for that matter. That part of his life was over. Anyway, he barely knew her. Though they chatted often at the gym, it was always just general small talk.

He'd always thought she was attractive, as did several of the Old Dudes–his nickname for Bill, Joe, Nate, and Corey. The Old Dudes were a group of lonely retired guys. Nate always said they were at the gym to work on their four sets of jaws. They usually followed Elle around the gym chatting, laughing, and flirting with her. She was always smiling and nice to the Old Dudes and took time to stop and say hi to Sean every day.

Damn. Poor Sean. Though, if you were going to go, there were worse ways. Like his own accident. He mentally shook his head. *Not going there today. Besides, you didn't die. You just wished you had.*

"I'll be right back. Going to the ladies' room," Elle said. She put her hand on Ryan's arm as she stood, glancing up at him. Blushing, she quickly pulled her hand away and looked down at her feet. "Back in a minute."

"You want to know the best advice I've ever heard?" Jack offered, coming over to lean on the bar next to Ryan as the two men watched Elle walk away.

"What's that?" Ryan asked, scowling, waiting for a smart-ass response.

"Life is short. And then you die," Jack said seriously. "So spend it living and not overthinking dumb shit." He winked at Ryan.

Ryan nodded. He looked down at where Elle had touched his arm and slowly let out a deep breath. Damn. He found himself wishing she hadn't pulled her hand away.

A few minutes later, Elle sat back down at the bar. Watching her, Ryan realized Jack was right. She was pretty–beautiful, actually. And naturally, not the typical Scottsdale type. No fake lashes, hair extensions, or lip injections unlike Kimberly, his ex.

Elle was beautiful without all that crap. She wore a little pink tank top and black leggings, her blonde hair in a messy ponytail. Her green eyes were a little sad and her cheeks flushed. Gazing at her full lips he again wondered how she would taste. He tore his gaze away. *Nope. Not going to happen. Not with Elle. Time to go.*

Ryan turned, signaling to Jack for the check. "Guess we should probably, ah, wrap this up," he said to Elle, pulling out his wallet.

Elle nodded, reaching for her purse.

"Put that away. I've got this." Ryan waved away her credit card as he pushed some cash in Jack's general direction.

"It sure was nice to meet you, sweetie. Hope to see you in here again soon," Jack said. To Ryan he added, "Think about what I said, son."

Ryan tipped his chin at Jack as he stood, then turned to Elle. "You ready?" he asked, offering his hand to help her up.

Elle nodded, taking his hand briefly and standing. "Thank you," she called to Jack with a smile and a wave as they exited the bar.

They walked out to Ryan's truck, his hand lightly resting against the small of her back.

Elle stumbled slightly in the parking lot. "Oops," she said with a giggle, reaching for Ryan's arm to steady herself.

"You okay?" Ryan glanced down at her.

"Yes, fine. Sorry about that," Elle replied quickly, letting go of his arm.

"I'm thinking maybe you shouldn't be driving." Ryan frowned, his arm a little tighter on her back as they reached his truck. "And maybe I shouldn't be either, at least not all the way back to the gym."

"Uber?" Elle asked, turning slightly and steadying herself against him. She blushed a little as she quickly removed her hand from his chest.

"Well, actually, I don't live very far from here." Ryan jerked his head over his shoulder, toward his place. "I could make us some coffee."

Jesus. Stop talking, Ryan chastised himself. *Did you seriously just invite her over to your house? What the hell are you thinking?*

"Um, okay," Elle replied slowly, gazing up at him. "Sure."

Ryan still had his hand on the small of her back. He thought back to Jack's advice. Maybe he was overthinking. He tightened his hand, pulling her until she was pressed up against him. His hand moved slowly up her spine to the back of her neck. God, she felt so good.

It had been a few months since his last one-night stand. No small talk, get-to-know-you, asking about the past. Just sex. And never at his house. Easier that way. But he was pretty sure Elle wasn't the one-night stand type.

"Ryan," she said, looking up into his eyes.

The way Elle said his name, soft and breathy, was all it took. Ryan couldn't fight it. He knew he probably should resist this urge, but the tequila muddied his thoughts. *Why not. Why the hell not?*

Her hands were back on his chest as he gazed into her eyes. They seemed darker than usual. He leaned down to meet her lips with his. He kissed her gently at first, softly exploring, then more insistently, pulling her closer. He loosened her ponytail, freeing her hair and running his hands through it. It was so soft.

Ryan's tongue found hers and fire ignited between them. *Oh God,* he thought. It had been too long since he'd held a woman in his arms. And she fit against him perfectly. He deepened the kiss and held her even tighter, moving his hands around her waist, then down to her slim hips. She felt incredible under his hands.

A small voice in the back of his head yelled, *Stop! You need to stop. This is a mistake. You know what will happen when she finds out about your past. What always happens. You're not thinking clearly. You're just going to get hurt again.* Elle wasn't a random woman he picked up in a bar. She'd want more than just sex.

Ryan let go of her suddenly. He put some space between them, breathing hard. "Fuck," he ground out with a scowl. He reached around Elle, wrenching open the passenger door of his truck. "Get in."

Elle dropped her hands, frozen for a moment, looking flushed and surprised at his sudden retreat.

"Please," Ryan added softly. He didn't wait for her to climb in. He turned, trying to calm his breathing as he walked around his truck. *What the hell was that? Fuck. You never should have kissed her. But damn, you were right about those lips, so good.* He sighed. He would make her some coffee and send her on her way. Anything else would end badly. It always did.

NOVEMBER 2021

"Get the fuck out of my apartment! I never want to see you again! How could you lie to me about something like that?" Kimberly yelled, furiously pushing Ryan away, her blue eyes cold.

"I'm sorry. I know I should have told you sooner," Ryan replied, his chest aching, his heart about to explode. He tried reaching for her hand. "Please, let me explain. I want you to understand exactly what happened. After Candi died, I –"

"No. Let go of me! I will never understand. How could you? You make me sick," Kimberly said, angrily pulling her hand away. "You don't think the fact that you were in fucking prison was maybe information you should have told me like, um, I don't know, eight months ago? Not right before we're about to move in together!"

"I know," Ryan said quietly. "I guess I was..." He paused, running his hands through his hair and blowing out a deep breath. "Dammit Kimberly, I was just so happy and excited about the future. I was scared. I didn't want to lose you. I love you."

"You love me? Please. You obviously don't know the meaning of that word. You're a liar. This is all a big lie," Kimberly replied, glaring at him and waving her arms at the half-packed boxes in her living room. "Jesus! You're a liar and a murderer and I want you out of my apartment! I'm not saying it again. Leave!"

"Wait, please," Ryan began, trying to fight the tears forming in his eyes. He knew he'd been wrong to keep his secret so long, but he'd known in his heart this would happen when he finally told her the truth. So he'd lied.

"No. We're done. Get out!" Kimberly yelled, her face hard and cold as she pointed at the front door. "I never want to see you again. Ever."

Ryan swallowed hard and sighed. "I am sorry," he said over his *shoulder as he walked to the door. He had to look away from the hatred he saw in her eyes, his heart breaking as she slammed the door behind him.*

Ryan and Elle pulled into his driveway a few minutes later. It had been a quick but strained ride from the bar. He knew it was his fault. She was probably thinking about what a jerk he was. It was for the best. He needed to sober her up and get her back to her car. Then they could go back to being gym friends. Though he suspected that wasn't going to happen now that he knew how good she tasted, how good she felt in his arms. He wasn't going to forget that any time soon.

Chapter Three

Elle watched Ryan turn the truck off and hop out. He walked around the hood to open her door. He didn't touch her this time. Ryan walked to his front door, unlocked it, and held it open for her to follow.

"I'll start some coffee," Ryan said, walking through the open living room to his kitchen.

Elle followed him in. Looking around the space, she found herself a little surprised and impressed. The designer in her could appreciate the work put into it. It was obviously an older home, but Ryan had done a damn good job remodeling. It had beautiful dark hardwood floors and two dark wood beams that ran along the ceiling, contrasting with the antique-white paint. Two huge sliding glass doors opened out to a large patio, which led to a pristine blue pool.

She took in the oversized, comfy-looking sectional and matching chairs facing a large TV hanging on the side wall. Everything was in its place. There wasn't any clutter on his gorgeous mahogany dining table with its dark upholstered chairs. The kitchen had dove-gray Shaker-style cabinets. White pearl granite countertops and a darker gray herringbone travertine backsplash pulled everything together.

Had he done the design work himself? This was nothing close to the bachelor pad she had briefly envisioned. It was a beautiful home.

Everything was basic and functional, yet elegant in a masculine way. There weren't personal pictures sitting out or any sign of a woman's touch. Interesting. Well, he did say his last relationship only lasted eight months.

Elle wandered into the kitchen where Ryan was making coffee. "Um, bathroom?"

Ryan pointed to a door to the right of the kitchen without looking up, busy setting a couple coffee mugs on the counter.

Elle found it, shut the door behind her and looked at herself in the mirror. *What the hell is happening?* She shook her head. *You need to get a grip. Have some coffee. Sober up and go home.*

Yeah. Home. Elle grimaced. If you could call the lonely Airbnb she had been forced to rent after her last fight with Todd "home." She'd caught him cheating and when she confronted him, it got ugly. She left the next day, going to a hotel for a while, where she decided she was never going back to him. She'd filed divorce papers the following day. When she returned home to throw him out, he'd had the locks changed and refused to let her in. She was still furious about everything he'd done.

It was her damn house. She'd bought it before they even started dating. Elle had such high hopes when she'd moved in. She'd finally made a big move on her own. No help from her father, who had helped buy her condo after college. And then she'd met someone new.

She sighed, remembering how Todd had made her feel on their first date. Like a princess. How quickly that had changed. He'd picked her up in a Lincoln Town Car complete with driver and a bottle of 2008 Louis Roederer Cristal Millesime Brut.

OCTOBER 2022

"You look so beautiful tonight." Todd poured a glass of champagne and handed it to Elle. "I couldn't have picked a better dress," he added appreciatively.

Elle glanced nervously down at her black Dolce & Gabbana dress. It was a little low cut for her taste, but her mother had insisted it was the hottest dress in the fall collection and perfect for a first date. The luxurious material hugged her curves. "Oh, thank you."

"We have a dinner reservation at Dominick's Steakhouse," Todd said, "but we could go somewhere else if you want."

"Oh, no, that's perfect," Elle replied, taking a sip of champagne and trying to calm her nerves. Todd was so polished; she felt like a little girl playing dress-up.

"Good. I only want you to be happy," Todd said, smiling at her. "Tonight is all about you, baby."

Elle blushed. Todd wore a black Armani suit with a crisp white shirt and a black tie. He looked like something out of a fashion magazine. His short blond hair was neatly cut, falling over his right eye. He had intense light-blue eyes and was clean-shaven with perfect teeth, straight and blindingly white. She was glad she'd worn the Dolce & Gabbana, though she would have been more comfortable in jeans.

"I'm so glad we're doing this tonight," Todd said, refilling their glasses. "The day after tomorrow, I have to fly back to London. I'm heading up the release of a new IPO for one of our biggest clients."

"Wow," Elle replied. "That's so exciting. My job is pretty boring compared to yours."

"I don't think so." Todd shook his head. "I think design is fascinating. You do something creative, artistic, beautiful. All I do is move money around."

"Oh, well, thank you," Elle said, smiling and relaxing a little. "I do *enjoy designing a new space in a client's home. It's always different, which is fun."*

"Maybe you can do my next house. My flat in London definitely needs some help. But I've also been thinking about buying something here in Scottsdale. Especially since I might be staying here for a while," Todd said, looking at Elle meaningfully as he took her hand.

"Oh." Elle was flustered, heat rising in her cheeks again. "Sure, yes. Of course. I would love that."

Todd leaned over, running his hand slowly up her arm. He caressed her shoulder and gently moved the strap of her dress just a little, leaning over to kiss the spot his fingers touched. He pulled away enough to look into her eyes.

"Elle," he said softly, his fingers brushing the side of her face. "Beautiful Elle." Todd leaned even closer, his lips lightly touching hers. "Is it bad that I'm more hungry for you than I am for dinner?"

Elle pulled away, nervously fidgeting with the hem of her dress. "Todd, I'm sorry I ..."

"It's okay. We can take this slow," Todd replied with a smile, putting his arm around her shoulder. "We have all the time in the world, baby."

ELLE RAN a hand through her hair, blowing out a long sigh. How had she made such a mess of her life? First Todd–talk about falling for the wrong man. She'd paid a dear price for that mistake. Was still paying. Her stomach tightened into a knot.

And now this man. Ryan. This beautiful, complicated, gorgeous man in whose house she was currently standing. She couldn't figure him out. He'd been so hot and cold. Maybe he was seeing someone.

She sighed. She was done trying to figure men out.

Okay. Go out there, drink some coffee and sober up for heaven's sake. The room spun a little and she grabbed hold of the counter. *Or better yet, book an Uber and go home now.*

Elle straightened her shoulders. Okay. Yes. That was a good idea. But her phone was in her gym bag which was on the floor by the front door. *Crap. Okay. You can do this. And whatever you do, do not touch him. Do not kiss him. Or even better, don't even look at him,* she thought, walking out of the bathroom.

"It's hot," Ryan said as she approached the kitchen. He set a steaming mug on the counter. "And black. I don't have any creamer, but I could probably find some sugar or stevia or something. Sorry, I always drink mine black."

"No, thank you. Black is fine," Elle said, leaning covertly against the counter to stabilize herself. Damned tequila. Ryan, impossible to read, watched her with dark eyes. She had to look away. Just looking at him now made her heart race. She wanted to reach out and touch him again. *Ugh. No.*

Instead, she reached for the mug and lifted it too fast, sloshing coffee on her hand and the counter. "Damn! Ow!" she exclaimed, setting the mug down quickly and spilling more.

Ryan reached for a hand towel, blotting at the spilled coffee. "I think I mentioned that it was hot," he said with a small smirk. He reached for her. "Let me see." He wiped her hand gently with the towel, inspecting it. "Just a little pink. I think you're going to live," he teased.

Ryan continued to hold her hand, gently rubbing his thumb over her palm. Suddenly, he pulled her into his arms and crushed her mouth against his. He pried her lips apart, forcing his tongue deep inside. He lifted her up, setting her firmly on the cool countertop, his mouth never leaving hers. Her skin tingled everywhere he ran his hands–up her arms, around her back, and through her hair.

Elle's mind raced. *You're supposed to be leaving, remember? Getting an Uber and leaving Mr. Hot & Cold.* But he was suddenly hot again. So hot.

Yeah, and you're going to get burned. But she was having trouble thinking straight at the moment. Her hands were busy reaching under his shirt, exploring around the waist of his basketball shorts. She moved her hands to his back, his skin hot under her touch. Hotter, even, than the now-forgotten coffee. She felt his sharp intake of breath.

Ryan sighed, pulling her closer. He deepened the kiss, his tongue hot and searching. It emboldened Elle. She reached for the bottom of his shirt and pulled it up, slowly running her hands up his chest. She broke away from his lips just long enough to get his shirt over his head and let it drop to the floor.

Oh my God, she thought, running her hands over his chiseled chest. He was cut like a Greek god. *How is this happening? How did I end up here?* In Ryan's house. In Ryan's kitchen. Her hands all over him. Hot with a fever she didn't think was all due to the tequila.

This is wrong. You never told him about Todd, a voice in her head reminded her. *You never told him you're still technically married.*

Well, it's a little late now. There's no turning back, she thought, wrapping her legs around his waist as his lips trailed down her neck. She felt his hands sliding under her tank and moving around her waist, setting fire to everything he touched. She wasn't stopping now.

After what Todd had done to her, she had thought it would be a long time before she'd feel safe with a man again. But it was so different with Ryan. He didn't scare her. She felt secure with his strong arms wrapped around her. Safe and wanted–two things she hadn't felt in a long damn time. So no, she wasn't stopping now.

Then the front door opened and closed with a thud, grabbing their attention.

"Oh," Ryan said, pulling away quickly and looking up. "Um, hey."

"Ahh, oh. Um, sorry."

Elle turned at the sound of the voice, staring at the tall, gorgeous woman standing in the entryway. She was holding a Tupperware container, looking about as astonished as Elle felt and staring back at her. *What the hell? He has a girlfriend? No. No, this can't be happen-*

ing. Elle felt the blood rush out of her face. She was suddenly aware of her hands, still on Ryan's naked chest, and she dropped them quickly. *Oh shit. This is bad. Shit. Shit. Shit.*

"Hey, sis," Ryan said sheepishly, backing away from Elle and putting a little space between them.

"I'm so sorry! I had no idea you had company. The door was unlocked and I made lasagna and we had leftovers and I, um, yeah ..." The woman paused her rambling holding up the Tupperware container. "I was just going to drop this off."

Elle was having trouble processing what was happening. Wait. What? This woman was his sister? Not his girlfriend. Now that she was looking, she noticed the striking similarities between them. This woman had the same dark hair and dark-brown eyes as Ryan. There was also an infuriating twinkle in her eyes. Elle blushed. *This is so embarrassing.*

"So, this is Elle," Ryan said, "and this is Lisa, my older sister."

"He just loves to say older," Lisa said, scowling at Ryan.

Hmm, they have the same scowl, too, Elle thought. "Oh, um, hi," she said awkwardly, hopping off the counter and straightening her tank. She was probably four shades of red, embarrassed to have been caught making out with Ryan in his kitchen. *Thank God Lisa didn't wait another few minutes to stop by.* She blushed harder at the thought of where they were headed before they were interrupted.

"Yeah, hi. Nice to meet you," Lisa replied with a knowing little smile. "I won't keep you, but ah, Ryan, could I talk to you for a minute?" She pointed at the front door. "Maybe out front?"

"Sure," Ryan replied, turning to Elle. "I'll be right back."

"Um, bye. Nice to meet you," Elle called after Lisa, who waved as she left.

Chapter Four

Ryan followed Lisa outside, pulling the door closed behind him. He knew exactly what was coming. He crossed his arms over his chest and leaned against the door, waiting for the lecture.

"Seriously? What the actual fuck are you doing?" Lisa began, narrowing her eyes.

"I think it was pretty obvious what I was doing," Ryan replied with a pointed look.

"Don't be an ass. You know what I meant. Who is she? How long has this been going on? What are you thinking?" Lisa demanded, gesturing wildly.

"Well, *Mom*," Ryan replied, knowing Lisa hated that. While she was only six years older than him, she had pretty much helped raise him while their parents were busy building their company. "I was actually thinking that maybe, just maybe, it is none of your damn business."

Lisa glared at him for a beat, then softened with a sigh, putting a hand on his arm. "You know it's only because I worry. And I mean, it kind of is my business. I don't want to have to pick up the pieces again after this one breaks your heart too. Besides, you know you're the only family I have left, besides Cayden and Charlie," she finished quietly, referring to her two young children.

Ryan sighed. He understood, it was partly why they were so close. Their older brother, Aiden, had died from leukemia at the age of eighteen. It had devastated the entire family. Not just Aiden's death, but the year of countless medical appointments and failed treatments leading up to it.

Their parents struggled with losing their firstborn son and had been emotionally unable to help Lisa and Ryan process losing their big brother. So the siblings had relied on each other. Then six years ago, their parents had died. They relied on each other yet again, on a whole new level. Now they really only had each other.

"What about George?" Ryan asked with a little grin. Lisa made a face. "Seriously? Stop."

Ryan knew Lisa's ex-husband was always on her shit list.

"George is fucking lucky to still be alive. But we're talking about you. Not George." Lisa frowned.

He sobered. "Sis, I really am fine. You don't need to worry. I know Elle from the gym. We just, ah, had a crazy day."

"Okay, I know you're fine right now. But you really scared me the last time, Ryan. After Kimberly. After the accident. After Candi died. You were so dark and angry. It was bad enough after Candi and well, you know ... I don't ever want to see you go through that again."

He nodded. Honestly, Ryan probably wouldn't be alive if not for his big sister loving him and kicking his ass simultaneously. Kimberly ending their relationship had wrecked him. He had thought he'd finally found a stable, loving, and mature partner.

Ryan had been excited to move on with his life, to start over after the dark, hard years after Candi's death. He'd wanted so badly to build something great with Kimberly and had been so damn happy. For the first time in years. But he'd screwed it up. He'd kept his secrets too long.

Looking back now, Ryan understood her reaction better. He never should have waited so long to tell her the truth. At the time, though, he'd been devastated. And angry. And bitter. He went through some dark days. Hell, dark months. It was so much easier to be angry than to be sad.

In hindsight, he knew his anger had almost destroyed him not once, but twice, recalling the accident. He shook his head, pushing the dark memories out.

He'd worked hard to let go of the anger. He'd learned to rely only on himself. He accepted that he was meant to be alone. After Kimberly broke his heart, it was hard to risk it again. Yet somehow Elle had managed to get inside a small part of it. Already.

"I'm fine," Ryan said, giving Lisa a hug. "I promise. It's all good."

"Are you going to tell her about Candi and all that?" Lisa asked, raising an eyebrow. "Or is this just a one-night stand type of thing?"

Ryan threw his hands up in exasperation. "Jesus, sis. I'm not talking to you about my sex life. Maybe. I don't know. This just kind of happened today."

"I do want you to be happy, you know," Lisa said softly.

"I know." Ryan smiled at his sister. "Now goodbye," he added, steering her toward her Mercedes, "and go home."

"Okay, okay. And don't forget to put that lasagna in the fridge," Lisa called over her shoulder as she got in her car. "And put a fucking shirt on. Good grief." She rolled her eyes, slamming her car door.

Ryan grinned and waved. "Love ya, sis!" he called. He turned and put his hand on the doorknob, then paused. What a crazy day. Elle was right about that. Crazy. He thought about the woman who waited for him inside and realized he felt something. He wasn't exactly sure what, but something. He definitely felt more alive than he'd felt in a long time. *Thank you, Sean,* he thought. *I might be cursing you later, but for tonight, thank you.*

"Everything okay in here?" Ryan asked, raising an eyebrow at finding Elle sitting on his bathroom floor. She was leaning against the vanity with her head in her hands.

"Tequila did me dirty," Elle replied, closing her eyes with a small groan.

Ryan knew he probably shouldn't be grinning, but she looked so miserable and beautiful at the same time. *What was it about this crazy woman?* he thought. He shook his head, leaning over to help her up. "You done? You okay?"

"Yes. No. Yes. I don't know," Elle replied with a weak smile, taking his hand and standing up.

"Maybe you should lie down," Ryan suggested. "You still look a little pale."

Elle nodded.

"Okay," Ryan said, lifting her into his arms. He turned, carrying her and headed for his bedroom.

Ryan gently set her down on the bed. "I'll bring you some water. Just close your eyes and relax for a few minutes," he instructed, covering her with a blanket after she laid down. He turned the light off and paused at the door, still able to see her in the dusky evening light. *Well, you finally got a woman back in your bed,* he thought. He closed the door halfway before walking back to the kitchen. Yeah, not exactly what he'd had in mind, but maybe it was for the best.

The events of the day had probably just got them carried away. And the tequila.

That's bullshit and you know it, Ryan argued with himself. He'd purposely not let people get close to him the last few years. It was just easier that way. But the shield he had around his heart had a crack in it. He knew he was in dangerous territory.

A few minutes later, Ryan brought back water and a couple of saltines and found Elle asleep. He set the glass and crackers on the nightstand and gently brushed a few stray strands of hair off her face. There was a strange ache in his chest from wanting her so much.

He'd been alone for so long now. He'd let himself imagine what it would be like to have Elle in his life as his woman.

You're dreaming. Why even pursue her? You know exactly how she'll react to your past. Just stop.

He left the room. *What a crazy day,* he thought, sinking down on the couch with a sigh, suddenly exhausted.

Chapter Five

It was dark when Elle woke up, vaguely disoriented. Then it all came flooding back. Sean. The tequila. The kiss. The *kisses,* plural. The sister. The bathroom. Oh God. She covered her face with her hands at the memories.

She had collapsed on the kitchen counter in mortification after Ryan followed Lisa outside. She had felt a little sick to her stomach, though the cool granite countertop had felt good against her hot forehead. The afternoon had been an emotional roller coaster ride. And her fuzzy brain hadn't been processing very well.

Then she *really* didn't feel so good. She ran for the bathroom, barely making it in time. Which was where Ryan had found her.

She had wanted to melt into the floor. She had never been so embarrassed. Oh yeah, except for the time Ryan's sister walked in on them. Yeah. Then too.

Wow, how sexy I was, she thought. She groaned internally, closing her eyes. Damn tequila. Damn. Damn. Damn. Her new mantra.

Then she recalled Ryan carrying her to bed and tucking her in. Ugh. Another of her finer moments. She glanced across the king bed, finding it empty. Getting up, she tiptoed to the bedroom door and peeked out. The house was dark except for the soft glow of a small under-cabinet light in the kitchen.

Elle walked quietly across the hardwood floor and found Ryan in the living room, asleep on the couch, his head on a throw pillow. Enough moonlight was coming through the front sliders that she could make out his features. *God, he's so damn good looking, even in his sleep,* she thought, gazing down at him. Maybe even more so with his face relaxed, his frown lines gone. She realized he scowled a fair amount.

It had taken six months of saying hi to Ryan at the gym before he actually started talking to her. He didn't let many people get close. Though she was one to talk. She had a ton of people in her life, but she could count on one hand the number of people she could truly confide in. She hadn't told anyone she was separated and divorcing Todd, just her parents. She was embarrassed to admit her marriage had failed so quickly.

MAY 2023

"Hey, so what's your name?" Ryan asked as Elle walked past him, pausing between sets on the Smith machine and taking out his earbuds. "We wave at each other all the time. Guess we should introduce ourselves."

"Oh, it's Elle." She stopped, surprised he wanted to talk to her. She always gave a little wave and said hi when she saw Ryan at the gym, but he'd never tried to talk to her before. She only knew his name because Sarah had mentioned it.

Elle and Sarah always chatted on the treadmill with their friend Paula, a petite older blonde with more energy than anyone else she knew. Elle had trouble keeping up with her. Paula called Elle and

Sarah her posse. They always joked together about strange people doing strange things in the gym. There was never a lack of material.

"Ryan," he said, reaching out to shake her hand. "Nice to officially meet you."

Elle shook his hand. "Nice to officially meet you, too," she said, slowly letting go of his hand and looking up into his dark eyes.

"What are you working on today?" Ryan asked, leaning casually against the frame of the Smith machine.

"Oh, it's leg day," Elle replied, making a face. "I have a love/hate relationship with leg day. I hate it while I'm doing it, but I love it when I'm done."

Ryan nodded. "I get that."

"Then I'm going to force myself to run on the treadmill. Not my favorite but since it's a hundred and five degrees out today, I'm definitely not running outside," Elle explained.

"Yeah, you don't want to get heat stroke. I can't run on the treadmill, at least not for very long. It's so boring," Ryan said, shaking his head.

"I agree. Most I can do is like thirty minutes and even then, I have to blast my angry music," Elle said with a grin.

"Angry music? What genre is that?" Ryan asked, grinning back at her.

"Oh, like Megadeth and Pantera."

"Really? I wouldn't have pegged you as a metal fanatic," Ryan said, raising an eyebrow.

"Just depends on my mood. I listen to all kinds of music," Elle said, shrugging. "Well, I guess I should go get on the treadmill." She felt a little flustered standing so close to him.

"Okay," Ryan replied, looking in her eyes. "It was very nice to officially meet you."

Elle nodded, giving a little wave as she walked away, her heart beating faster. Damn, he's good looking, she thought. She sighed as she walked away, wishing for the millionth time she had never married

Todd. He'd been acting differently lately. The honeymoon phase was definitely over.

ELLE LOOKED AT HER WATCH. She really should leave. Time to order that Uber. She found her phone in her gym bag. Thank goodness she hadn't left her bag in Ryan's truck. She didn't want to wake him up. She'd embarrassed herself enough for one day. *He'll probably wake up and be glad your crazy ass is gone.* She pulled up the Uber app. Eight minutes away. Okay.

She wandered around quietly, tracking down her shoes and glancing at Mr. Hot one last time.

She silently opened his front door, closing it just as quietly behind her. As she waited for her Uber on the front porch she suddenly felt torn. Maybe she shouldn't be leaving like this, slinking away in the dark. *Coward,* a voice in her head accused.

No, this is for the best, she thought. Elle had so many confusing emotions swirling in her. She really liked him, and they obviously had incredible chemistry. She shivered thinking about kissing him, her hands all over him, her heartbeat accelerating.

Stop. You're acting like some lovestruck teenager. Do you really want to drag him into the shit show going on in your life right now? Not only does he not want that, he doesn't deserve that. Elle suddenly felt exhausted. Climbing into the Uber, all she could think about was falling into her bed and sleeping until she could put Ryan out of her mind.

Yeah, the voice in her head taunted, *good luck with that.*

"Todd, stop talking. Hello! You need to–," Elle tried to interrupt, giving up as he continued. She held her cell away from her head. Six minutes so far, and she'd barely been able to get a word in as Todd continued to yell. She set her phone down on her desk, still able to hear him.

Elle sighed, picked up her coffee mug, and took a sip, thoughts of Ryan popping into her head. She regretted leaving the way she did last night. She should have at least left a note. *Damned tequila,* she thought again, wishing their evening had ended differently. She felt warm at the memory of kissing him in his kitchen and running her hands over his chest, his shoulders, his arms.

"Elle? Do you hear me? Are you listening?" Todd yelled, startling her out of her thoughts.

Elle set her coffee down, frustrated with herself, Ryan, and Todd. She picked her phone up. "Stop! I'm done talking to you. Enough! Just talk to my attorney," Elle yelled into the phone. Not waiting for a response, she ended the call. She put her head on her desk, banging it a couple times on the file she had been working on. She just wanted Todd out of her life. For good.

"Everything okay here?"

Elle sat up. Her dad stood in the doorway of her office, a concerned look on his face. "Yes, sorry. Three guesses who that was," she said.

"I'm sorry, sweetie." Tom Campbell was a no-nonsense guy unless it came to his daughter. He came into Elle's office and leaned against her desk, looking down at her. "Your mother and I are worried about you."

Elle raised an eyebrow, leaning back in her office chair. Her mother only worried about herself.

Tom laughed, his deep voice filling the office and his sharp jawline softening into a smile. "Okay, okay. *I'm* worried about you," he admitted, holding up his well-manicured hands. "Why don't we go to dinner tonight? Your mother has some charity thing she's going to with your Aunt Ann, so I have no plans. And I worry about you staying at that Airbnb. Wouldn't you rather come back home and stay with us until this mess is over?"

"Mother would have a fit. You know anything that interrupts her daily schedule upsets her," Elle said ruefully. Actually, she'd much rather be at the Airbnb than argue with her mother daily. About her clothes, her shoes, her diet, her friends. The list went on and on. Nothing was ever good enough for Ava, unless it was her own idea.

"Well dinner, then. Okay? I have a meeting at four this afternoon, but it shouldn't take too long, and I have nothing scheduled after that. I'll make a reservation at Ancala," he said, referring to the country club they belonged to.

"Sounds good, Dad, thank you," Elle said, standing to give him a hug. "I'm sorry I've made such a mess of my life."

"Todd fooled us all, Elle," Tom replied. "I only wish I'd seen through him sooner, before you married him."

"It's because you're too nice. You always want to believe the best of everyone," Elle said with a smile. That would be the only way he'd been able to put up with her mother for thirty-five years.

"Shh, don't tell my clients. I've got an image to uphold," Tom said, smiling. "I'll see you at the club at six thirty."

Elle nodded. "Yes, I'll be there." She sat back down at her desk, watching her father leave her office with a little wave. Her mother might be a nightmare on a good day, but at least she could always count on her dad.

Being an only child, she'd always dreamed of having a sister or a brother, a big family. But her dad had devoted his life to his business. *And Mother devoted her life to herself,* Elle thought wryly. Elle had always suspected that she was an accident. That her parents never planned to have any children.

She didn't doubt they loved her, in their own way. But she'd always felt like they loved her like a pet they were always a little surprised to see and not quite sure what to do with. Since she'd started working at her dad's firm after graduating with a degree in design from the California Institute of the Arts, she had grown closer to him. Her mother, on the other hand, was still more interested in her socialite friends and the charity work they patted themselves on the back for.

Elle had learned to be self-sufficient at an early age, handling everything from cooking for herself to doing her own laundry. Maybe that's why when Todd came along and actually took care of her–brief as that time was–she'd been so desperate for attention that she'd let herself be fooled.

She'd had a few relationships, but nothing that set her soul on fire. Thoughts of Ryan immediately popped back into her head. He set more than just her soul on fire. Dammit. Two men, so different. One she couldn't wait to get out of her life. And one she wished was in her life more. Maybe once her divorce was finalized, she could think about pursuing something with Ryan. If he even wanted that.

She looked at the files piled on the corner of her desk, sighing. Well, she might be terrible at relationships, but at least she was good at her job. She pushed thoughts of both men out of her head, reaching for a file. She just needed to focus on work.

Chapter Six

Ryan poured more coffee into his mug with a sigh. Damn. He'd woken up around midnight and discovered Elle had gone. No goodbye, no note. Just gone. *Did I dream the entire thing?* he wondered, taking a sip of his coffee.

No, he definitely remembered Elle sitting on this very counter last night, pulling his shirt off, touching him, kissing him. Not a dream. He blew out a breath.

He'd been alone for so long. How long was he supposed to suffer for his mistakes? How much penance was enough? He admitted a little part of him wanted to share his life with someone again, have someone hold him, someone to wake up next to. To feel something. Something besides loneliness and anger. *Elle is never going to be that,* a voice in his head whispered. *When she finds out what you did, she'll hate you. Just like the others. Just like Kimberly.*

Shut up, Ryan commanded the voice. *I already know that.*

He sighed. Elle was probably relieved nothing had happened between them. Well, not nothing. Something had happened. He smiled a little, remembering her pouty lips. How they tasted. How they felt.

Enough. She obviously couldn't wait to leave. Besides, it's easier this way. No need to explain his past, explain Candi.

If only he'd never met Candi. His life would be so different.

FEBRUARY 2009

"Hey, handsome."

Ryan looked up from his shot to see a cute blond in a short skirt leaning against the side of the pool table, holding out a bottle of Coors Light.

"Hey," Ryan replied, setting his cue stick down.

"Buy you a beer?" she asked with a flirty smile. "Thanks," Ryan said as he accepted the bottle. He took a long drink as he appreciated her low-cut pink crop top paired with a white mini-skirt, high heels at the end of her shapely legs. Okay, she had his attention.

"I'm Candi. I'm in the sorority that your frat invited to this party, but honestly, it's kinda lame."

"Is it now?" Ryan asked, raising an eyebrow and taking another sip. "Sorry you think so."

"I was really hoping there would be a band or something. I love to dance," Candi said. "At least your DJ is playing decent music. Do you want to dance?"

Ryan looked around the room, frowning. The DJ was playing Tupac. A few people were doing shots at the bar. Small groups of people were talking and laughing, but she was right. It was a lame party.

This was supposed to be his welcome-back party. He'd been out for eight weeks recovering from knee surgery after getting taken down hard on the football field at Arizona State's homecoming game. But frankly, he was in a shitty mood and not really feeling a party, espe-

cially a lame one. He looked back at Candi. She was definitely the highlight of the evening so far.

"Well?" Candi asked again. "Or do you want to give me a tour of this place? I've never been here before."

"Sure, why not?" Ryan replied, draining the beer and setting it down on the side of the pool table. "What do you want to see?"

"How about your room?" Candi replied with a wink, taking his hand.

"Okay." Ryan shrugged. He led her up the stairs and down the hall to his room.

"Aren't you that quarterback who got tackled at the homecoming game?" Candi asked. "I remember that game. Holy shit, that was brutal. Didn't you have to have surgery or something?"

"Yeah," Ryan replied, opening the door to his room and leaning against the doorframe.

"But you seem all recovered," Candi said softly, pushing herself up against him and putting her hands on his hips. "Everything in good working order?"

"Knee is still rehabbing, doing PT, gonna take some time. But trust me, everything else is one hundred percent operational," Ryan replied, running his hands slowly up her arms. So soft. She smelled damn good. His recovery had been spent at his folks' house in his old bedroom. A long, boring eight weeks cooped up. He was more than ready for Candi.

"Well, that is very good news," Candi replied with a coy smile. She leaned in to kiss him, her hands moving up to his chest.

Ryan pulled her closer and kissed her soft, pliable mouth. His tongue found its way inside. He reached around her back, his hands making their way under her top. Just as he thought—no bra.

"If you're wondering if I'm wearing panties, I'm not," Candi whispered. "Want to see for yourself?"

Ryan reached under her skirt, sliding his hand up just enough to glide over her hip. Nope, no panties. Well, this night was looking up.

He slammed his door shut with his shoulder and moved them toward his bed. They fell onto it together, her lips and hands all over him.

"Here baby," Candi said as she leaned back and reached into a little pocket of her skirt to retrieve a baggie with a few pills in it. She put one in her mouth, then pulled another one out and held it up to Ryan's lips. "Your turn."

Ryan looked at the pill then up to Candi. He opened his mouth and let her put it on his tongue. Why the fuck not, he thought. Maybe it would be nice to feel something besides pain and anger—the only things he'd felt since the tackle during the homecoming game that officially ended his dream of a career in the NFL. Anything has to be better than that, he thought. He closed his eyes and let the warmth flow through him, finding Candi's lips again as the rush consumed them.

"HEY BOYS," Lisa called, walking through the hangar to the back where Ryan was showing Cayden some moves on the heavy bag he'd recently put up. They were both shirtless.

"Mom, watch this," Cayden said excitedly, turning to throw a cross at the bag followed by a hook and a roundhouse kick. "Uncle Ryan just taught me that. It's called a combo."

"Kid is pretty good," Ryan said, bumping gloves with Cayden. "He's light on his feet."

"Nice job. But Cayden, I know there's some homework waiting for you in my office," Lisa said, pointing over her shoulder. "I think it's time to go get it done."

"Okay. Fine," Cayden replied. Taking his gloves off with a little pout, he turned back to Ryan. "Can you show me some more moves after I finish my homework?"

"Sure thing, buddy," Ryan replied, pulling his own gloves off and tossing them on the counter behind him.

"Yes!" his nephew replied, pumping his fist in the air as he grabbed his tee shirt off the counter.

"So, how did the rest of your evening go last night?" Lisa asked, watching Cayden skip across the hangar to her office.

"It didn't," Ryan replied. He took a long drink from his water bottle.

"What?" Lisa asked, surprised, looking over at him. "It didn't?"

"Elle ended up getting sick. Too much tequila, I guess." Ryan shrugged.

"Tequila, huh? Well damn," Lisa said, frowning. "That sucks."

"She fell asleep, and I crashed on the couch. Then, when I woke up, she was gone," Ryan said.

"Oh. Huh. So, are you going to see her again?"

"I'll probably see her at the gym." Ryan shrugged again. "No big deal."

Lisa narrowed her eyes at him. "You sure about that?"

Ryan nodded, though that ache in his chest was still there, reminding him how alone he was. As if he needed a reminder. "Is the Bravo going out today?" he asked, changing the subject.

"Yep," Lisa replied, "at seventeen hundred hours. Emma is scheduled to fly today. She should be here in an hour or so.

"Okay. It will be ready," Ryan said, pulling his shirt over his head. He just needed to focus on work. He definitely shouldn't go looking for Elle. Or think about the past.

MARCH 2009

"Do you want another drink?" Ryan asked in Candi's ear, his arms

wrapped around her, holding her close. They swayed together to the loud music.

"Sure, but let's make a pit stop by the bathroom first," Candi replied with a grin and a wink. Taking his hand, she led him through the crowd of people dancing in the frat house's living room.

"Here baby," Candi said with a grin, closing and locking the bathroom door. She shook a little baggie of coke between her fingers. "You know the only snow in Arizona goes up your nose. I told you this party was going to be fun."

"Here, let me," Ryan said, taking the baggie and carefully making a small pile on a mirror Candi pulled out of her purse. He arranged the little pile into four neat rows.

"God, baby, the last month has been the best month of my life," Candi purred, licking Ryan's ear. "I can't believe we didn't meet before this. But I'm so glad we finally did."

Ryan looked at Candi. She wore a low-cut black dress that clung to every curve. He already knew she wasn't wearing panties. "Me too...here," he said, pulling a twenty-dollar bill out of his pocket, rolling it up. "You go first."

Candi took the rolled-up twenty he offered and leaned over the bathroom counter. She inhaled two lines, then straightened up and pulled him toward her to run her tongue over his lips. "Oh fuck. This is some good shit. You're going to love it. Your turn, baby."

Ryan leaned over the counter and did the other two lines. He stood back up, closing his eyes for a second. "Damn," he said. He finally felt something again. Something besides the constant cold, angry ache in his chest that had taken hold after that damn game. Something hot and powerful.

"Right," Candi replied, giggling. "I told you! First rate. My mom got this stuff on her last trip to Aspen. She'll never notice that I took some."

"Yeah, it's really good," Ryan replied, rubbing his thumb over Candi's lips and licking his own.

"Fuck me. Right here. Right now," Candi said softly, running her hands down the front of his jeans to rub his crotch. "I want you so bad, baby."

Ryan grabbed Candi, one hand on her ass, one in her hair. He plunged his tongue deep in her mouth, hard and fast. His heart was beating out of control. He wanted her with a fire that took his breath away. He had to have her. Right now. Right here. He couldn't even think, all he could do was feel.

Everything was bright and intense. And so hot. The coke made him feel everything—every kiss and every touch intensified. He reached under her skirt, pulling her dress up, and lifted her. He set her on the counter, his fierce need making it hard to breathe.

"ELLE!" Ryan called across the parking lot, walking toward her car.

"Ryan!" Elle exclaimed, turning with her hand over her heart, surprise evident in her tone.

"What the hell happened to you? I woke up and you were gone. What the hell was that?" Ryan asked hotly, putting his hand on her arm. "You were gone from my bed. Gone from my house." He had conflicting emotions. He was relieved to see she was okay, but he was also angry. Angry that she'd made him worry about her, angry with himself for letting her get to him, and angry that he wanted to kiss her again, too.

"Ryan, please," Elle said, nervously looking around the parking lot.

"Come on," Ryan said, his hand still on her arm, leading her over to his truck. "If you don't want anyone to hear this conversation, then get in the damn truck." He opened the passenger door.

"Please," he added softly.

Elle looked into his eyes and nodded. He motioned toward the passenger seat and she climbed in. Ryan walked around the hood of the truck and got into the driver's seat.

"Look," he said, rubbing his jaw. "I'm sorry. I just spent the last two days worried about you. I mean, I woke up and you were just gone. I had no way to get a hold of you, no number. I had no idea where you'd gone, how you'd gotten there, if you were okay." Ryan paused, inhaling deeply through his nose.

"How you were feeling," he added with a knowing look. Elle blushed.

"I've been at the gym the last two days, sitting in the parking lot just waiting for you to show up. Hell, I thought for a minute that I dreamed the entire thing." Ryan let out a short laugh.

He ran a hand through his hair, leaning back in his seat and exhaling slowly. "I am sorry about how I acted just now. I should have handled that better." He paused again. "I guess you should know that I've only been in one healthy–well, healthy-ish–relationship in my entire life. I've made a lot of mistakes in the past and I'm still learning and growing. Though that's not really an excuse, but I am sorry."

"I'm sorry too," Elle said, her green eyes meeting his. "I should have at least left a note. I didn't think you'd worry. I guess I just, um, wasn't thinking clearly."

Ryan nodded. What the hell was he even doing right now? He had to look away. Shit. She looked so damn good sitting in his truck. Blonde hair under a black baseball cap, red tank top and black shorts, long tan legs. He sighed. He'd just been so frustrated–and yeah, worried–when he woke up and found her gone. Now sitting here, he felt like an idiot. He shouldn't have confronted her.

It felt like a sign the other morning. She was gone, and it was all for the best. No need for hard conversations. But he hadn't been able to stop thinking about her. About the way she said his name. The way she kissed him. The way she touched him. Now, sitting beside her, he was questioning his sanity. *Just let her go. This is a mistake. You're not relationship material, remember?*

"I think the tequila may have pushed us where we shouldn't have gone," Ryan said quietly, looking out the window, breaking eye contact.

Even if they shouldn't have gone there, he knew it was exactly where he had wanted to go.

"Oh," Elle replied, chewing on her lower lip.

"There are a few things you should know about my past, I guess," Ryan said. "I want to be honest with you right now because that's why my last relationship ended. I kept secrets that I should have been honest about."

"The eight-month one?" Elle asked, looking up.

Ryan nodded. "Yes. Kimberly. And that was almost two years ago now. But also, I was married. Years ago, just after college. But she–Candi–well, she died."

"Oh, Ryan, I'm so sorry," Elle said softly.

"So, with those relationships, plus a few disastrous dates since, I don't have a very good track record, so to speak," Ryan said wryly. "I've really just been trying to work on myself. After it ended with Kimberly I was in a very dark, angry place and I never want to be like that again.

"But honestly, I'm not sure it's a good idea for us to be ..." Ryan trailed off, clearing his throat and looking down at his hands resting on the steering wheel. "Getting involved. My life is–well, complicated, and I'm not really looking to start anything."

Ryan could barely look at her because he knew if he did, her lips would distract him. He wanted to go back to before they were interrupted in his kitchen. Back to her hands on his chest, pulling his shirt off. Back to her lips against his. Damn Lisa.

But he knew this was for the best. Elle was sweet and kind and, God, beautiful. He glanced at her again.

She deserved someone better than him. Besides, she would probably never understand what had happened after Candi died. Hell, no one else ever did.

"I should probably–I mean–I've got to, um ..." Elle stammered. She turned and reached for the door handle, choking out, "... go."

"Elle," Ryan said. He wanted to reach out for her, to pull her back into his arms. He knew he'd just hurt her. *Better now than later,* the voice in his head said.

"I'm sorry," he said lamely.

Elle nodded and Ryan watched her climb out of his truck, slamming the door. He watched her Jaguar back out of its parking spot and drive off. He immediately regretted pushing her away. He closed his eyes. Fuck. But better that she hated him for being a jerk now. He'd made so many mistakes. He was doing his best to not make any more.

JULY 2009

"What the hell, Candi? Who are all these fucking people?" Ryan asked, finally finding her in his kitchen where she was mixing a huge batch of margaritas. He looked again at his crowded living room. The dining room table was set up for beer pong and music blasted from the speakers. People he didn't recognize were standing around drinking and laughing.

"What? I just invited a few friends over," Candi replied, pouring the margaritas into several glasses. "I've hardly seen my sorority sisters since graduation."

"And you decided to do this at my apartment, why?" Ryan asked angrily. "I'm tired. I just want some dinner and to go to bed."

"But baby, it's Friday night! And my roommate's parents are in town, so she's making them some big dinner at our condo. Boring. I had to get out of there," Candi explained, turning to line some tequila shots up on the bar.

"Seriously, I'm really not in the mood for this. I had a super

stressful day. We had some engine trouble with the Beechcraft. Luckily, Dad was able to fix it, but the charter ended up getting rescheduled for tomorrow and it was a big mess," Ryan said, blowing out a long sigh.

"Baby, you work too hard." Candi handed him a drink. "Here, drink this. There's pizza on the counter. And I have a little something else for you too," she added with a wink.

"Candi, I'm tired," Ryan said, setting the drink down on the counter with more force than necessary. "I'm not in the mood to party. Can you please just ask everyone to leave?"

"What the fuck, Ryan?" Candi hissed at him. "You're always tired and you never want to party anymore. Christ, you're making me crazy. And what are you even thinking? I'm not asking people to leave–are you nuts? My friends came here to have a good time."

"Come with me. I can't think, it's so loud in here," Ryan said, grabbing her hand and leading her out of the kitchen.

"No. Dammit, Ryan. Wait," Candi said exasperatedly, reluctantly following him down the hall to his bedroom.

"I'm not asking, Candi. I want those people out of my apartment," Ryan said, slamming the bedroom door and blocking some of the noise from the party. "Do you hear me?"

"No, I won't ask them to leave!" Candi yelled. "Stop being such an asshole!"

"I'm an asshole?" Ryan yelled back, grabbing her by the arms and pushing her against the door. "I'm an asshole?"

"Yes!" Candi shouted, pulling him against her. She grabbed his right hand and forced it under her top to cover her breast. "Yes, you are, but you still make me so hot," she added softly.

Ryan glared at her, breathing hard. He wanted to pull his hand away but couldn't force himself to do it.

"I know what you need," Candi whispered, reaching into her pocket and pulling out a pill. "You know you'll feel better, baby. Please."

Ryan sighed, then nodded. He let her put the pill on his tongue, closing his eyes.

"See baby?" Candi purred, wrapping her arms around him and running her hands under his shirt. "We're meant for each other. No one knows you better than I do."

Eyes still closed, Ryan felt a slow warmth start in his chest, then spreading down his arms, his legs. He exhaled slowly before opening his eyes and looking at Candi. At her brilliant blue eyes. And her mouth—those lips made him crazy. An intense feeling consumed him, blocking out the anger and emptiness. He felt alive again.

"Yes baby," Candi said, licking her lips. "I want you so much."

Ryan leaned in, placing his lips on hers. He roughly forced her arms over her head, holding her wrists in place with one hand while his other pulled her skirt up to reach underneath. "Is this what you want?" he ground out harshly.

"Yes," Candi moaned against his lips. "Yes baby."

Ryan managed to get his jeans undone with one hand, heat spreading through his body, taking over. He couldn't think straight, only feel. Feel Candi's body hot against his. He had to possess her. Now.

Chapter Seven

Oh thank God, Elle thought, trying to catch her breath. Finally, the trailhead was in sight. She slowed to a walk, taking a drink from her almost-empty water bottle. She'd come out to the McDowell Sonoran Preserve to run off some frustration. Six miles later she didn't feel any less frustrated. Hot, tired and sweaty, but still frustrated. Elle took her earbuds out–even blasting her favorite Smashing Pumpkins playlist hadn't helped.

You know you can't avoid the gym forever, a little voice in her head nagged.

Maybe not, but running into Ryan was the last thing she wanted right now. There's no way she could make small talk with him like nothing had happened. There was a strange little ache in her chest. She missed him. She wanted to see him again. Kiss him again.

Stop–no you don't, she told herself firmly.

Elle wasn't sure if she was more hurt, angry, or just plain morti-fied recalling the conversation they had in Ryan's truck the other day.

She'd just gotten out of her car in the gym parking lot. Elle hadn't been to the gym the previous two days because she had been afraid to run into him. Afraid things would go back to how they were before, but also afraid they wouldn't. Her mind had been on Ryan, wondering if she'd see him. And there he had been, next to her car, looking down at her with those dark, unreadable eyes. She'd been so distracted she hadn't even noticed his truck when she entered the lot.

She had gotten in his truck and watched as he climbed into the driver's seat. His features were dark and hard. He had clearly been angry.

Elle had swallowed, remembering the tequila-fueled day. Hell, she hadn't been able to get it out of her mind. Maybe she shouldn't have left the way she did.

Ryan was wearing another compression tee, this time black, with black basketball shorts. Elle recalled admiring his chest. Remembering her hands all over it. When he turned to look at her, she had looked away in embarrassment.

Ryan had been honest with her about his past. Elle had felt guilty as he talked, fidgeting with the strap of her gym bag. She hadn't told him about her husband, Todd, or their separation and pending divorce. There Ryan was, wanting to be honest with her, and she hadn't been truthful with him. A lie of omission was still a lie. She should have told him about Todd that day at the bar.

But when he said he wasn't looking to start anything, Elle had felt crushed. She had felt a strange rush of disappointment. Almost thirty-three with one failed marriage under her belt, and Ryan wasn't interested in her either. She had decided there was no point in telling Ryan about Todd if things weren't going anywhere.

She'd felt tears form and commanded herself to get out of the damn truck before she embarrassed herself. Her feet had barely touched the pavement before tears had sprung from her eyes. Mortifying.

Before Todd, she was fine being alone. Maybe growing up as an only child had something to do with that, but she'd never been someone who had to be in a relationship just so she wouldn't be alone. She enjoyed having her own space and doing what she wanted, when she wanted.

Elle blew out a deep breath as she wiped the sweat from her brow. She wasn't sure who she was more irritated with, Todd or Ryan. Seriously–he wasn't looking to start anything right now? Bull. She didn't believe him. Not with the way he kissed her. She frowned wondering why he was really pushing her away. Ugh. Men. She shook her head. And they say women are complicated

Fine. I'll go back to the gym tomorrow, Elle decided. *But if he's there, I'm not talking to him.* He doesn't want to start something, then fine. Fine with her. His loss. She'd never thrown herself at a man before and she sure as hell wasn't going to start now.

"Hey, are you okay?"

Elle looked up. Sarah stood next to the exercise bench where she was sitting. She'd been lost in thought, oblivious to the noise and activity of the gym around her.

"I was on the treadmill over there and saw you sitting here for like ten minutes looking like you just lost your best friend," Sarah said, concerned. "Everything okay? I don't think I've seen you for over a week."

Elle shook her head, looking up. "Yeah, sorry. Didn't sleep very well last night, I guess." It had been a week since Ryan had dumped her in his truck. *Dumped you? That's a little bit melodramatic. It's not like you were even dating.*

She'd been avoiding the gym–avoiding Ryan. She couldn't stop thinking about him, but she didn't think she could manage going back to being casual friends. Not when all she could think about was the way he kissed her, the way he touched her, the way his body felt against hers. She sighed. Maybe she should switch gyms.

"Did you hear about Sean?" Sarah asked, sitting down on the bench next to Elle.

"No, how is he doing?" Elle asked, hoping for good news.

"Turned out he had a heart attack, but he made it. He's got a long road to recovery, but he's going to be okay. Tough old guy," Sarah said, shaking her head.

"Oh wow, damn. But I'm glad he's going to be okay. And no, I hadn't heard. So thank you for letting me know," Elle replied.

"Nate and I are coordinating with Sean's daughter to have some meals delivered for him, through Uber Eats or something, just to help out while he's recovering," Sarah explained. "If you want to do a dinner too, let me know."

"That's a great idea," Elle said, nodding. "Yes, I definitely want to contribute. Thank you for doing that."

"Okay, once we get the details figured out, I'll let you know," Sarah replied. She paused. "Are you sure you're okay?"

"Yes, I'm fine. Just have a lot going on." Elle forced a smile.

"All right, well, let's get lunch or something next week, okay? We need to catch up. I've got to fill you in on some changes in my life. Um, having to do with Nate, actually," Sarah said with a smile.

"Nate?" Elle asked, surprised, finally noticing how happy her friend looked. She knew both Sarah and Nate were widowed. "What? You two?"

Sarah blushed. "We ended up spending a couple hours at the hospital with Sean's daughter, just providing moral support. He drove me home after that and we talked for hours. I never realized how much we had in common. Then he asked me out to dinner and, well, we've had two dates since then."

"Aww, Sarah, I'm so happy for you two," Elle said, giving her friend a hug. She didn't think she knew two nicer people. They both deserved happiness. "Yes, I will text you later. I want all the details."

"Good. I've got to run now. Gotta pick my son up from school," Sarah said, standing up.

"Sounds good, have a great rest of your day," Elle said as her friend walked off. Her heart was happy for Sarah and Nate. Now, if she could just find a way to make her heart happy in her own love life.

Chapter Eight

September 2009

Ryan straightened up, blinking a few times. He brushed the tiny bit of coke dust left off the men's room counter of the nightclub. He put the small baggie with the rest of the coke back in his jeans pocket.

"Jesus, where did you get that stuff from?" Ryan asked Candi. "It's even better than the shit your mom brought back from Aspen that time." He closed his eyes for a second as she reapplied her lipstick in the mirror.

"I'd like to know the answer to that, too."

Ryan turned to see a man coming out of the end stall holding up a badge identifying him as a US Narcotic Agent. "Fuuuck," he replied, looking over at Candi, then dropping his head in resignation.

"You're both under arrest for possession of a controlled substance," the officer said.

"What the hell?" Candi exclaimed, turning around to glare at the cop. "This is total entrapment."

"Candi, shut up," Ryan said quickly, putting a hand on her arm.

"No. I won't. This is bullshit," Candi replied hotly, shaking his hand off.

"Tell it to the judge at your arraignment. I don't give a shit. Now turn around and put your hands behind your backs," the officer instructed.

"Jesus, just do it," Ryan told Candi, turning around slowly and putting his hands behind his back. "Don't make it worse."

"How am I making it worse?" Candi yelled. "We've done nothing wrong. We were just having a little fun."

"I'm not telling you again, missy, turn around and put your hands behind your back," the officer instructed again, narrowing his eyes at her as he pulled cuffs out of his back pocket. "Or I can add resisting arrest, if you'd like."

"Fuck you," Candi replied, turning around in a huff and finally putting her hands behind her back. "Fine. Whatever. My dad will bail me out and then go after your job, asshole."

"Christ, shut up. Stop talking." Ryan glared at her as the officer put the cuffs on him.

Candi glared back at him. "Nice. Way to have my back. Thanks."

"This is me having your back," Ryan responded. "Don't make any trouble and you'll be out soon enough."

"Listen to your boyfriend, sweetie," the officer said, putting the cuffs on Candi. "Being difficult is only going to make your stay with us that much longer."

Candi's face was dark with anger, but she kept her mouth shut as the officer led them out of the nightclub.

Ryan sighed, getting into the back of the patrol car. Shit. His dad was going to kill him.

RYAN POPPED the top off a Coors Light and sank down onto his patio couch, putting his feet up on the wicker coffee table and taking a long drink. He set the beer down with a sigh and looked up at the evening sky, which was just turning dark blue as the sun set behind the hills. His thoughts immediately turned to Elle.

He blew out a breath and silently admitted to himself that there was obviously something between them. And maybe had been for quite a while. Ryan knew he hoped to see her every time he went to the gym. Elle's smile and the cute, shy way she tilted her head at him when they talked always made his day.

He'd spent so many years pushing people away that he forgot how to let anyone in. But he wasn't sure he could open his heart again. It had so much damage that he wasn't sure it would survive any more.

NOVEMBER 2009

"I think we need some space," Ryan said, holding his aching head in his hands on the side of his bed. Another night of drinking, getting high, fighting, and making up and having sex. Jesus, it was basically all they'd done since he'd gotten out of jail three weeks ago.

Candi got off with a year of probation. But he'd been sentenced to thirty days in jail along with a year's probation since the baggie of coke had been in his pocket. A Class 4 felony.

Ryan was sick of it. The roller coaster of getting high, feeling free and light, and then the crash. The anger and the coldness coming back. The highs weren't as high anymore and the lows were even lower. He knew he had to stop this vicious cycle. He'd just have to learn to live with the emptiness.

Thirty days sitting in a cell had made him question what he was doing with his life. But as soon as he was out, Candi sucked him back into party mode. Celebrating, she'd said. Celebrating his release.

It was ridiculous to be celebrating any of that mistake. More mistakes like that and he'd be sitting in jail for a lot longer than thirty days.

"What?" *Candi asked, sitting up behind him, her naked body pressed against his back. She wrapped her arms around him, stroking his chest.* "I don't think I heard you correctly."

"Stop." *Ryan shook her off, standing up and pulling his sweats on in harsh movements.* "You heard me. I need a break from you. I can't do this anymore."

"You need a break from ME?" *Candi yelled, climbing out of his bed. She elbowed him out of her way as she stood up.* "Maybe I need a break from you. Christ, all you do is mope around. Okay, so you had to do thirty days in jail. Big fucking deal. And so your football career didn't turn out the way you wanted. Get the hell over it."

"Get dressed and get out," *Ryan said, his face hard, yanking his shirt over his head.* "I'm done."

"Done? You think we're done? We're done when I say we're done. Not one minute before that," *Candi said, raising her voice with every word and shoving his shoulder.*

"Stop," *Ryan said, grabbing her hands to stop her from pushing him again.* "Control yourself. This is over. Just get your shit and leave."

"No, I won't," *Candi said, quieter this time. She freed her hands to caress his chest.* "Please. I love you, baby."

"No, you don't," *Ryan replied with a tired sigh, letting go of her and turning toward the door.* "This isn't love. This isn't how love is supposed to feel. All we do is fight and—"

"And have amazing make-up sex," *Candi purred, reaching for him. She slid her hand in the waistband of his sweats.* "I know you want me."

"I don't. This is ridiculous," *Ryan said roughly, twisting his body to keep her hands out of his pants. He pushed her away.* "Stop."

Candi reached up suddenly and slapped him. "You're ridiculous. From football star to mechanic. Fine. I can do better anyway. Fuck you!" she yelled.

Ryan forced himself to hold his hands at his sides. He was breathing hard, trying to control himself as a slow rage burned in his chest. "Get out. Now," he said through clenched teeth.

Candi pulled her shorts and tank on. "You'll never do better than me! You'll look back and regret treating me this way! Asshole!" she yelled, slamming the door behind her.

"You've been quieter than normal the last few days," Lisa said, leaning up against the G550 in the hangar as Ryan went over the preflight checks for Emma.

Ryan shrugged without looking at Lisa.

"Did you ever talk to Elle?" Lisa asked.

"Briefly," Ryan replied, still going over his outside run-up.

"Why briefly? What happened?" Lisa asked, frowning.

She didn't mean to mess things up for her brother.

"Nothing. I ended it," Ryan answered. "Not that there was even anything to end. We just agreed that starting a relationship right now is not a good idea."

"You agreed? Or you made the decision for both of you?" Lisa inquired. "Because it looked like something was happening when I, um, interrupted you guys."

"Nothing happened," Ryan said, his dark eyes hard, practically glaring a hole into the clipboard in his hands. "What does it matter anyway, we both know how it would have ended. Why bother? Why put myself through it again? I just want to be alone, okay? I've got to get this preflight done."

"Ryan." Lisa placed a hand on her brother's arm. "I feel a little responsible. I shouldn't have reacted the way I did the other night."

"No, you were right," Ryan replied. "I'm in a good place right now. I don't need to jeopardize that."

"Shit." Lisa sighed. "No, actually, I was wrong. And you know how much I fucking hate admitting that." She scrunched up her nose.

Ryan finally looked up from his preflight checklist to raise an eyebrow at Lisa.

"I was only thinking about myself. I wasn't thinking about you. You've been alone too long, little brother. I'm sorry. I'm partly to blame. I just worry about you and, well, I know how hard it is with everything you've been through," Lisa admitted. "But Elle seemed nice and cute and, well, maybe you should rethink things. Maybe you should ask her out."

"Why?" Ryan asked harshly, not waiting for a reply. "She doesn't need me and my past complicating her life. No, it's better this way. Now, I really need to finish this, if you don't mind."

Lisa nodded, turning and walking back to her office. There was no point trying to push the issue if he'd made up his mind. *Damn you, Candi*, she thought for the millionth time. *Why couldn't you just destroy your own life? Why did you have to destroy Ryan's too?*

December 2009

"I'm pregnant."

Ryan was having trouble processing what Candi was telling him. He'd opened the door of his apartment to find her standing on his doorstep. "What did you say?"

"I said I'm pregnant." Candi looked into his eyes. "With your baby. Our baby," she added softly. "Can I come in?"

"Yep," Ryan replied, opening the door wider to let Candi pass.

He closed the door behind them and leaned against it, crossing his arms over his chest and frowning in disbelief. "Mighty convenient."

"Seriously, Ryan," Candi said quietly. "Believe me, I didn't plan this. The last thing I want right now is a baby."

"So then what's the problem?" Ryan asked calmly, though he felt anything but calm.

"Jesus, do you hate me that much?" Candi asked, tears welling in her eyes. "I know we broke up, but I thought you'd at least want to know that you're going to be a father."

"So you're keeping it?" Ryan asked, refusing to let himself feel anything. He wasn't sure how he wanted her to respond.

"Yes, I'm keeping IT. IT is a baby–OUR baby!" Candi yelled. "Fuck, Ryan. You are so cold. Never mind, let me out. I'm leaving."

Ryan blew out a deep breath, reaching out to put his hands on her shoulders. "Wait. I'm sorry. I'm just in shock. It's kind of the last thing I expected. Give me a minute to process this."

"Tell me about it. It's the last thing I expected, too. I took like eight tests yesterday," Candi said with a rueful smile. "And yeah, all positive."

"So now what?" Ryan asked, looking at her guardedly.

"Look." Candi let out a deep breath of her own. "I just wanted you to know. I don't expect you to marry me or anything. But I do want you to know that I'm sorry. I'm sorry about our fight. I'm sorry about the things I said. I never should have said any of that shit. You just took me by surprise. I was hurt and angry and I lashed out at you."

"I'm sorry, too. I just need to start making some changes in my life. We can't go on the way we have been," Ryan replied, shaking his head. "We just can't."

"I know, things have gotten out of control," Candi agreed. "But I want you to know, I flushed what was left of the coke that was in my condo. And the pills. I'm not drinking either. A baby wasn't in my plans, but now, well, I just want a healthy baby."

"Okay," Ryan replied, reluctantly wrapping his arms around her. "That's good. That's what I want, too."

RYAN SAT down in the cockpit of the Citation Bravo, checking his maintenance manual for the third time. He kept getting distracted by thoughts of Elle. What was it about that woman? He'd slept like shit the last couple nights, tossing and turning. He couldn't stop remembering her hands on his chest, her lips on his, the way she said his name.

He'd also been dreaming about Candi lately, which was unsettling. He just wanted the past to stay in the past. He was tired of the ghosts haunting him, reminding him of things he wanted to forget.

"Ryan," Lisa called through the open side door, "are you in there?"

"Yeah sis, cockpit. Trying to fix the terrain awareness warning system. Emma said it was having issues the last time she flew, but I'm not finding the problem," Ryan replied as Lisa entered the cockpit.

"Well, it's not scheduled to go out again until next week. So you have time to figure it out," Lisa said, climbing into the right seat.

"That's good," Ryan said with a tired sigh.

"You seem distracted," Lisa said, raising an eyebrow. "Any particular reason?"

"Mind your own damn business," Ryan said, flipping through the manual again and avoiding eye contact. His sister was a little too perceptive sometimes.

"Hmm, thought so," Lisa replied with a knowing smile.

"What?" Ryan slammed the manual closed. No point in trying to focus on this problem right now.

"Christ, Ryan, just take a chance," Lisa said, smacking him on the shoulder. "It's pretty obvious you can't stop thinking about her. Why don't you ask her out?"

"Why?" Ryan asked with a small shrug, resigned. "It will just turn into Kimberly 2.0. Once she finds out about Candi and what happened after she died, it will be just like every other time, with every other woman I've ever told."

"So you're just going to be alone for the rest of your life? Come on," Lisa said, "maybe it's just that you hadn't met the right woman until now."

"So Elle is the right woman now? Geez sis, I barely know her. What makes you think she can handle my past?" Ryan asked, rubbing his hands over his face.

"What makes you think she can't?" Lisa countered. "Kimberly wasn't the right woman for you, and I think you know that now, looking back."

Ryan nodded. At the time he'd been so happy to be in a healthy relationship. No games. No drama. No drugs. No problems. Maybe he'd craved that normalcy so much that he'd built Kimberly up to be the perfect woman, and he'd tried to be the perfect partner. But that wasn't reality. It was doomed from the start. It was a make-believe world that came crashing down hard when the truth came out.

Did he want to take the chance with Elle? Tell her how his wife had died and explain what he went through after. Would she understand? Was he ready to risk his heart again? He'd lost so much already. He was afraid he couldn't handle much more loss in his life.

April 2010

"Candi," Ryan called, coming in through the garage door. "I brought dinner." He tossed his truck keys on the counter next to the washer and dryer as he walked through the utility room. He pushed the door to their kitchen open and found Candi lying at the bottom of the stairs, blood oozing from the side of her head. "Jesus! Candi! Oh God." Ryan dropped the bag of takeout on the kitchen counter.

"Candi...shit," Ryan rushed over to her. Kneeling next to her, he

took her pulse. Finding a weak one, he reached for his cell and called 911.

"Ryan," Candi said softly, opening her eyes. Tears ran down her cheeks. She reached up to touch his face. "I fell. I'm so sorry. I tripped on the stairs."

"Shhh, don't talk. An ambulance is coming. Lie still. You're fine, you're going to be fine," Ryan assured her, blinking away his own tears. He could see blood between her legs. Oh God, no. Not the baby.

"No, it hurts," Candi sobbed. "I feel it. The baby. I was scared to move. Oh God. Something is wrong. Please, no. Ryan, is our baby okay?"

Ryan couldn't see, he had to brush the tears out of his eyes. He leaned down and gently put his arms around her, rocking her slowly. "It's okay. It's going to be okay," he repeated over and over while his heart shattered into a million tiny pieces.

Chapter Nine

Elle set the weights back on the rack with a sigh. *This is pointless,* she thought. *Might as well just leave. I'm not getting any real workout done.* All she had done since getting to the gym was keep an eye out for Ryan. Every time someone came through the front door, she looked over to see if it was him. She'd been hoping to work off some nervous energy from the last few days. Maybe a quick thirty-minute run on the treadmill would help.

After her run, she walked across the parking lot to her car, lost in thought. The run hadn't helped her feel any less anxious. She checked her watch. Four thirty. Maybe she'd just go back to her Airbnb and open a bottle of wine. It's technically happy hour.

"Figured I'd find you here."

She looked up to see Todd standing next to her Jaguar. "Move. I have nothing to say to you," Elle said firmly, gripping her gym bag a little tighter. She felt nauseous looking at him and backed up to put a little space between them. She motioned for him to move away from the driver's door.

"Too bad, because I have a few things to say to you," Todd

replied, eerily calm as he moved closer to her. "Why haven't you signed the papers yet? You've got a lot of nerve!"

"No, I won't. Get away from me. I'm not signing those papers. I'm not giving you another dime. Especially after what you did," Elle said, glaring at him, her heart pounding and her whole body shaking a little. She didn't want to be this close to him. "I've got a lot of nerve? You've got to be kidding me. Now get away from my car."

Todd grabbed her arm. "What do you mean, after what I–"

"Everything okay here?"

Elle and Todd turned.

Oh God no, Elle thought, immediately turning bright red. Ryan stood there, watching them. She shook Todd's hand off, backing away from him again. *Ugh. This is not happening.*

"Mind your own fucking business, asshole," Todd spat at Ryan, then turned back to Elle.

"Elle," Ryan said, walking closer to stand next to her, "are you okay?"

Elle looked up into Ryan's concerned eyes. *Shit. Shit.* In the middle of an argument with Todd, Ryan still had the power to melt her insides. "Yes, yes. Fine. Fine," she managed to get out.

Todd dropped his hand and narrowed his eyes at Ryan. "What the fuck? Who are you?" He didn't wait for an answer. "Whatever, I don't care. We're having a private conversation. Get lost."

"Actually, I think you need to leave Elle alone," Ryan replied, frowning at Todd. He draped an arm around Elle's shoulder, turning her. "Let's go."

"Wait, where do you think you're going?" Todd asked angrily, reaching for Elle's arm again.

"You really don't want to do that," Ryan said with fire in his eyes, calmly looking down at Todd. "Let go of her. Now."

Todd let go and held up his hands. "Fine," he replied, calling after them as they walked across the lot to where Ryan had parked his motorcycle. "We'll talk later, Elle."

"You okay?" Ryan asked, stopping next to his motorcycle and looking down at her.

"Yeah," Elle replied, mortified that Ryan had seen her arguing with Todd. *Shit*. She had to explain, right now.

"Who was that asshole? An ex?"

Elle swallowed hard, not making eye contact with Ryan. "My husband, Todd," she admitted quietly.

"What?" Ryan asked, his eyes widening in surprise. "You're married? To that guy?"

"Yes, but ..." Elle began.

"You never said anything the other day," Ryan accused, narrowing his eyes, his features suddenly hard. "You should have told me you were married. Why didn't you say anything?"

"I know, I should have," Elle said, glancing at his dark eyes. She quickly looked away from the anger she saw there. "I'm sorry. But you don't understand, we're–"

"And what the hell was going on just now?" Ryan interrupted.

"Todd and I–" Elle started.

Ryan's cell phone rang. "Shit. Sorry, just a minute." He turned away to answer the phone. "What's up, Lisa?"

Elle bit her lip, waiting for him to finish his call. Ryan was silent, listening to Lisa.

"Yeah, I'll be there in a few minutes." He ended the call and turned back to Elle. "I'm sorry, there's a problem with the Beechcraft and it's scheduled to go out later. I have to get back to the hangar." Ryan reached for his helmet.

"Oh, um, sure, okay," Elle said, nodding even though she didn't want to leave things this way. "It's just that, well, I just want you to know that–"

"I really have to go," Ryan interrupted, getting on his bike and looking away.

"Okay." Elle backed away from Ryan. "Umm, see you later, I guess." She watched as he started his motorcycle and headed out of the parking lot.

She couldn't imagine what he must think. Dammit, if only he'd let her explain.

At least it looked like Todd had left. She didn't see him or his Beemer anywhere. Thankfully.

Well, shit. Now she really wanted that bottle of wine. *Another fine mess you've made.*

Chapter Ten

"So what's this kid's story?" Ryan looked at the tall, skinny kid using a push broom across the open gym. The kid had a deal, cleaning in return for gym privileges. Ryan started volunteering at 4th Street Boxing Gym right after he was released from prison. He enjoyed working with the kids so much that he'd continued to volunteer even after his required community service hours were done.

"Owen Harper," Logan replied, leaning against the back counter. "Kid is only seventeen and he's already had a hard life. His mom overdosed a year ago, and his dad is a serious piece of shit. Beats the kid up all the time. That's why he came here. He wants to learn how to protect himself. Fucking sad state of affairs that a kid needs to learn how to fight to protect himself from his own father."

"Damn," Ryan said, shaking his head and glancing back at Logan.

Logan Litchfield was a legend. As a former professional heavy-weight, he'd fought some big names in his day. Even at seventy-one years old, he was a six-foot-six, two-hundred-and-seventy-pound force to be reckoned with. Like Ryan, Logan was an ex-con. He'd been heavily involved in a gang in his younger years. He was busted after a failed bank robbery, during which a security guard had been killed.

After Logan got out of jail, he changed his life. He got out of the gang and took up boxing. After retiring from a very successful career, he opened his own boxing gym, catering to underprivileged and troubled youth. He wanted to help a younger generation navigate the future with more success and support than he'd had.

Ryan thought Logan was doing a pretty incredible thing here. He loved helping broken, damaged kids turn into strong, independent adults. He was proud to call Logan a friend.

"Kid's got a quiet strength about him," Logan said. "He just needs some guidance and support. Two things I don't think he's ever had."

"I've got some time. Want me to work with him?" Ryan asked. He needed a distraction so he would stop thinking about Elle. He had been shocked to learn she was married. Well. Guess it was a good thing nothing more had happened between them. Now there was no need to tell her about his past. There was no way he was getting involved with a married woman. He'd made a lot of mistakes in his life, but he'd never made that one before and he didn't plan to now. He shook his head to clear his thoughts. *Enough.*

"Yeah, I think that's a great idea. Thanks, Ryan. I appreciate all your help, you know," Logan said, putting his hand on Ryan's shoulder.

"Well, you've done more for me than you'll ever know. So anything I can do to help, I'm here," Ryan said. "You helped save my life when I thought I was beyond saving, and these kids need that, too. It's the least I can do."

Logan nodded. "I'll send Owen over to talk to you when he's done cleaning up." He headed over to talk to Owen.

"Sounds good," Ryan called after him.

About thirty minutes later, Ryan was working the heavy bag when Owen approached him. "Are you Ryan?" he asked.

"Yes." Ryan took his gloves off and set them on the bench behind him before holding his hand out to Owen. "Ryan Daley. Nice to meet you, Owen."

Owen shook Ryan's hand but avoided eye contact.

"So, Owen, why do you want to learn to box?" Ryan asked, leaning against the counter.

Owen shrugged, looking down at the floor. "I don't know if I want to box, really. I just want to learn to fight." He finally looked up and made eye contact with Ryan. "I want to look like you. You're buff as shit. I bet no one messes with you."

"You might be surprised," Ryan said with a wry laugh. "I can teach you to fight, but there's more to it than just throwing a punch."

"What do you mean?" Owen asked.

"Answer me this...what do you think the definition of a warrior is?"

"A strong man who can fight anyone," Owen replied without hesitation, standing up straight.

"Well, that's part of it," Ryan agreed. "The definition of a warrior is someone, a man or woman, who can fight to protect themself. But it is also someone who is capable of setting goals and has the skill, strength, and knowledge to accomplish those goals."

Owen frowned a little.

"What else do you want to learn, besides fighting?" Ryan asked. "What are you interested in? What do you like to do?"

Owen shrugged again, his eyes dropping back to the floor. "I don't know. No one's ever asked me that before."

"Well, I want you to think about it and have an answer for me next time we meet," Ryan said. "Come by after school tomorrow and we'll go over a few basic skills. You still have to make time for cleaning here and homework, okay?"

"Okay," Owen agreed. "And thank you." He gave Ryan a shy smile. "See you tomorrow."

Ryan smiled as Owen practically skipped across the gym. Logan was right. Kid had heart–it was just sadly buried under years of abuse. Time to fix that.

Chapter Eleven

Tom pushed his empty dinner plate away. "You're quiet tonight, Elle," he said, taking a sip of his old-fashioned.

"Oh," Elle replied, glancing over at her dad. "Sorry. Just a lot on my mind, I guess."

"You do look a little tired, Elle," her mother said, picking up her wine glass. "You really need to start taking better care of yourself. Why don't you let me make an appointment for you at the spa?"

Ava Campbell looked casually elegant in a black Armani dress, not one hair out of place.

Elle knew a lot of work went into her mother's carefully curated style, but at fifty-eight, Ava could still hold her own against a woman half her age. She was always doing barre classes, hot yoga, appointments with her aesthetician, Botox. The list went on and on.

Elle had zero interest in any of that. If she remembered to get her hair trimmed every six months, it was a miracle. She sighed. "No, that's really not necessary. Thank you, but I'm fine."

"All right. If you say so. Darling, you really should have worn that red Gucci dress I bought you last week," Ava said, frowning at Elle's black jeans and black sweater. "Elise's son is here visiting, and I wanted to introduce you to him."

"Mother, I'm not even divorced yet. Good grief," Elle replied, biting her tongue. She wished she could tell her mother to mind her own business. There was no way she was letting Ava play matchmaker.

Elle had dated her fair share of polished businessmen from the club. They all had one thing in common–they were boring, competing with each other over who played a better golf game or had a more expensive car. She loved that Ryan drove a truck and had a motorcycle–

Shit, seriously, stop thinking about him, she chided herself. Every thought she had inevitably circled back to him. She sighed.

"Well, it doesn't hurt to make some introductions, now does it?" Ava responded. "Elise and Jeff are well respected at the club."

Elle tried not to roll her eyes. She knew that was code for wealthy.

"Stop frowning, dear," Ava commanded. "You're so much prettier when you smile."

Kill me now, Elle thought. *Why did I let Dad talk me into dinner at the club? Just nod and smile. Then you can go home.* Ha. Home. The empty Airbnb actually sounded worse than suffering through dinner with her mother. All she did there was mope around and think about Ryan.

She wanted to tell him about Todd, but she didn't know how to get a hold of Ryan outside the gym. *You know where he lives,* a little voice reminded her.

Yeah. Not happening. There was no way she would just show up on his doorstep. However, Jack's wasn't that far away. She could swing by there on her way home. He might be there. Maybe she could explain everything.

Chapter Twelve

"You're even more mopey than usual," Jack said, setting another beer on the bar in front of Ryan.

Ryan scowled. "Mopey? I'm not fucking mopey."

"Yeah, you are," the bartender insisted. "How's Elle?"

"How would I know?" Ryan said dismissively. "Maybe ask her husband."

"Huh," Jack replied, frowning. "Didn't see that one coming. Really?"

Ryan nodded. He frowned at the memory of how Todd had treated Elle the other day. Maybe there was more to the story. She didn't seem very happy. *Doesn't matter,* he thought, *not going down that rabbit hole.* That kind of trouble was the last thing he needed. Nope. Not getting involved.

Jack shrugged, moving down the bar to help another thirsty customer.

"Is this seat open?"

Ryan turned. A cute brunette stood next to the bar, smiling up at him. He nodded. "Yep," he replied, turning back to his beer.

"I'm Mia. Come here often?" she asked with a grin. "Sorry, is that the worst pickup line ever or what?"

Ryan shrugged and looked away, not really in the mood to make conversation.

"What's good here?" Mia asked. "Is there a drink menu?"

Ryan snorted. "Ha. The beer is cold and the whisky is decent." *And so is the tequila* he thought, remembering that day with Elle. "Beyond that, you're in the wrong bar."

"What will it be?" Jack came over, wiping his hands on a towel.

"Well, I hear the beer is cold, so I guess a beer it is," Mia replied with a smile. "Thanks."

"You got it, honey," Jack replied, reaching into the cooler behind the bar and grabbing a cold beer. He popped the top off a Coors Light, setting it on the bar in front of her. "Let me know if you need anything else."

Mia nodded to Jack before turning back to Ryan. "Cheers," she said, holding up her beer bottle.

Ryan looked at Mia again. She was cute enough, wearing a little white tank top and a pair of tight jeans. She had shoulder-length light-brown hair, brown eyes, and a cute little smile. *Maybe Mia will help you forget about Elle.* Doubtful.

Aloud, he replied, "Cheers. I'm Ryan." He lightly tapped her bottle, then took another drink.

"I'm here visiting some friends, but there's always drama with two of my girlfriends and I needed a little break. So I thought I'd come check this place out." Mia looked around the bar.

Ryan just nodded. Mia was attractive and seemed nice, but he couldn't concentrate on her. His thoughts kept jumping back to Elle.

Shit. Maybe he should talk to her again. Looking back, it was obvious she'd been fighting with her husband. In the moment, Ryan had been so shocked to find out Elle was married that everything else faded into the background. Todd. Guy seemed like a dick. Now he regretted leaving her there with him.

Stop. What are you thinking? No.

"So, are you single, Ryan?" Mia asked, interrupting his thoughts. She put a hand on his arm and lightly ran her fingers up to his shoulder.

"Speak of the devil," Jack said quietly, coming closer to Ryan and nodding toward the door as Elle walked in.

Ryan turned to find Elle staring at him from just inside the door. "Shit," he said quietly. He shook Mia's hand off his arm, but Elle had definitely seen it. She turned and bolted out the door.

"So, not single," Mia said wryly, dropping her hand to her lap. "Too bad."

"Sorry," Ryan replied, pulling some money out of his pocket and tossing it on the bar. "Keep the change, Jack." He jumped up from his seat and headed across the bar to the door. "Elle, wait," he called.

"Elle," Ryan called again as he stepped outside, spotting her hurrying across the parking lot to her car. "Hey, will you wait?" he asked. He reached her just as she was about to open her car door.

"Why?" Elle asked impatiently. "What do you want? You seemed to be having a good time back there."

"That was just some girl. I don't even know her," Ryan explained. He moved in front of her car door, blocking it.

"Well, for not knowing her, you two looked cozy enough," Elle retorted, trying to reach around him for the door handle. "Will you move please? I was just leaving."

"Seriously, Elle, I'm not the one who is married," Ryan replied heatedly, cupping his hands around her biceps. He was torn between wanting to shake her and wanting to kiss her.

"I'm sorry. But you wouldn't let me explain the other day," Elle said angrily, trying unsuccessfully to shake his arms off. "I'm separated and getting a divorce, but whatever ... it doesn't matter. Just never mind. Go back to your little hottie. Now move."

Ryan paused for a second, then grinned. *Is she jealous?* "You're actually pretty damn cute when you're angry," he said. So there was more to the story after all. He wanted to know what it was.

"What? I am not! Get out of my way." Elle glared at him.

"Yes you are," Ryan replied, looking at her lips. He definitely wanted to kiss her.

"No, I'm–"

Ryan couldn't stop himself. He didn't care about anything but kissing her. He pulled her against him firmly, one hand moving around her waist and the other cradling her head with his fingers in her hair. He leaned down to find her lips, interrupting her mid-sentence.

Elle clamped her lips tightly together, refusing to kiss him back. He continued to apply pressure, gently forcing her lips open. He heard her let out a sigh as she relented, starting to respond and finally opening to him. *Oh God.* It was just as good as he remembered.

"Ryan, dammit," Elle said softly, pulling away. "We need to talk. Please."

Ryan nodded. "Follow me back to my place, okay?" "Okay," she agreed.

Ryan kissed her again briefly before opening her car door for her. Once she was settled in the driver's seat of her car he headed to his truck.

Chapter Thirteen

Ryan closed his front door behind them, taking Elle's hand and leading her to his couch. "Have a seat." Then he went to the kitchen while she settled in, returning with wine. Elle accepted a glass. He took a sip from his own as he sat down.

They sat diagonally across from each other on his sectional. Neither making eye contact, neither wanting to talk.

"So you are–" Ryan began.

"I need to–" Elle started at the same time.

They smiled at each other. Ryan took another sip from his glass.

"Sorry. I'm really sorry about ... um, I didn't mean to ... um, over-react back at Jack's," Elle said, looking down at her wine. She was a little embarrassed at her behavior.

Ryan smiled. "It's been a long time since I've had a woman get jealous over me."

Suddenly, she just wanted to get it out. Tell Ryan everything and see his reaction. See if there was anything there, besides the electricity she still felt between them. He'd said before that they shouldn't get involved, but Elle felt like they already were, well ... something. Something was definitely going on between them.

Elle sighed. "Okay. Well, here goes. So I met Todd about a year ago. He was like Prince Charming. He wined and dined me and basically swept me off my feet. My parents, especially my mother, loved him. My girlfriends were all jealous. It seemed so perfect." She paused.

"Until it wasn't."

"We married six months after we met, and soon after that I discovered that he was a fraud. He lied about everything. He didn't come from a wealthy family in Europe. He wasn't the high-stakes investor that he said he was. He didn't actually work for a big firm out of London. It was all a big lie. He was flat broke with a ton of debt."

"Damn," Ryan said.

"Todd said he loved me. He said he lied because he knew I would leave him if I knew the truth. He apologized and begged and pleaded, saying he wanted me and this marriage more than anything. He could be very convincing when he wanted to be," Elle explained wryly. Todd could be so charming when he wanted to be. "So I forgave him. I withdrew money from a trust that my paternal grandfather had left me and paid off his debts."

Ryan raised his eyebrows.

"Yeah, I know. I was an idiot," Elle said, shaking her head. "But I took my vows seriously. I didn't want a divorce. I wanted to believe him. I wanted to be happy. I wanted a family, maybe. I guess I believed him because I didn't want to believe the alternative and admit that I fell for a damn con man."

"Wow. I'm really sorry that all happened," Ryan said somberly.

"Well," Elle replied, "there's more."

"Okay, go on," he said.

Elle picked up her wine glass and took a sip. "So things, I don't know, maybe got a little better for a bit. He got a job in my father's architecture firm, though I couldn't tell you exactly what he did. Schmooze clients maybe and play a lot of golf. He certainly didn't know anything about architecture." Elle looked around the spacious, beautiful room again. Ryan obviously knew a lot more about the design end of things than Todd ever would.

"Anyway, he just drifted further and further away. Late meetings, early breakfasts. Always gone on the weekends. Never showing affection or wanting to spend time with me, unless he wanted something," she said.

"A little over a month ago, we had a huge fight. He had walked out of the firm and said he was done–he didn't want to work there anymore or work anywhere else," Elle said with a snort. "As if he'd ever done any actual work. But he also seemed to have some money coming in from somewhere, which made me suspicious. New golf clubs, expensive suits, new shoes, et cetera. So, I followed him one afternoon. He went to the club, the Ancala golf course, off Vía Linda. Anyway, he met this woman getting out of a Mercedes and they started kissing as the valet drove her car off."

"Oh damn," Ryan said, his eyes widening.

"I guess I knew he was cheating on me; he probably had been the entire time. I just didn't want to admit it. He must have been pretty much done with me at that point. He had another sucker in his sights." Elle paused, remembering how angry she had been that day. "When Todd finally showed up back at the house that night, I accused him of having an affair. I told him I'd seen him with her, and he just calmly admitted it. He shrugged like it wasn't a big deal. Said I needed to mind my own fucking business. Jesus, I couldn't believe it.

"I told him to get out, but he refused," Elle paused, looking down at her lap. She'd never told anyone what had happened that night.

AUGUST 2023

"*The fuck I will. I'm not going anywhere,*" Todd said angrily, grabbing Elle by the arm and squeezing hard.

"*Stop!*" Elle cried out in pain, trying to wrench her arm away. "*You're hurting me. Let go.*"

"*No, I won't,*" Todd snarled, his eyes cold. "*I'll hurt you if I want to. Christ, you've been a whiny fucking bitch lately. I'm not sure how I've put up with you this long.*"

"*What?!*" Elle exclaimed, her heart pounding at his words and the dark look on his face. "*Stop Todd, you're scaring me.*" She tried to back up and failed, Todd's firm grip unrelenting.

"*Good,*" Todd replied harshly, reaching a hand up to grab her chin hard. "*Maybe that's what you need. Then maybe you'll stop doing stupid things like following me around. It's pathetic.*"

Elle tried to pull away again but he pinned her against the kitchen counter. "*I'm sorry. I won't follow you ever again,*" she said as evenly as she could, willing to agree to anything to get him to calm down. Fear grew in her chest as he pushed her harder against the counter. "*Please, let me go. I just want to go to my parents' house. You stay.*"

"*You're not fucking going anywhere, baby,*" Todd said quietly. "*In fact, I think I need to teach you a little lesson.*" He reached up and slapped her hard across the face.

She gasped in shock. "*Todd. Stop. What are you doing?*" Tears sprang to her eyes, her cheek stinging.

"*Something I guess I should have done a long time ago,*" Todd replied, hitting her across the mouth this time. Then he reached his hand up, winding it in her hair, and jerked her head back.

Elle twisted, trying to get away from him, but he only pulled her hair harder.

"*Stop. No, Todd. Please stop!*" she cried out, terrified by his sudden cruel behavior.

"*I'm your husband. You don't get to tell me no,*" Todd said, stepping back, yet leaning forward to whisper in her ear. "*You're mine to do with as I please.*"

"*Please, can't we just talk? I'm sorry,*" Elle begged, trembling. "*I'm sorry I followed you. I'm sorry I told you to get out. I don't want you to–"

"I don't really care what you want, baby," Todd replied, a little thoughtfully. "I never really cared, actually." He hit her hard in the stomach.

Elle gasped again, the air rushing out of her lungs. She tried to suck in a breath as Todd let go of her hair. He roughly pushed her down on the floor, falling on top of her. He grabbed her face, hitting her head against the floor.

Elle saw stars and blinked a few times to clear them. "Todd. No!" Panic consumed her as she fought, struggling to get him off her. "Stop. Jesus, just stop. I can't breathe," she choked out. The weight of his body pushing down on hers crushed her lungs.

"You are my wife, and you will never give me any more grief about how I choose to live my life. Do you understand?" Todd yelled, slapping her again.

"Stop fighting me," he growled. "Do you understand that I am in control?" He grabbed her face again roughly. "Say it."

Elle nodded, sobbing quietly. "Yes. Yes, I understand," she said as tears rolled out of her eyes.

"Good. I'm glad we were able to come to an understanding, baby." Todd got up off the floor and looked down at her. "Now go clean yourself up and let's go to bed," he said as he walked out of the kitchen. He didn't look back.

Elle slowly and carefully got to her feet. Her ribs were on fire, her chest burning and her head pounding so much she was dizzy. Walk, she commanded herself, putting a hand out to stabilize herself against the wall as she moved. Just walk. You can do it.

She limped into the bathroom and found a face-cloth, wetting it. She gingerly wiped the blood off her face as tears continued to fall down her cheeks. She'd never have thought Todd was capable of that kind of behavior. She looked at her reflection in the mirror. She had married a monster.

"He hit me," Elle said quietly, not looking at Ryan, ashamed that she had married a man that could do that.

"He did what?" Ryan asked.

"I had a black eye and a split lip and a swollen cheek. Took a lot of concealer to cover that. Also, a couple of bruised ribs and a knot on my head," Elle explained, looking anywhere but at him.

"Jesus," Ryan breathed out.

"The next morning when he left the house, I packed a bag and went to a hotel. The next afternoon I went to try to get a few things from the house and he'd had the locks changed. I spent two weeks in a hotel before finding the Airbnb where I've been ever since. I filed for divorce right away, and of course he's fighting me on every small detail. I'm ready to just give him whatever he wants just so I can get him the hell out of my life." Elle paused, chewing on her lower lip. "So. Now you know. The mess my life is."

Elle stood and walked over to the slider, looking out and rubbing her arms. Telling her miserable story left her feeling defeated. She didn't want to look at Ryan's handsome face. Didn't want to see the disgust in his eyes. She was so ashamed. Falling for a con man who beat her. She'd made so many mistakes—not being honest with Ryan right from the start being another huge one.

Ryan got up and went to her, turning her to him and wrapping his arms around her. He held her against him as they looked at the darkness outside. "I'm so sorry you went through all that. That you're still going through it," he said.

Elle buried her face in his shoulder, tears forming in her eyes. *Stop it,* she thought. *You are not crying in front of Ryan. Pull yourself together, dammit.* "I can't imagine what you think of me," she said softly. "I've made one terrible decision after another, and then the other day and how I acted. I mean, I am still technically married. I should have told you, and I'm sorry. I hope you can forgive me."

Chapter Fourteen

Ryan held Elle away from him. His heart hurt at the pain he saw on her face. He brushed a tear away from the corner of one eye.

He knew Todd's type. Lisa had been entangled in a similar situation years ago, but at least she hadn't married the guy. Lisa's ex-husband and the father of her two kids, George, might be a lot of things but he was a hardworking, honest man. He could be an asshole sometimes. But Ryan knew Lisa could be an asshole, too.

Ryan had watched Elle's face as she talked. He knew exactly what she was feeling. He'd been there with Candi. She'd cheated on him—once that she had admitted to, but he was sure there had been more. Always begging for his forgiveness after coming home drunk and high at two in the morning. Always saying she was sorry, that she would change, be better. When he'd finally been ready to leave her, done with her lies and unable to single-handedly save their marriage, she'd told him she was pregnant again. He closed his eyes for a moment, pushing that memory out of his mind and focusing on Elle.

He opened his eyes and met her gaze. "Elle. I am the last person who would ever judge you. And what happened between us the other day was just as much my fault, if not more. You don't have to apologize." His gaze traveled to her lips. He wanted to kiss her until her pain went away. *What was it about this woman?* She deserved so much better. Better than Todd for damn sure. But better than him, too.

Ryan realized Elle had a sadness in her eyes. It had always been there, even when she smiled and laughed at the gym. *Maybe that's why we're so attracted to each other. We're both damaged. We've both been hurt the most by people who were supposed to love us.*

He felt ... not sure what, exactly. His conflicting emotions confused him. He had decided after Kimberly he was done with relationships. It wasn't worth putting his heart out there only to get it broken.

But Elle made him think about trying again. He was having trouble keeping to his rule about no relationships when she was everything he had ever wanted in a woman–sweet, smart, sexy.

He pulled her back to him. Leaning down, he found her lips with his. They were soft and yielding, opening to him. He realized they'd started something here, something he wanted to pursue. Yes, she was technically still married. But Ryan decided he didn't care. He wanted her. *Hell, I need her,* he finally admitted to himself. Maybe it was time to let someone in again.

Ryan kissed her harder, his hands tangled in her hair. He then slowly moved them over her shoulders and down her back, pulling her closer against him. He pulled back from her lips just enough to murmur, "If this isn't what you want, tell me and I'll stop."

He kissed her again, deeper. His tongue found hers, hot and yearning. Pulling away again slightly, he caressed her cheek. He slowly and gently brushed his thumb over her lips where he'd kissed them. "If I'm not what you want, tell me and I'll stop. But tell me now. Because otherwise, I'm not going to stop," he said.

"This is what I want," Elle breathed out. "You are what I want."

Hearing Elle say those words, Ryan came undone. Words he hadn't heard in so long. He leaned down to lift her up. She wrapped her legs around him, her lips still on his, and he turned, heading for his bedroom. *No interruptions this time,* he thought, *please.*

If I only get one night with Elle, I'm going to make it memorable. Ryan carried her to his bed. No thinking about the future, no what-ifs. He deserved this—hell, they both deserved this. At least one night together. They'd been through so much. So much shit from people in their lives who were supposed to love them the most but treated them the worst.

Chapter Fifteen

L isa slammed the door of her Mercedes. *Fucking asshole,* she thought to herself, wondering for the tenth time that night why she was bothering to try dating again. *Well,* she thought, glancing at her watch, *now what?* She had optimistically hired a babysitter until ten, and it was just now eight o'clock.

Hell, I'm not going home yet. I'll just go by Jack's, she decided, *have a couple beers and maybe play some pool. I deserve a mommy break. It's been a long week already, and it was only Wednesday.*

"Hey Lisa, the usual?" Jack asked as she came in, sitting down on a rickety stool at the nearly empty bar.

"Hell yes!" Lisa exclaimed, blowing him a kiss. "Thank you, honey. And keep 'em coming." She checked her phone while Jack got her beer, then took a long drink. *Good. Nothing from the babysitter.* She could relax and try not to dwell on another disastrous date.

Jesus, the fucking men in this town weren't even men. *Where did all the cowboys go?* She was sick of corporate types with their perfect hair, teeth, and nails. She'd give anything for a tall, dark, and handsome man. Maybe in Wranglers with a Stetson. Who drove a truck, for fuck's sake. Not a damn Beemer or Mercedes. A little voice reminded her she drove a Mercedes. *Yeah, well, I'm a woman. And I've earned that fucking AMG.* But seriously. Screw Scottsdale, maybe she needed to move to Texas. Or Montana.

"Anyone sitting here?"

Lisa turned, ready to tell the stranger to fuck off, and gaped instead. *Jesus. Prayers do get answered.* Was she dreaming? Already drunk? She'd had two vodka sodas with dinner–the only way she got through the date.

"Sorry," the stranger said, "I didn't mean to startle you."

Lisa swallowed. She was never at a loss for words. Ever.

"Yeah, whatever," she finally choked out. She waved at the barstool next to her, picking up her beer to take a long swallow.

"I'm Conor," the stranger said. "Conor Hayes."

"Good for you," Lisa replied, finally finding her voice. She took another long pull on her beer.

Conor smiled, sitting down. "Can I buy you another beer?"

"I'm perfectly capable of buying my own beer, thanks," Lisa replied tartly, though her throat was dry and she was having trouble making eye contact.

Good Lord almighty, he was gorgeous. Tall, dark, and handsome didn't even begin to describe him. He had brown hair, piercing blue eyes and, fuck, he was wearing jeans, boots, and a Stetson. Had she been granted three wishes that morning?

She glanced at his left hand. No ring, which surprised her. He was definitely in his late forties. Suntanned skin and a few wrinkles around his eyes that only made him sexier. *A lot of men don't wear a ring,* she reminded herself. He was probably married. She tried to decide if she cared. *Nope. Not tonight.*

"Whatever you have cold in a bottle is fine," Conor told Jack. "Thanks. And one for the lady." He nodded toward Lisa, who scowled at him.

Christ, Lisa thought. He didn't order a martini like her stupid date–he actually ordered a beer. And wasn't even picky about it. *I'm going to fuck this man tonight. Maybe in his truck. Oh sweet Jesus, please let him have a truck.* All her fantasies were coming true. She was suddenly having trouble breathing. It had been too long.

It's been three whole weeks, a voice in her head reminded her.

Yeah, exactly, too damn long. And that had been George. Her ex-husband was actually good at one thing. And only one thing.

Jack set a beer down in front of Conor and another in front of Lisa with a playful warning. "Play nice, Lisa." Then he winked at Conor. "Careful of that one. She'll eat you up and spit you out."

"Oh really?" Conor took a drink of his beer and turned to Lisa. "Well, I'm not scared," he said, looking her straight in the eyes.

"No? Well, you should be," Lisa replied, though she was sure her cheeks were pink.

Conor laughed. "Hot date tonight?" he asked, looking her over.

"There was not one fucking thing that was hot about my date," Lisa replied, making a point of slowly looking him over from head to toe. "Pretty much the opposite of what I'm looking at right now." She raised an eyebrow at him.

Conor blinked. "Sorry to hear that," he replied.

"So, how long are you in town for this time, Conor?" Jack asked.

Lisa glanced at Jack and then back at Conor. *Well, damn. He's not from around here.* Though she should have realized it by his appearance. Not a lot of cowboys in downtown Scottsdale. Sadly.

"I head back to the ranch in the morning," Conor replied to Jack, finishing his first beer. "Horse sale took longer today than I anticipated." He explained to Lisa, "I own the Black Diamond Ranch out between Casa Grande and Tucson. It's a cattle ranch. I had two older horses that are no longer able to work the ranch, so we sold them to a local ranch here in Scottsdale that works with kids with disabilities."

"Mm, that's cool," Lisa said, pushing aside her empty beer and reaching for the fresh one. "So, not playing cowboy, but an actual cowboy?"

"Well now, I guess I am," Conor drawled with a little smirk and a tip of his Stetson. "Ma'am."

Lisa rolled her eyes. Sarcastic asshole. Sexy, sarcastic asshole. Damn. She felt a little flushed.

"What about you? It's Lisa, right?" Conor asked. "What do you do?"

Lisa looked at him without answering right away. She took a drink of her beer.

"Look. I don't want to chat about innocuous bullshit. How about you tell me something interesting about yourself instead? Then I'll decide if I'm interested enough to tell you about myself."

Conor laughed. "You mean, more interesting than being an actual cowboy?" he asked with a twinkle in his eyes.

"Yes," Lisa replied. She'd asked her earlier date the same question and he had seemed to think that meant she wanted to know all about his golf handicap. Wrong answer. *Let's see if Conor can do better.*

"Well," Conor replied, "let's see. I have five older sisters. I used to rodeo and bull ride, and I'm also a pilot. I have my private pilot license."

"Did you say five older sisters?" Lisa asked in surprise, though the fact that he was a pilot also registered in her brain. "Your folks must have really wanted a boy."

"Apparently," Conor replied with another wink.

"But you are so ..." Lisa paused, waving her hand at him. "So, um, well, masculine. I would never have guessed that you grew up with five older sisters."

"Well, thank you, ma'am." Conor smiled. "Let's just say that my father was a very influential and masculine male role model."

I bet he was, Lisa thought, breaking away from his piercing blue eyes and taking another sip of her beer. Damn, he had a sexy mouth. She wanted to know what it tasted like.

"And my sisters are all tomboys. We all grew up on the ranch. When you have six kids, you put 'em to work young. Riding, roping, wrangling, cleaning stalls and, well, just generally doing whatever needs doing. It used to be a much bigger production than it is now. Now that my folks have both passed."

Lisa nodded. Something they had in common.

"So, did I pass the test?" Conor asked with a grin.

Lisa shrugged nonchalantly. God, that smile was making her flustered. She was normally in control, never giving a fuck what anyone thought. She looked at Conor. She gave a fuck what he thought. Was he as attracted to her as she was to him? Did he want to kiss her as much as she wanted to kiss him?

"All right, yes, I'm Lisa," she began. "I've been divorced for four years, have two kids, a boy and a girl, eight and ten. I run a flight charter service out of the Southwest Jet Center here in Scottsdale. Similar story to yours, I guess. My parents built a pretty big company then they were both killed in a car accident six years ago. After that, I sold a big chunk of the company. My younger brother wasn't in a position to help out at the time, and it was way more than I could handle with two babies. So basically, my life is work and kids and the occasional terrible Tinder date." She let out a small, self-deprecating laugh.

"So yeah, that's the sixty-second biography, but the most important thing about me is that I don't play any fucking games. I don't have time in my life for that. I'll always tell you exactly what I want." She deliberately looked at his lips. *And I definitely want you.*

"Want to dance?" Conor asked suddenly as a slow George Strait song came on the jukebox.

"What? Here? No." Lisa frowned, shaking her head. "I mean, where?" Jack's place had a few scattered tables and a pool table. Definitely no dance floor. People came here to drink, not dance.

Conor stood up, set his Stetson on the bar, and took her by the arm. "Right here," he said as he pulled her up from the barstool. He took her hand in his and held it firmly against his chest. His other arm went around her waist, pulling her close against him.

Holy shit, he feels good, Lisa thought as they moved together slowly to the music. Tall, with hard muscles and strong arms. Her earlier date had looked decent in his Tinder profile but was soft and lacking in person, not to mention boring. Nope. This right here was what she wanted. A real fucking man.

She looked into Conor's eyes, finding a little tease in them and a half smile on his face. She raised an eyebrow at him, then narrowed her eyes. "What's funny?"

"I never expected to walk into this bar and meet ..." Conor paused. "Well, meet you."

He let go of her hand and moved his hand behind her neck, reaching under her hair, pulling her to him. "But I am damn glad I did," he added softly. He leaned in and kissed her, his lips on hers strong and demanding.

Lisa pulled away suddenly. "Do you drive a truck?"

Conor laughed. "Yes. I do," he answered. "Why?"

"No reason," Lisa replied. This time she reached for him, finding his lips and running her fingers through his hair. It was a little longer than she'd thought it might be when it was under his Stetson. The silky strands felt so good in her hands. *Hell yes,* she thought. And thank God. She would have been so disappointed if he drove a sports car or an SUV.

This man has no idea how lucky he's going to get tonight, she thought, moving her hands over his shoulders and down his arms. She loved the feel of his muscles through his denim shirt.

What the hell, why not? I want this man. Tonight. Right now. She'd been divorced four years now and rarely allowed herself to date. Partly because of her kids and partly because the dating pool sucked. She slept with George occasionally because he was convenient. And safe, she admitted to herself.

But tonight she didn't want safe. She wanted dangerous. She wanted this handsome stranger. *Not exactly a stranger anymore,* she thought as her mouth explored his. No strings attached. No expectations about the future. No lame small talk. Just sex. Lisa was certain he would be good. He definitely knew how to kiss. How to touch her.

She was already hot for him. His kisses set her on fire, a slow burn running through her as he touched her skin.

"Your place or mine?" Conor breathed into her ear.

"Definitely your place," Lisa replied, breathily. *If we make it that far*. Finally, a man who knew how to take charge. A man she had waited a long time to find. Finally, a man who knew how to set her on fire. And the fire was raging.

Chapter Sixteen

The song ended and Conor wondered how they had gone from zero to sixty so fast. If this was what she wanted, then he wanted it, too. He was already having trouble controlling his hands, wanting to move the strap of her dress aside and kiss her neck down to her full breasts. He wanted his mouth all over her.

Actually, there was little doubt about how much he wanted her. Their bodies pressed hard together even though they weren't dancing anymore.

Conor pulled away enough to turn toward the bar. He never took his arm off her back, keeping her against him. Reaching in his pocket, he grabbed some money and laid it on the bar. "Thanks, Jack," he said, picking up his hat and putting it back on his head.

"Let's go," he commanded Lisa, guiding her toward the door.

Outside, Conor led Lisa around the building and across the parking lot to his truck, which was parked out back with the empty horse trailer behind it, still holding her tight to his side and trying to control himself. *Christ. Is this actually happening?* Where had this woman come from? He was still waiting for the punchline.

When they got to his truck, he reached around her, turning her in his arms and pushing her, none too gently, her back now against the door of his black Chevy pickup. He pressed himself hard against her with one hand wrapped up in her hair, pulling it back to force her face up toward his. Then he kissed her with a passion he hadn't felt in a long damn time.

"I'm at a hotel. The, um, Hilton over on Princess," Conor managed to mumble a few minutes later, kissing her neck, her ear, and moving down her throat as her hands tangled in his hair.

"I don't care," Lisa responded, breathing hard, her hands pulling up his shirt and running around his waist, then back to his chest. She unbuttoned his shirt as she kissed him. "We don't need a hotel. I want you now."

Conor grinned again. He was pretty sure whatever Lisa wanted, she got. And he was damn happy she wanted him. He continued down her throat, trailing kisses as he explored, holding his hat on his head with one hand and Lisa firmly against his truck with the other. So, she didn't care, huh? What did she want, to have sex here, behind the bar in the parking lot, up against his truck? Hell, he probably could. No, he definitely could, but he wasn't looking to get arrested tonight.

He pulled her away from the truck, wrenching the door open. Breathing hard, he said, "Get in." Without waiting for her to react, he reached his hands around her slim waist and lifted her into the truck, setting her on the seat. He pushed the seat control button down, tossing his Stetson on the dash as the seat lowered backward. Then he climbed into the truck and lowered himself on top of her, slamming the door behind him.

"I DON'T THINK I've done that since I was in high school," Conor said, still trying to catch his breath and calm his heartbeat. He'd managed to get his jeans back on and was pinned between Lisa and the truck's console, trying not to crush her as he looked around trying to locate his shirt.

"What? Had sex?" Lisa teased, grinning at him as she straightened her dress.

"Ha ha. Very funny. No ... had sex in my truck," Conor replied. "Can we please do it somewhere else next time? Like a couch or a bed? Something comfortable? I'm too old for this shit, though it was pretty damn incredible." He leaned over and kissed her again. "Do you see my shirt?"

"Um, I think it's behind the seat," Lisa replied as she sat up, flipping down the visor to check her reflection.

"Found it," Conor said, rescuing his crumpled shirt from the floor of the back seat and shaking out the wrinkles.

Lisa reached for the door handle.

"Wait," Conor said, reaching to stop her, putting his hand on hers. "Are you leaving?"

"Why, do you want to do it again?" Lisa asked as she raised an eyebrow, grinning.

"Yes. Yes, definitely. Just not in the damn truck," Conor said with a smile.

Lisa looked at her watch. "I have to go, but yes. Next time we can do it in a bed, old man," she replied. Then she opened the door and hopped out, grabbing her purse off the floorboard.

"Hey, wait," Conor said, trying to scramble out of the seat and reaching for one of his boots, laying discarded on the floor, while trying to pull the other on. He didn't even remember kicking them off. "How do I get a hold of you? I want your number. Hell, I don't even know your last name."

"If it's meant to be, you'll find me again," Lisa said, blowing him a kiss as she ran barefoot across the parking lot to her car, carrying her boots.

Conor stared after her. He slowly got out of the truck, got his other boot on and his hat back on his head, then shut the door and leaned against it. He exhaled a deep breath and watched her car roar out of the parking lot. Damn.

Wow. He was still stunned. In the span of about an hour, he'd met the woman of his dreams, danced with her, kissed her, and had sex with her. In his damn truck, no less. *Hell,* he thought, *if it's the last thing I do, I'm gonna find you. And then I'm never going to let you run away again.*

In fact, Conor promised himself, *I'm gonna marry that woman.*

"You're awfully quiet this morning, Boss," Riley said.

Conor shrugged, taking a swig of coffee from his travel mug and setting it back in the cup holder, focusing on the highway before him. Riley Clarke was his foreman and his oldest friend. They'd grown up together on the ranch, back when Riley's old man had been the ranch foreman.

"I know you're worried about the sale coming up," Riley said, "but it's gonna work out."

Conor nodded, but he wasn't thinking about the upcoming cattle sale or the ranch. He'd lain awake most of the night with thoughts of Lisa. He could hardly believe what had happened between them. Christ, he'd woken up this morning wondering if it had been a dream. That woman was a four-alarm fire. She was unlike anyone he'd met lately. He got a little warm remembering the things they had done in his truck last night.

This truck, he thought, glancing at his passenger seat. Unfortunately, now Riley sat there, his six-foot-six, two-hundred-and-eighty-pound frame filling the seat, drinking coffee, and eating a bagel he'd snagged from the hotel breakfast bar.

"What did you end up doing last night, Boss?" Riley asked. "I sat at the hotel lobby bar having a few beers after dinner. Never saw you come in."

"Mind your own business," Conor said with a half smile.

"Oh shit!" Riley exclaimed. "What's her name? I know that look. And damn, 'bout time you moved on from Chloe."

Fucking Chloe. She'd broken his heart and his bank account. It had been over a year, and he was still recovering from the pain of catching her cheating with one of his wranglers in the barn. He'd invested way too much time and money in that relationship. Flying her to Dallas for shopping trips, Vegas for weekend getaways that cost him thousands. He'd even bought her a Jeep. Christ, he must have been out of his mind.

Looking back, he recognized that he had been over-compensating. He hadn't spent enough time or money on Maggie, but he went way too far with Chloe. It had been a totally one-sided relationship, he realized now. Though the sex had been pretty damn good. But it was nothing compared to last night with Lisa.

Damn, that was one cool lady. But spicy. Definitely spicy. She had looked so good, her long dark hair falling in soft curls down her back, lively dark eyes mocking him, full lips painted with red lipstick. *Definitely sexy, too.*

Conor remembered thinking she was a little overdressed for Jack's dive bar. She had been wearing a low-cut black dress that ended high on her thighs, showing off long, shapely legs ending in black boots. Nice boots. He didn't see a lot of women in downtown Scottsdale wearing cowboy boots, unless they were playing dress-up when the rodeo was in town.

He had understood enough to know that she was a woman who needed to be kissed properly, maybe even a little roughly. He recalled her passion as she had kissed him back. Bold and searching. So hot. He had been right–there was nothing timid about that woman.

"Her name is: none of your business," Conor replied with a grin, wondering again how he was going to track Lisa down. There was no way in hell he would let that one get away.

Conor had let one incredible woman get away years ago. He'd put the ranch first and Maggie second for years until she finally gave up and let him go. One of the biggest regrets of his life. She was now happily married to some pediatrician in Phoenix and had a couple of kids.

That should have been us. Always the damn ranch. Maybe it was time to let it go. His sisters were all married now, except Cari, with families of their own and pursuing their own careers. They all still had a vested interest, but he'd been running the show for almost twenty years now. Hell, his oldest sister, Cate, was talking about retiring. Twenty years was a long time–he might be ready for something different in his life.

An image of Lisa flashed in his mind. She'd been on top of him in the truck last night, skirt shoved up to her waist, her arms around him, calling out his name over and over. Damn. *That was one of the hottest nights of my life,* he thought, adjusting his jeans.

Maybe Jack would know how to get a hold of Lisa. *Wait,* Conor remembered suddenly, *Southwest Jet Center!* She'd told him how to find her. He smiled. It was almost like she planned it.

As they got closer to the ranch, he thought, *gonna dump the trailer, drop off Riley and head back to Scottsdale.* Then he remembered the meeting with the auction house this afternoon. Fuck. He sighed. *Tomorrow is Friday–I'll go then. If I can wait that long.*

Chapter Seventeen

"How'd your date go last night?" Ryan asked, leaning on the door of Lisa's office.

"Fucking terrible," Lisa said with a big smile.

"Really? Cuz you look unusually happy," Ryan replied, raising an eyebrow.

"Oh, I am. But it wasn't from my Tinder date."

"Care to elaborate?" Her brother looked confused.

"Do you really want to know that I met a super-hot cowboy at Jack's last night and then had sex with him in his truck?" Lisa asked, grinning behind her coffee mug.

"Jesus Christ, sis," Ryan said, covering his ears with his hands. "Stop! For fuck's sake." Then he put his hands down with a scowl. "Oh, you're joking. Very funny."

Lisa smiled.

"Wait, you are joking, aren't you?" Ryan asked slowly, raising an eyebrow.

Lisa shrugged. "Maybe."

Ryan shook his head, making gagging noises.

"What about you?" Lisa asked. "I heard you out in the shop. Were you actually singing along with the radio?"

"Don't be jealous that I sing better than you," Ryan said.

She knew when her brother was deliberately avoiding her real question.

Lisa narrowed her eyes. "Speaking of unusually happy. What's going on with you? Elle? Did you ask her out?"

"Not exactly," Ryan replied slowly, not making eye contact.

"What does that mean?" Lisa asked.

"Elle, well, she's been through some hell herself," Ryan explained, finally meeting her gaze. "I ran into her in the gym parking lot the other day and this asshole was hassling her."

"What?" This surprised Lisa. "Who?"

"Her ex. She's going through a pretty nasty divorce right now and—"

"What? She's fucking married?" Lisa exclaimed, standing up and slamming her hands down on the top of the desk. "What the hell are you thinking? A husband? What if he—"

"Sis, wait," Ryan said, coming over to Lisa and putting his hands on her shoulders. "You don't understand what she's been through. Remember Tate?"

Lisa sat back down in her office chair with a sigh. "Like I could ever forget. Shit. That bad?" she asked.

"Worse. She married the guy. Todd." Ryan leaned against her desk. "Guy is a piece of work. Lied, cheated, treated her like shit and took a bunch of her money from a trust from her grandfather. It's a big mess."

"Damn," Lisa said. "So she's divorcing this guy ... Todd?"

"Yeah, trying to. Apparently, they had a really big fight and he beat her up pretty good. She left him after that and spent two weeks in a hotel before moving into an Airbnb," Ryan explained.

"Holy shit. What an asshole," Lisa replied, shaking her head.

"I know," Ryan agreed. "So yeah, she's just trying to get the divorce finalized so she can get him out of her life for good."

"Hope she has a really good attorney," Lisa said wryly, remembering Tate and the hell he'd put her through. Thank God she hadn't married him. He'd managed to fool her long enough to get her bank account information and clean out her checking account, along with cash she'd had in a safe and some of her mother's jewelry. She was still pissed off about it.

Getting the cops involved and hiring a lawyer had been a mistake. She should have just let him go and moved on. But she'd been so angry at the time. After he was released on bail, he stalked her for the next six months, making threats and harassing her.

Six months of restraining orders, constantly looking over her shoulder, and trips to the police station before the cops finally caught him in her garage with a baseball bat waiting for her. Luckily, her neighbor had seen him break a window and climb into the garage and called the cops. Turned out, she had been far from his only victim.

She shuddered. After Tate had been released, he'd followed her to Jack's and attacked her in the back parking lot. Luckily, Ryan had found them and beat the shit out of Tate. Lisa had no remorse for how that had turned out for Tate. Asshole got everything he deserved. Though she did still harbor a lot of guilt about how that had turned out for Ryan.

"So, you haven't told her anything about Candi or your prison time yet?" Lisa asked.

Ryan shook his head. "Not yet, but she's coming over for dinner tonight and we're going to talk more," he replied.

"Well, maybe she's been through enough shit herself that when you explain everything you went through, she'll understand," Lisa said, squeezing Ryan's hand.

"I hope so," Ryan said, nodding slowly. "I really hope so."

"Shit, you've already fallen for her, haven't you?" Lisa accused, blowing out a sigh.

Ryan shrugged.

"Well, I hope it goes well, I really do," Lisa said, praying fervently that it did. She didn't want Ryan sliding back to that dark place again.

"But in the meantime, why don't you get some fucking work done?" She pointed toward the hangar.

"Yes, boss," Ryan replied with a grin and a little salute. "On it."

Lisa watched him walk out of her office while thinking about the crazy week the Daley siblings were having. She put her chin on her hands. Lord knows they deserved some fucking happiness eventually, she just worried that wasn't ever going to be in the cards for them. Were happy days in their future or was it all about to blow up in their faces again?

MARCH 2013

"Not this time, Candi. It's over," Ryan said angrily, grabbing a few tee shirts and haphazardly packing them in a duffel he'd tossed on their bed.

"But I showed you the test," Candi protested, grabbing Ryan's arm. "I really am pregnant again."

"I know. I believe you. But I told you already," Ryan replied coldly, shaking her hand off. "I will never turn my back on my child, but you and I are done. I cannot go through this with you anymore. I need my life back."

"What are you talking about? This is our life, Ryan!" Candi cried, trying to grab his arm again.

"No. This is over. This life you're talking about is a joke. You haven't been home before two a.m. in weeks," Ryan said harshly, shaking her off again. "I don't know what you're doing, who you're doing it with, where you're going. I'm over all of it."

"But it's going to be different now," Candi begged. "I'm going to be different. I promise, baby."

"It's not different. Jesus! You're pregnant again and you're still partying. You're still doing coke and drinking, aren't you?" Ryan

seethed with rage. "Deny it," he dared, grabbing her by the arms. "You can't, can you?"

"I stopped, Ryan, I stopped. I promise!" Candi wailed.

"I'm done listening to your promises. It's been almost three years, Candi," Ryan said, raising his voice as he picked up his duffel and headed out of their bedroom. "Three fucking years of this bullshit. You are never going to change, and I cannot take any more of this game with you."

"But it's not a game," Candi sobbed, following him. "I know I've made mistakes before, but this is different. Please Ryan. Don't leave! Where are you going?"

"I just need to get out of here," Ryan replied, opening the garage door, walking to his truck, and throwing his duffel in the back. "I need to get away from you."

"The fuck you do! You're not going anywhere, Ryan!" Candi yelled, following him into the garage. "No!"

"Stop," Ryan said, anger consuming him as he pushed her back, away from his truck. "Go back in the house."

"No, I will not!" Candi yelled, trying to grab his keys out of his hand. "Stop. You can't leave me! I won't let you!"

Ryan turned, shaking her off harder and getting in the driver's seat, slamming the door. Candi raced around the truck and opened the passenger door, climbing in.

"You're not going anywhere without me," Candi yelled, slamming the passenger door closed.

"No," Ryan said, raising his voice, trying to reach around her for the door handle. "Get the fuck out of my truck. We're over."

"No! Never!" Candi screamed, pushing his hands away and slapping him on the side of the head with both hands, over and over. "Never!"

"Jesus, Candi, stop!" Ryan exclaimed, grabbing her wrists, pushing her back to the passenger side roughly. "Fine. Whatever. I'm still leaving. I'm done fighting with you."

"You always were a quitter. You're pathetic. I honestly don't know

why I wasted so much time on you anyway," Candi said contemptu-
ously, flopping back in the passenger seat and glaring at Ryan.

"Stop talking," Ryan said through gritted teeth, pulling out of the
driveway and heading down the side street toward the highway.

"No! I won't. You want to know what I've been doing and who
I've been doing it with, well then I'll tell you," Candi replied hotly.
"I met someone. Someone who knows how to treat a woman. I've
been fucking him. He's way better in bed than you've ever been. He
knows how to make a woman scream. In fact, Ryan, this baby probably isn't even yours, so I guess it really doesn't fucking matter what
you do. If you want it to be over so damn bad, then that's fine
with me!"

Ryan made it to the highway. The more Candi talked, the faster he
drove. He was trying to drown out her scathing voice and the horrible
things she was saying by pushing the Chevy's engine as hard as he
could. Maybe, if he drove fast enough, he could outrun her cruelty.

"Everything was always about you. Jesus, I'm actually fine with us
being over. I hate you, Ryan! I hate you! I want a divorce and I never
want to see you again. And don't even think about ever seeing this
baby, because that's never going to happen," Candi said, raising her
voice again. "Hey asshole! Are you listening to me?"

Ryan ignored her, focusing on the highway and the noise of the
engine. He could almost block her out. There was a dark pressure in
his head, like he was traveling down a black tunnel. The only thing he
could see was the road in front of him. The only thing he could hear
was the Chevy's motor.

"Hey, where are we going?" Ryan barely registered Candi yelling.
"Stop! I said, stop!"

Candi couldn't reach him in this tunnel. In fact, if he went far
enough back, back in time to before he met her, before the drugs and
the games and the lies, he could escape. Flee this life before it turned
bad. He was in a race to avoid the words coming out of her mouth. He
just needed to drive faster, and he could get away.

"Ryan!" Candi screamed, punching him in the arm, trying to hit

him in the head, slapping him and then grabbing the steering wheel.
"Turn this fucking truck around right now! I want to–"

Ryan jerked the wheel back out of her hands, but he felt the Chevy turning and skidding. He was going too fast and he couldn't control it. The wheel shook in his hands. He broke out of the dark tunnel in his head, seeing the concrete embankment directly ahead of them and slamming on his brakes.

"Ryan! Jesus! No!" Candi screamed. Then everything went black.

Chapter Eighteen

Em, get a drink with me tonight? Lisa texted her friend, restlessly walking around her office. Thoughts of Conor and the night before were making it hard to focus on her work.

Jack's @ 7 came the reply.

Lisa texted back a thumbs-up emoji, sitting back down at her desk. Okay. Time to concentrate. The Citation jet was due for its twenty-four-month scheduled maintenance and the King 200 was due for its biannual. She needed to make sure all the paperwork was in order for Ryan. *You can daydream about Conor later,* she told herself.

"WAIT. What? Let me get this straight. You did what? Here? How? And with who? A cowboy? No way," Emma blurted out in a rush, her mouth hanging open in shock. She had been flying for Lisa for the last four years and they had become good friends. Daley Charters had gone through several other pilots over the years, each claiming Lisa was impossible to work for. But after twenty years in the air force, Emma Larsson thought Lisa was a dream boss. She loved flying for Daley Charters.

"Can you maybe say all of that a little louder please? For fuck's sake," Lisa replied, playfully smacking Emma on the shoulder.

"Sorry," Emma replied quieter, her blue eyes still wide. "Jesus, just when I think you'll never shock me again, you do. Way to step up your game." She'd been single for two years now after a nasty divorce and lived vicariously through Lisa's crazy dating life. Her stories never failed to provide entertainment.

"Well, I didn't plan it, but yeah, that happened," Lisa said, grinning. She took a drink of her beer. "Maybe the best sex I've ever had in my life."

Emma sighed. "Figures. You go on a shitty Tinder date and end up meeting a hot cowboy and I go on a shitty Tinder date and end up crying in my pillow. Does he have a brother?"

"Five sisters." Lisa shook her head. "No brothers."

"Damn. Five sisters, huh? Just my luck," Emma said, brushing her red hair out of her eyes. "I definitely need another beer. Shit. Story of my life."

"Oh stop," Lisa said. "There's someone out there for you. Maybe Conor has a hot friend."

"Yeah, I'm going to be forty-five next week, and all I've got to show for it is one cheating ex-husband," Emma replied, frowning into her beer and slouching on the bar.

"You've gone on two dates in six months, Em," Lisa said. "What do you expect? You've got to put yourself out there more. Prince Charming isn't going to just come knocking on your door. Besides, you know it's because you're just too badass for all these Scottsdale pussies. They show up to a date in a Beemer and you show up in leathers riding a motorcycle. Add in being a badass pilot. They just can't fucking compete."

"True. I don't know. Maybe it's time to sell the bike," Emma replied, shrugging.

"What? Don't you dare!" Lisa exclaimed. "Don't you dare go changing. It's what I love about you. You don't fit into society's neat little box of how a woman is supposed to behave. Fuck that. We live life on our own terms."

"Yeah, I think we kicked the door to that box down a long time ago," Emma agreed with a grin. She'd followed in her father's footsteps, getting a rare spot at the Air Force Academy. She'd graduated with honors and went on to be one of only a handful of women trained to fly some of the elite fighter aircraft. So yeah, she'd been kicking doors down for a long time.

"Speaking of people who live life on their own terms, how is your brother?" Lisa asked.

"He's good, I guess," Emma replied, looking over at Lisa and raising an eyebrow. "Raif is back in Arizona." Lisa had an affair with her brother years ago that had not ended well. Rafael had just gotten out of the army and had been restless. After about a month of seeing Lisa, he'd suddenly left one morning. A week later he sent both Lisa and Emma a text saying he was on his way to Croatia to work a security job and then basically disappeared, showing up every few years to crash on Emma's couch for a few days before taking off again.

"Huh, that's nice. I only wish him well, you know. We were over a long time ago. Definitely not going back down that road. Besides, I found me a hot cowboy." Lisa winked. "Hey, maybe there's a meet-a-hot-cowboy app," she added with a laugh.

"Or a hot motorcycle dude," Emma replied, looking up with a grin. "So, are you going to see the hot cowboy again? Conor?"

Lisa shrugged. "No idea. I definitely dropped some hints. Guess we'll see if he tries to track me down. I mean, I know the name of his ranch, and Jack could probably tell me how to find him, but I'd much rather he come looking for me, you know?"

"If I had to put money on it, I'd say the odds are in your favor," Emma mused. "Sex like that will definitely have a man coming back for more. Maybe that's what I need to do. On my next date, I'm just gonna channel you. Play the what-would-Lisa-do game."

Lisa laughed. "Yes! I love it, Em! That's exactly what you need to do. Cheers."

"Cheers," Emma replied, tipping her beer bottle at Lisa's, smiling and shaking her head. Like she'd ever have the balls to follow through on that. She was fierce in her career, but she'd never had much luck with men. Most of them were intimidated by a woman who flew jets and rode motorcycles. She sighed. She could go for a hot cowboy right about now.

Chapter Nineteen

March 2013

Ryan moaned, trying to open his eyes. Every movement was a painful, throbbing struggle. His body was on fire. Every nerve ending screamed at him as he tried to move.

"Ryan, can you hear me? Lie still, okay? Don't try to move," Lisa said from beside him, gently holding his bruised hand.

Ryan nodded and tried to speak, but all that came out was a croak. He managed to get his right eye open. Everything was blurry. He cleared his throat as best he could and tried again. "What happened? Where am I?"

"Don't try to talk, little brother," Lisa said softly. "Just listen."

Ryan nodded, though it was almost impossible. Something around his neck forced his head to stay in one position.

"You were in an accident," Lisa explained. "You're going to be okay, but you're pretty messed up. Don't try to move. You're going to need surgery on your neck. Do you remember what happened?"

Ryan pressed his eyelids shut as it all came rushing back. The fight with Candi at the house. In his truck. More fighting. Candi hitting him and grabbing the steering wheel. Oh fuck. No. He opened his right eye *again, this time managing to get the left one open a little too.* "Yes. Kind of. Candi and I were fighting. She was hitting me. Then I couldn't stop. I couldn't make the truck stop."

"You're going to be okay. But Ryan ... it's Candi," Lisa said, her voice thick with tears. "She's messed up. Pretty bad. She's in surgery right now."

Ryan blinked several times. Everything was still blurry. The pounding in his head made it hard to hear what Lisa was saying. He couldn't process anything, images flooding into his mind—nothing made sense. He closed his eyes again. "She's pregnant. Tell the doctors she's pregnant," he said before slipping back into the darkness.

Chapter Twenty

Elle sat at her desk, looking out the window. She picked up her coffee mug and took a sip. She'd hoped to see Ryan before now but had just signed a new client and had been busy all week getting their initial design plan done. The client would be traveling while their house was being worked on, so she had to meet with them as much as possible while they were still in town. But Ryan had invited her over for dinner at his house tonight and it was all she could think about, unable to focus on her new project.

She loved their flirty texts all week. He was subtly funny and his humor never failed to bring a smile to her face.

Elle felt a little flustered recalling everything they had done during their night together and how he'd made her feel. Sex with Ryan was like nothing she had ever experienced before. He was strong yet gentle. She hadn't been able to stop thinking about the way he kissed her and touched her, the way his body felt against hers. A perfect balance between rough and soft.

Elle blushed. *Damn. All I can think about is ripping his clothes off.*

She glanced at her watch. Three more hours. She set her coffee mug down with a long sigh. She couldn't wait to be back in his arms. But first, she had to get through the rest of this paperwork.

Chapter Twenty-One

November 2013

Ryan let out a long sigh, looking at his phone again. Lisa was late. "Hey Jack, guess I'll have another beer," he said.

"It's not like Lisa to be late. No word from her?" Jack asked, setting a fresh beer down on the bar in front of Ryan. "No. Nothing. I left the hangar this afternoon around five thirty. Had to wait for Emma to bring the G550 back and then ran home to shower and change. Lisa left around five and said to meet her here at six thirty." Ryan glanced at his phone again. 6:46.

Ryan took a drink of his beer. He knew why she wanted to meet. She had another lecture prepared, he was sure of it. He was so sick of it, yet he was more than a little surprised she was late to deliver said lecture. It had been six months since Candi OD'd. Six months of hell. Trying to recover from the accident. Trying to recover from her death. His body had healed, but he knew his heart would take a lot longer.

Ryan knew he deserved a lecture. He'd pushed everyone away, his parents, his sister, his friends. No one understood the darkness he was feeling inside. He had so much guilt over Candi's death and the loss of another baby. Another baby that would never be born. Because of him.

After the accident, Candi had to have her spleen removed. She'd also suffered a broken pelvis and had lost the baby, along with a broken arm and numerous stitches in her forehead and cheek. They'd both had to spend several weeks in the hospital recovering. Afterward, he didn't have the heart to leave her. Candi had been beyond devastated losing a second baby. She was a ghost of her former self. Sleeping most of the day and waking up screaming in the night from nightmares.

Ryan had been at work one afternoon when Candi's mom had called him. Val had gone over to the house to see how Candi was doing and found her unconscious. She'd overdosed on pain pills. Val had called an ambulance, but Candi had died on the way to the hospital.

He took another drink of his beer. At least her suffering was over. He wished his was. He'd endured so much loss he wasn't sure how he was even functioning. Ryan set his beer down, contemplating finding something stronger.

He shook his head. No. No way was he going back down that road. He'd die first.

"Hey Jack, there's some sort of ruckus going on in the back parking lot."

Ryan looked over to see Chris, one of Jack's regulars, coming in the door.

"What sort of ruckus?" Ryan asked, immediately knowing it had to be Lisa. What the hell was she getting herself involved in now? For fuck's sake. "Never mind. I'll go investigate. Someone probably cut Lisa off in traffic and she's giving them hell."

Ryan went out the back door, looking around the almost empty parking lot, frowning. He stood there for a moment, listening. He saw a parked truck in the back of the lot and what looked like Lisa's Audi. Closing the door behind him, he headed across the parking lot. Might as well check it out.

"What the fuck?!" Ryan exclaimed as he came around the back of the lifted Chevy pickup. He didn't quite understand what he was seeing. "Tate? Is that you? What the hell are you doing?"

Tate turned around, glaring up at Ryan. "Go away. This is between me and Lisa. We have some business to handle."

"The hell I will," Ryan replied, pushing Tate out of the way to see Lisa lying on the ground, her nose bloody and her right eye almost swollen shut.

"What did you do?" he ground out, reaching for Tate's collar. He grabbed the other man with both hands and picked him up off his feet. It looked like Lisa had given as good as she'd gotten. Tate had a bloody nose and a split lip. "What the fuck?" he asked again.

"Ryan," Lisa moaned, trying to sit up.

"Stay there, sis," Ryan commanded. "I'm handling this."

"I don't want to fight you, Ryan, but I will. My beef is with Lisa. I went to jail because of that bitch and it's time she paid," Tate responded angrily, pushing Ryan back.

"You know I'm never going to let that happen," Ryan said. Rage consumed him, seeing Lisa beat up. He slammed his fist into Tate's face and pushed him hard against the truck. All the pent-up anger from the last six months unleashed itself as he hit Tate again.

Tate was no stranger to violence. The man was six foot three and at least two hundred and fifty pounds–Ryan knew he'd have a fight on his hands, but the anger he felt seeing Lisa lying helpless on the ground only fueled his rage.

Tate threw a punch to Ryan's gut, then a cross to his jaw. Ryan barely felt it, immediately throwing a cross, catching Tate in the jaw. Tate staggered back, but recovered quickly, catching Ryan and pushing him up against the truck, smashing his head against the door. Ryan blinked, seeing stars. He managed to avoid Tate's next cross and punched him again in the face. Ryan felt Tate's nose break. Tate swung again, catching Ryan in the right eye.

The blinding pain only enraged Ryan more. He hooked a leg around Tate's, dropping the other man to the ground. Falling on top of him, he pounded his fists into Tate's face. Over and over.

"Ryan, stop!" Lisa cried, crawling over to where they were fighting, *trying to pull Ryan off Tate. "He's had enough. Stop. You're going to kill him."*

Ryan could hear her, but he couldn't make himself stop. The fire burning in him was out of control. He couldn't see, he could barely breathe. Fighting was all he could do. He felt arms on him, trying to pull him off Tate. He heard voices yelling but he couldn't stop. The darkness had taken over completely.

Chapter Twenty-Two

Ryan opened the door and saw Elle standing on his porch. She wore a blue sundress and sandals, her long hair falling around her shoulders in soft curls.

"Hi," Elle said with a shy smile, holding up a bottle of wine. "I brought a bottle of Petrus. It's a cabernet, hope that works."

"You look beautiful," Ryan said, taking the bottle of wine and setting it on the table just inside the door before pulling her into his arms and kissing her. He'd been marinating steaks, but they might not make it onto the grill. The only thing he was hungry for right now was her.

Suddenly a black sports car roared into the driveway and squealed to a stop next to Ryan's truck.

"What the hell?" Ryan said, quickly letting go of Elle and moving in front of her, holding her protectively behind him. "Who is that?"

"Oh no. Oh shit. It's Todd. He must have followed me. I'm so sorry!" Elle put a hand on Ryan's arm.

Todd jumped out of his car, shaking his head as he walked toward them. He looked at Elle, then at Ryan, then back to Elle, narrowing his eyes. "Well, well, well. I knew it. Thought I'd follow you just to be sure. After seeing you two together the other day I should have guessed it then. You're fucking him, aren't you?"

"Todd, no, stop it," Elle choked out, turning bright red.

"Wow, you don't waste any time," Todd replied, smiling tightly. "I'm actually a little impressed. Payback for Samantha, right?"

"What? Oh, so that's her name," Elle said "But no—"

"Whatever, I don't really care. You need to just sign the divorce papers," Todd said angrily. "I'm done playing games with you. Fucking cheating whore!"

"Stop. You need to get off my property," Ryan said calmly, clenching his teeth, livid at what this asshole was saying to Elle now— and what he had done to her in the past. Ryan took a deep breath.

"Or what?" Todd sneered. "Going to punch me, big guy?"

"Ryan, wait," Elle begged, trying to pull him into the house. "Don't do anything. He wants you to hit him. He's trying to provoke you. Everything is a game to him. He wants to call the cops and have you arrested. Nothing would make him happier. Please don't give him the satisfaction."

Ryan turned ice cold at Elle's words. The cops. Fuck. He looked at Todd. The other man looked pretty fit, probably around six feet tall, but he was wearing an expensive suit and looked like the type that would back down if Ryan started to move on him. Todd had a snarl on his face, but Ryan knew he would have no trouble kicking his ass—hell, he'd held his own against much bigger men. But he couldn't take the chance of the cops coming, finding his rap sheet, possibly arresting him. He hesitated, wanting nothing more than to rub this guy's sneering, ugly mouth into the ground.

"Nice job, Elle," Todd taunted. "I see you found yourself a giant pussy!"

"Get inside," Ryan said as calmly as he could, pushing her gently into the house.

"No, Ryan, please. Don't let him get to you," Elle begged, her hand still on his arm.

"I'm not doing anything. That piece of shit isn't worth it," Ryan said. He turned back to Todd. "Now get off my property before I call the cops."

Ryan stepped through the door, pulling it closed behind him and locking it.

"I am so sorry," Elle sobbed as Ryan wrapped his arms around her. "Didn't think, I didn't think he ..."

"Shh, it's okay. You're okay," Ryan said. She was shaking in his arms, and he was feeling a little shaky himself. Ryan heard a car door slam and then Todd's car peeled out of the driveway. "He's gone."

"Shit. He knows where you live now. I never should have–"

Ryan didn't let her finish, taking her face in his hands. "Elle. Listen to me very carefully. You did nothing wrong. You have done nothing wrong, okay? You have nothing to be sorry about."

Elle nodded, still trembling.

"Come on," Ryan said, taking her hand. "Come sit down and I'll pour us each a whisky."

Elle nodded, following him across the room, sinking down onto the couch.

Ryan poured two fingers each of Laphroaig into a couple of cut crystal cocktail glasses, handing one to Elle while taking a drink of his. "I think we can both use it."

Fuck, Ryan thought. *That was close.* He closed his eyes for a moment, thankful he was able to control himself. Thankful the cops weren't here hauling him away in cuffs. It was time to tell Elle about everything before this went any further.

"Elle," Ryan cleared his throat, steeling himself for what was coming, "this probably is terrible timing, but I need to tell you some things about my past."

"Okay," Elle said, taking a sip of her whisky.

"So, I told you about my wife, Candi, that she died. But I need to tell you about how she died and, well, what happened after that." He paused, looking down into his glass, not wanting to make eye contact. *Shit. Okay. Just tell her.*

Elle nodded and took another sip of her whisky. "Okay," she said again, looking a little confused.

Ryan sat next to her on the couch, wanting to hold her hand but not trusting himself to touch her, not wanting to be distracted. He had to get this out. Now. Somehow.

"Sorry, this is hard. I guess I might as well just start at the beginning," Ryan said, looking at her sweet face and praying to God she didn't hate him after this. "So, Lisa and I had an older brother, Aiden. I was ten and Lisa was sixteen when he died from leukemia. He was only eighteen."

"Oh Ryan," Elle said, her eyes wide.

"Please, just let me get this all out," Ryan said quietly, holding up his hand briefly, then continuing. "Aiden had played sports his whole life and excelled at everything he did, until he got sick. After he died, I felt like I needed to step up and be the golden boy. I started playing sports, first soccer and then baseball. Finally found my niche with football. Turned out I was pretty good, could run fast for being a big kid and had a good arm. Could throw the ball sixty yards, easily. My dad was so proud of me.

"He and my mom both had a difficult time after Aiden died and they basically threw themselves into their business. But when my football career started to take off, my dad finally seemed happy again. He came to every game. I was All-American my junior and senior years of high school, our team was All-State, and then I landed a full ride to Arizona State. I was starting quarterback for the Sun Devils my junior and senior years.

"I was lifting weights and really focusing on fitness, being the best athlete I could be. I didn't care too much about school itself, though I was a decent student. Didn't care much about partying, either. Football was my life. I wanted my dad to be proud of me. I wanted him to be happy.

"My senior year at ASU, I'd been courted by some NFL teams, the Cardinals, the 49ers, and a couple others. I was in the running for the Heisman Trophy; my future was on fire. We were set to go to the

Rose Bowl. Then I got tackled in the last game of the season, second quarter, and blew out my knee. It all came crashing down. I had to have surgery on my meniscus and ACL. After I recovered, the phone stopped ringing. My professional football career was over before it began."

Ryan took a deep breath and got up. "Refill?" he asked. Elle nodded. He took her glass, walked over to the bar, and poured some more whisky in their glasses. *Well, you got through the easy part. Now for the hard part,* he thought, sitting back down and taking a drink before continuing.

"It was a really hard time for me. I was lost. I started partying and drinking, anything to numb the pain. That's when I met Candi. She was beautiful and fun. She was a non-stop party. She was everything I thought I needed. There was no time to feel sorry for myself. I honestly don't know how I managed to graduate. We spent the next four months either in bed, drunk, or high," Ryan looked down at his hands, unable to meet Elle's gaze. "I'm sorry. This is hard to tell you."

Elle reached for Ryan's hand, squeezing it.

Ryan finally looked at Elle wondering at her ability to make him feel stronger. Well, no going back now. *We'll see if she still feels the same way when I'm finished.*

"Well. There's more," he said, squeezing her hand back.

"Right after graduation we had been partying one night at a club downtown. Candi had swiped a little bag of coke from her mom. Anyway, we were doing some lines in the bathroom of the club. There were a bunch of people around. Hell, we didn't even try to hide it. Suddenly this guy comes up and says, 'You're under arrest.' He was an undercover vice cop that had been working the club. We were both arrested for possession.

"Candi's dad bailed us out. My father was so mad he refused to bail me out but he did hire an attorney for me. Candi lucked out and got a year of probation but because the coke was in my pocket, I served thirty days, followed by a year's probation.

"When I got out, we went right back into party mode. But after a couple weeks of that, Candi and I had a big fight and it made me see a different side of her, an ugly side. I broke up with her the next day. It made me realize that I needed to get my shit together, that we'd been spiraling out of control, heading down a really bad road. Then a week later she showed up at my apartment and announced that she was pregnant. With my baby."

Elle's eyes widened in surprise.

"There was no question that I was going to do the right thing. We were married two months later." Ryan ran his fingers through his hair. He'd been excited about the baby, excited to be a father. "Candi actually settled down. We stopped the booze and drugs. She seemed happy and excited to be a mother. Things were, if not perfect, at least, better.

"I patched things up with my dad, told him we'd stopped partying. I started working for him again around that time. I got my airframe and powerplant certification and things settled into some normalcy." Ryan stopped, took another drink, and let out a deep breath.

Here we go, he thought. He braced himself and somehow managed to tell Elle everything. Candi, the lost pregnancies, the accident, Candi's OD. Elle was quiet for the most part, occasionally starting to say something but Ryan always cut her off. He couldn't lose steam now.

"After Candi died, well, I guess it was my turn to go off the deep end. I was so angry. So fucking angry at how my life had turned out. So many wasted years. I lashed out at everyone in my life. Pushing people away as hard as I could. I would just feel this burning rage all the time.

"I was at Jack's one night. I was supposed to be meeting Lisa there. She had the patience of a saint back then. She's the one person who never gave up on me. But she had an ex, similar to Todd, I guess. Tate. Guy was an asshole and a con man. He stole a bunch of money from her a few years previous and she had him arrested. Turned out, she wasn't his only victim, and he ended up doing a few years in jail. When he got out, he wanted revenge on Lisa.

"I found them in the parking lot behind the bar. He had grabbed her from her car and beat her up pretty badly. Honestly, I think I found them just in time. I got Tate off her and, well, we fought. All of that rage that I'd been holding inside just came out. I couldn't stop. I was out of control. Someone came out from the bar and pulled me off him before I could kill him. But he died at the hospital from his injuries," Ryan confessed, looking down again, not wanting to make eye contact with Elle or see her reaction.

"My dad hired the best lawyer," Ryan continued. "Between the trial prep and continuances and finally the trial, it took a year all told. One of the most miserable years of my life. Or so I thought then. I was found guilty of third-degree murder, manslaughter. The judge sentenced me to six years in prison."

Elle gaped at him.

"I ended up serving just over three. I got out early because of good behavior and overcrowding." Ryan stopped taking a deep breath. He saw the shock on Elle's face. *Here it comes*, he thought. *Here's where I lose her. No one wants an ex-con as a boyfriend.* A possession charge for coke was one thing. Being a felon who killed a man was another.

Elle sat there stunned. Ryan's anxiety spiraled with each silent minute.

Ryan stood up, turning away from Elle. "I've told exactly three women that story, you're the fourth. You know how it went over with Kimberly. The second woman I told calmly got up from the table at the restaurant, grabbed her purse, and walked off. I never heard from her again.

"The third, well, I didn't even make it all the way through to the part about Tate before she walked out. So we know how they all feel about me. Kind of why I gave up on dating. No one wants to get involved with an ex-con. I won't hold it against you if you want to leave now. I'm sorry I started something with you that I probably shouldn't have ... it wasn't fair," Ryan said, looking out the slider at the setting sun.

Elle stood up from the couch, set her glass down firmly, and walked over to Ryan. She grabbed his arm and pulled him to her. She took both of her hands and framed his face, forcing him to look down at her. "Fair? Fair? You think I want to leave? That's not fair. Don't ever assume to know how I feel. You obviously don't know me very well. Because love isn't about running away. It's about holding on to each other even harder, especially when things get hard," she said. "Especially because no one else ever fucking did."

Ryan looked at Elle, her face strong and confident, her eyes glowing with unshed tears. She was smiling at him. He felt his heart pounding. *Did she say love?* Ryan couldn't even respond. Elle's reaction was so far from what he had expected that he was having trouble keeping up.

"I couldn't give two shits about your past. I only care about now. I know the man you are now. What happened back then was terrible, horrific even, and traumatic. I can't even begin to understand everything you've gone through and survived. But it doesn't change anything that's happening between you and me," Elle said. "Now is where our story begins. Not in the past. Now."

Ryan took her in his arms tightly, closing his eyes with a relieved sigh.

"Ryan," Elle said as she held him, "I forgive you, but you don't need my forgiveness. You need to forgive yourself." Ryan held her for a moment longer before pulling away.

"So I might as well tell you the rest, which isn't much, but I want you to know it all."

Elle nodded, taking his hand and sitting back down on the couch with him.

"After I got out of prison, I had two years of probation," Ryan explained. "I was lucky enough to be able to live with Lisa. I truly wouldn't be where I am today without her love and support. But while I was in prison our parents were in a car accident. As I think I told you when we were at Jack's, they didn't make it.

"Lisa had it rough for a while. She had two toddlers, and now, this huge business to run," Ryan said. "She made the decision to sell part of the company to bring it to the size it is now, with five private jets and a small crew at Daley Charters, which is where I've been working ever since I got out." Ryan so rarely talked about those years to anyone, it was hard for him to say the words out loud. His time in prison had been dark and difficult and he wanted nothing more than to forget they ever happened.

"Lisa put most of the money from the sale in trusts for her kids, paid off her house, and is doing really well now. Though she still works too hard.

"After my probation was done, Lisa bought this house. She said it was an investment in my future. I didn't want it. Didn't think I deserved it, but she convinced me, said it was the only way she was ever going to get me the fuck out of her house," he finished with a small smile.

Elle smiled back at him.

Ryan couldn't believe she was still there, sitting on his couch, holding his hand, after he had finished telling her. *This is the woman I've been waiting for all along,* he realized.

"So, I've basically been fixing this house and fixing myself at the same time for the last three years. It's been a long road." Ryan paused. "If I had known you'd be waiting for me at the end of that journey, it would have made it a lot more bearable."

"This is all so crazy," Elle said. "Just like I said the other day. Everything you've been through. Everything I've been through, which doesn't even compare." She reached out and gently touched his face, saying again slowly, "Crazy."

"Yet here we are. Together," Ryan said, pulling Elle onto his lap, leaning back on the couch, and wrapping his arms around her like he never wanted to let go.

He held Elle in his arms and kissed her like his life depended on it, because it one hundred percent did. Elle. This incredible woman now knew all about his tortured past and, despite it, was still here, holding him. Since she had been able to forgive him, maybe he'd be able to start forgiving himself.

Chapter Twenty-Three

Lisa slammed the phone down. "Fuck," she said. Her secretary, who wasn't supposed to do any booking, had double-booked two charters for the following week and they were short a pilot. After spending all morning trying to sort it out, she still had made no progress. Her assistant, Jenny, was off for the day and now her secretary was out too, probably getting her nails done or some shit. Time to find a new secretary.

She blew out a long breath and glanced up to find Conor standing in her doorway with his hat in his hands and a little smile on his face. "Conor!" Lisa exclaimed, standing up in surprise.

"Howdy ma'am," Conor drawled, leaning against the door frame. "Sorry to startle you–I didn't want to interrupt your phone call. Turns out you're a hard woman to track down."

"Where–how did you–" Lisa was having trouble forming a complete sentence. Conor was standing there, in her office, in Levi jeans and cowboy boots. Wearing another denim shirt, this one black, holding his Stetson. He looked like a snack she wanted to eat for lunch. Damn.

"How did I find you?" Conor finished for Lisa as he came in, setting his hat on one of the two chairs facing her desk. He looked her over as he sat down in the other chair, and it was all Lisa could do to keep herself from fidgeting with the gold necklaces she had paired with her low-cut white silk blouse. "Let me tell you, it wasn't easy," he admitted.

Lisa sat back down slowly, trying to calm her heartbeat. She had hoped Conor would track her down, but she hadn't held out much faith. She was used to being disappointed by men.

"Turns out there are twelve charter companies out of Southwest Jet Center. I've now visited ten of them," Conor explained with a little grin.

Lisa smiled back. "I'm actually pretty glad you didn't find me on the first stop. You should have to work for it. Makes you appreciate it more," she said with a wink, finding her cool.

Conor laughed and cleared his throat. "Do you have plans for tomorrow night?" he asked.

Lisa shrugged. "Why?" she asked coyly, crossing her arms across her chest and leaning back in her chair, though what she really wanted to do was climb over the desk and tear his clothes off. She looked at his lips and licked her own.

"I thought we could have dinner. Can you get a babysitter overnight?"

Lisa blinked at him. *Overnight,* she repeated to herself. Conor was assuming an awful lot. "Kids are actually at my ex's until Sunday evening," she replied.

"Perfect," Conor said, standing up and walking around Lisa's desk. He pulled her up out of her chair and into his arms, his lips finding hers for a quick, searing kiss. "So are you going to give me your phone number now, Lisa Daley?"

"Maybe," Lisa replied, pulling him to her and planting her lips back on his, exactly where she wanted them.

She felt Conor's grin against her lips as he kissed her back. His hands ran around behind her neck, through her hair, and down her back. She shivered, deepening the kiss and pulling him closer.

After about a minute he pulled away, a little breathless. "Pack an overnight bag. I'll pick you up here at four thirty p.m. tomorrow," he instructed as he turned, picking up his Stetson and putting it back on his head.

"Here?" Lisa asked, surprised, feeling flushed.

"Yes ma'am," Conor replied, tipping his hat to her. "I'll see you then."

Damn, Lisa thought, watching him walk out of her office. She felt an excitement she hadn't felt in a long time, her heart racing. He had actually searched for her and found her. The next twenty-four hours better fucking fly by.

"I'm guessing that's the cowboy," Ryan said with a scowl, coming into Lisa's office from the hangar and wiping his hands on a shop towel.

"That's the cowboy," Lisa said dreamily, watching Conor's truck drive away.

"Sis," Ryan said, snapping his fingers near her face as he sat down in the chair recently vacated by Conor. "Did you hear me? I asked what he was doing here."

Lisa startled back to reality. "Sorry, yeah, what?"

Ryan laughed as he leaned back in the chair. "Wow. I haven't seen you this lovestruck in a long time."

Lisa scowled at him. "Shut up. You don't know what you're talking about."

Ryan laughed again. "Okay, okay. Whatever you say."

Lisa finally focused her attention on Ryan and his smile. "Oh God, how did it go with Elle? Did it go well? How did she respond?" Lisa asked in a rush pausing before wryly adding, "Though from the smile on your stupid face, I'm guessing it went well."

Ryan nodded, still smiling. "Yeah, it went well."

"Sweet Jesus hallelujah!" Lisa exclaimed, feeling a huge relief wash over her. She'd been so worried about how Ryan would react if another woman rejected him. Thank God Elle hadn't. "When can I invite you two over for dinner? I need to get to know this woman who will be my sister-in-law."

"Jesus, sis, calm down. Don't go planning the wedding just yet. Elle still has to get Todd out of her life. It's still complicated," Ryan reminded Lisa.

"I know. And don't you go getting involved in any of that. I don't want anything to jeopardize your future," Lisa said sternly, pointing a finger at him.

"Yes, *Mom*," Ryan replied. "So, what was the cowboy doing here?"

"Asking me on a date," Lisa responded. "He's picking me up here tomorrow."

"Here?" Ryan asked. "That's a little strange." Lisa shrugged. "Guess I'll find out."

Chapter Twenty-Four

Lisa glanced at her watch for the second time since arriving back at Daley Charters. 4:25 p.m. She'd parked her car in front of the office, which was dark and locked up. She got out and looked around, frowning. No black Chevy pickup anywhere in sight. Lisa sighed, glancing at her watch again. Conor had exactly five minutes to make an appearance or she was leaving.

She turned at the sound of a plane landing on the runway closest to her hangar. It was a Cherokee Six 300. Great older plane, very reliable, though not luxury enough for Daley Charters. When people booked charters they wanted all the bells and whistles. Leather recliners, flight attendants, bar service, and charcuterie boards.

Leaning against her car, Lisa glanced at her watch again. Two minutes. She looked back at the Cherokee and realized that it was slowly taxiing toward her. *What the hell,* she thought, frowning. *Are they lost? This is a private hangar.*

The plane rolled to a stop. The side door opened, and Lisa gaped as Conor hopped down. What the hell? Oh right–Conor had said he was a licensed pilot at Jack's. And apparently, he also had his own plane. His ranch must do well, she thought as he strode toward her, looking sexy in what must be his standard attire of Stetson, denim shirt, Levi's, and boots. Lisa became a little warm thinking about spending the night with him. *In a bed this time,* she remembered with a smile.

"Hello beautiful. Ready?" Conor asked with a grin, coming up to her. "Did you pack a bag?"

Lisa nodded, still surprised he'd shown up in a plane to pick her up for their date. She opened her trunk and grabbed her duffle.

"Let me," Conor said, taking her bag in one hand and her hand in the other. He tossed the bag into the plane on a rear seat then turned to Lisa. "Hi." He pulled her in for a quick kiss. "Hope you're hungry," he added before helping her up into the Cherokee.

Definitely hungry for something, Lisa thought as Conor settled himself in, buckled up, and handed her a headset. "Where exactly are we going?" she asked, buckling her safety belt and putting the headset on and adjusting it.

"The ranch," Conor replied as they taxied to the runway. As they waited for clearance, he turned to Lisa. "It's about a forty-minute trip."

Lisa nodded, taking in the scenery as they lifted off, quickly leaving the city behind. She did love Arizona. A landscape of cracked land, crumbling rock, and vibrant desert blooms in the wild, desolate hills. The canyons and washes formed by years of monsoons exposed harsh wind-worn rock formations with rough sides in different shades of browns and dark reds. The solitary, stark beauty always took her breath away. "Beautiful," she breathed.

Conor said, "So, Black Diamond used to be over fifty thousand acres. My grandfather, John Hayes, started it as a cattle ranch back in the forties, slowly buying up surrounding land and cattle until it was one of the biggest in Arizona. My father, James, grew up there and officially took over running it in the eighties.

"I think I told you that my folks both passed many years ago. It's just me and my older sister, Cari, who live there now. And Cari is gone a lot. She's a photographer and travels a lot for her work.

Anyway, so yeah, that's where we're going. And yes, if you're wondering, Cari is currently out of town," Conor added with a grin.

"That's quite the history," Lisa replied, purposely ignoring his last comment. "So none of your other sisters stayed on the ranch?"

Conor nodded. "For a while, yes. They all came and went over the years. And we all grew up working the ranch. It's a hard life. It's a lot of work. After my folks passed, we sold off some of the cattle and some of the land and downsized quite a bit. Eventually, my sisters all decided they wanted to pursue other careers. Then about eight years ago we all made the mutual decision to sell off another big chunk of the ranch. It was just too much, even with help. My sister Cassidy and her husband, Bob, and their two kids lived there until just over a year ago. Then Bob got transferred to Texas, so they moved out. And now it's just Cari and me left."

"I have a ranch foreman, Riley, who runs the stables and the ranch hands. He's got a small house on the property. And there are only eight hands now, full time, that live in the bunkhouse. They do everything from mending fences to watering and moving cattle from one field to the next. In the last year I've had to take over more of the day-to-day business of running the ranch. Cassidy used to handle most of that, but now that they've moved, I've had to step up and deal with that side," Conor explained.

Lisa glanced at Conor as he concentrated on lining up the plane to land on a narrow runway, impressed. He was obviously a very hardworking man. She looked back out the side window and spotted a huge house set back in some trees. They must be at a higher elevation than Scottsdale. Lisa couldn't see even one palm tree.

Instead, there were two beautiful huge jacaranda trees flanking the main house. A bunch of autumn blaze red maple trees separated the main house from a big white barn, stables, and corrals, giving it some privacy. It was pretty, very functional, and laid out orderly.

Conor pulled into a small hangar behind the barn, shut the engine off, and turned to Lisa. "Well, here we are."

Lisa nodded, letting him help her out of the plane to a golf cart parked just outside the hangar. "A golf cart? Here I was expecting a horse," she said with a grin.

"Maybe later, you're not really dressed for it," Conor replied with a smile, gesturing to her heels.

Lisa flipped her hair and got in the golf cart. "True," she replied, taking in the beautiful, old but well-maintained main house as they approached. Two stories with what looked like two wings spreading out on each side of the main front section. It was painted white with a dark-red tile roof. Lots of windows and a huge front porch with an old swing and Adirondack chairs scattered around in little groupings. She could absolutely picture Conor growing up here with his family.

Lisa had a pretty, little Spanish-style stucco house on a quarter of an acre back in North Scottsdale. It was about ten years old now and had four bedrooms with a pool, but it paled in comparison to this beauty. "Wow. This is gorgeous," Lisa said as Conor stopped the cart in front of the grand porch.

"I can give you the full tour later, but Jimmy made me promise to be back by five thirty," Conor said, opening one of the two massive wood front doors. He set Lisa's bag on a chair just inside the door and hung his Stetson on a rack on the wall. "So, welcome to Black Diamond."

"It's stunning," Lisa said, taking in the giant foyer with a sweeping staircase off to the right and a large open hall that connected to the rest of the house. The dark wood of the staircase contrasted with the cream-colored paint on the walls. A huge chandelier hung from the ceiling, its lights twinkling in the dusk, giving the spacious area a welcoming glow. Well-maintained hardwood floors gleamed, and the big picture windows on each side of the front door let in the warm evening glow of the sunset. "Who is Jimmy?"

"Jimmy is the cook," Conor explained. "Normally, Cari and I fend for ourselves and Jimmy takes care of Riley and the bunkhouse, but sometimes, for special occasions, he'll cook in the house."

"And this is a special occasion?" Lisa probed, raising an eyebrow.

"Well," Conor replied, "Riley has a big mouth and when Jimmy found out I was bringing a woman home, he insisted on cooking something special."

Lisa smiled. "Does that mean you don't bring a lot of women home?" she asked coyly.

Conor pulled Lisa into his arms and said, "Let's just say it's a rare occurrence." He found her lips with his, brushing his fingers through her hair and deepening the kiss, his tongue finding hers.

"Ah-hem."

Conor pulled away from Lisa. A man stood in the hall, a huge grin on his old, wrinkled face. "Sorry, Boss," he addressed Conor. "Don't mean to interrupt, but dinner is almost ready. I'll meet you in the main dining room." Ah. This must be Jimmy. The man smiled at Lisa as he exited the room. "Ma'am."

"Guess that's our cue," Conor said, leaning in for one more kiss. "To be continued."

Lisa took Conor's hand, letting him lead her through several open, and spacious living areas until they arrived in the main dining room. She could fit her entire kitchen, dining room, and nook in this room, she thought, looking at the antique walnut table that seated twelve. There were only two places set, though, and Conor led her over to a chair at the end of the large table, holding it for her as she sat.

"Wine?" Conor asked as he sat next to her, reaching for the bottle on the table.

"Yes, please," Lisa replied, taking in the built-in antique cabinets filled with crystal and china lining the inside wall. She knew she had a box of good china that her folks had given her and George for a wedding present somewhere, but she wasn't sure where exactly. The Fiesta tableware she used was much safer with the kids. The outer wall of the dining room was almost completely floor-to-ceiling windows looking out to a manicured courtyard filled with fall-blooming flowers.

Jimmy brought out two salads and a basket of warm bread, setting them in front of Lisa and Conor. "Enjoy," he said before heading back to the kitchen.

"Slainte." Lisa held up her glass to Conor's. At his confused look, she explained, "It's Irish. It means 'to your health'."

"Slainte," Conor repeated, then took a drink.

"My actual name is Laoise—that's L-a-o-i-s-e," Lisa said, then dug into her salad. "It's pronounced *Leesha,* but I guess my mom got tired of always having to spell it and Americanized it to just Lisa."

"Laoise," Conor repeated. "I like it, it suits you better."

"Thank you. My father, Liam Daley, was second-generation American from Ireland. My mom, Sofia, was Italian. Let me tell you, those two knew how to fight," Lisa said with a laugh. "If my mom was mad at my dad, you ran and hid—it was much safer. But they were just as passionate about their love for each other. They could be very romantic also," she added. "Lucky for you, I have both the Irish and the Italian blood."

Conor broke off a piece of French bread from the loaf. "You said they were killed in a car crash. I'm so sorry."

"Yeah, so now my brother, Ryan, and my kids, Cayden and Charlie, are all the family I have left," Lisa replied. "I had an older brother, Aiden, who died when he was eighteen, from leukemia."

"Damn," Conor responded.

"It was a long time ago," Lisa said with a shrug, moving her empty salad plate to the side as Jimmy brought out a big bowl of linguine in a white wine bouillabaisse with steamer clams. "Wow, that looks amazing."

"Thanks, Jimmy," Conor said.

"So, you obviously have a big family—sisters, brothers-in-law, nieces, and nephews—but you never married?" Lisa asked.

"No," Conor said after Jimmy left, dishing up noodles and clams for them both. "There was someone significant in my life for a long time, Maggie, and I guess I should have married her, but I was so wrapped up in running the ranch, I let her get away."

"And she had no interest in helping you run the ranch, in being a partner?" Lisa inquired, twirling some noodles on her fork. If it had been her, she would have wanted to be a partner. That was a big reason why she had divorced George. He didn't understand why she didn't just sell the entire charter company and retire, be a stay-at-home mom. Why she had wanted to keep part of it and run it herself. Not understanding that it was her and Ryan's heritage their parents had built for them. Cayden and Charlie's heritage, too. And then he'd had no interest in helping her run it, wanting to just stick with his small welding business.

Conor looked up, surprised. "No. I mean, I guess we never talked about it, but she had no interest in"–he waved a hand around–"this. She ended up marrying a doctor and lives in Phoenix. That's the life she wanted. It can be very quiet out here; it's definitely a slower way of life."

Peaceful, Lisa thought. *I like it.* Maggie had been a fool to let Conor get away, but Lisa was glad she had, or she wouldn't be sitting here right now. She smiled. Maybe her luck was changing.

She watched Conor eat his dinner. What was it about this man? Obviously, they had smoking-hot chemistry, but there was more. Lisa supposed if he just wanted sex, he could have taken her to dinner in Scottsdale and they could have gone back to her place. But he brought her here, to his family home.

Lisa didn't want to think about it too much. After everything she and Ryan had been through, it was hard to believe in happy endings.

"So, who is a better cook, you or Jimmy? Because this might be one of the best dinners I've ever eaten in my life," Lisa proclaimed, pushing her empty plate away with a contented sigh.

"I definitely don't do anything fancy, but I do a mean steak. What about you?"

"Well," Lisa said, finishing her second glass of wine. "I make a mean peanut butter and jelly sandwich. Oh, and chicken nuggets and mac and cheese."

Conor laughed. "I love peanut butter and jelly," he said with a grin.

"No, I do cook a little, but between work and raising two busy, active kids, cooking comes down to what is quick and easy," Lisa explained.

"Dessert?" Jimmy asked, coming in to remove their plates.

"Not for me, I'm so full. It was excellent, though. Thank you, Jimmy," Lisa said as Conor shook his head, too.

Jimmy grinned. "My pleasure. Well, if you two want a snack later, there's cheesecake in the fridge," he said before heading back into the kitchen.

"Thanks," Conor said, standing up and taking Lisa's hand. "Good night, Jimmy. See you tomorrow." He turned to Lisa. "Thought we'd move to the library."

Lisa followed him down another set of hallways. *Library? Of course this house has a library.* Conor led her into another large, open room. In this one, three of the four walls were lined with bookshelves, filled from top to bottom. A big oak desk stood to one side, piled with papers. A large stone fireplace stood against the outside wall, flanked by French doors leading to a small patio. A big, worn-leather sofa faced the gas fireplace in which a small fire was burning. Two upright chairs faced each other at either end of the sofa.

Lisa curled up on the couch, kicking off her heels and tucking her feet under her as Conor walked to a small bar cabinet.

"More wine?" he asked, holding up a bottle.

Lisa nodded, watching as he made short work of getting it open and pouring them each a glass.

"Thank you," Lisa said, taking a sip after he handed her a glass and sat down next to her.

"So, after your folks died, you took over running the charter company?" Conor asked.

"Yes. It was rough for a while, handling everything by myself. I ended up, well, similar story to yours, I guess. The company was just too big, too much to run alone. I ended up selling most of the planes. I now have two Gulfstreams, a G550 and a G200, a Citation Bravo, a

Beechcraft King Air 200, and a smaller single-engine Piper Saratoga," Lisa explained.

"Very nice planes," Conor replied, impressed.

"Thanks," Lisa said with a little smile. She was pretty proud of the company. Even though the business was much smaller now, it was still successful. She didn't pat herself on the back often, but she was proud of how hard she had worked. Her parents' legacy was very important to her.

"Why did you have to handle everything by yourself? Ryan wasn't involved?" Conor asked.

"No, not initially," Lisa said, looking down at her wine glass for a moment, thinking. "I—well, I don't normally share this information with very many people, but Ryan was in prison at the time."

"Prison?" Conor asked, looking up from his wine glass in surprise. "Your brother? What did he do?"

"Nothing. He didn't do shit. He saved my life. And ended up paying a steep price, which I blame myself for," Lisa said bitterly.

Conor gave Lisa a confused look.

"I'm sorry," Lisa said, blowing out a deep breath. She took a sip of wine. "I still get so angry about it.

"My ex-boyfriend, Tate, attacked me in the parking lot behind Jack's and Ryan beat the shit out of him. Tate ended up dying a couple of days later, mostly from his injuries, but it turned out he also had a heart condition. The state charged Ryan with third-degree murder, manslaughter, and he was sentenced to six years in prison. He ended up having to serve just a little over three years," Lisa explained.

"Damn," Conor replied softly.

"Ryan never should have gone to prison. It was so unfair. I still feel guilty as fuck, because he was only protecting me. Tate absolutely would have killed me. I feel zero remorse that Tate died. He deserved everything he got," Lisa said fiercely.

"Ryan did not.

"It almost broke him," she continued. "Everything he went

through. I honestly don't know how it didn't. But we Daleys are tough and stubborn. I refused to let him give up. And he's been in a much better place the last few years, and now he's finally met some-one, Elle. I just want him to be happy, you know?" She finished her last sip of wine, then set her empty glass down. "Well, now you know the dirty family secret."

Conor took Lisa's hand. "Every family has its share of those. If you think it changes anything between us, it doesn't. I've been through some shit of my own–are you going to judge me?"

"Maybe," Lisa replied with a little smile, "but I'll save that deci-sion for later." She shifted her position on the sofa, moving onto her knees and facing Conor, slowly unbuttoning her top. "Are you ready for dessert now?"

Conor swallowed hard. "Yes ma'am, I do believe I am," he replied with a smile.

Chapter Twenty-Five

"I'm so glad you were able to meet today," Elle said, pausing as the server brought two glasses of wine and set them on the table.

"Me too," Sarah replied. "I feel like I've barely seen you lately. But I figured you've been busy."

"Well, yes and no. And that's kind of what I wanted to talk to you about," Elle replied, fidgeting with her napkin. "Some changes in my life."

"What's going on, honey?" Sarah asked, taking a sip of wine.

"So, I haven't told very many people, but Todd and I are separated and I've filed for divorce," Elle admitted. There. She'd said it out loud to someone besides her parents and Ryan.

"Well, honestly," Sarah said slowly, setting her glass down, "I'm not surprised."

"Really?" Elle asked in amazement. "Why is that?"

"I've seen a few relationships in my time. For one thing, you never talk about him. And when I went to that grand opening party at your dad's new office building downtown last spring and met Todd for the first time, I was actually pretty surprised he was your husband. He just didn't seem your type."

"Turns out, he wasn't," Elle said with a wry little laugh.

"He just didn't seem, um, well, attentive or loving," Sarah tried to explain. "I'm sorry, I should just keep my big mouth shut."

"No, please! You can say anything to me," Elle encouraged. She valued her friend's opinion.

"Well, you guys were still newlyweds, so the way he acted just didn't make sense to me. It was a big evening for your family, and I saw him at one point, well, it looked like he was hitting on some woman who was there," Sarah admitted.

"He probably was," Elle agreed. "Hence the divorce."

"Oh shit, so he really was cheating? I'm so sorry. What an ass," Sarah said, shaking her head. "Frankly, you're better off. You deserve better than that, honey."

Thoughts of Ryan immediately popped into her head. She was pretty sure she was turning pink.

"Elle?" Sarah asked, leaning in, her eyes widening. "Have you already found better?"

Elle nodded, blushing harder.

"Who?" Sarah asked excitedly. "Anyone I know?"

Elle choked on her wine. She hadn't planned on telling Sarah. She'd been hoping to space telling people about the divorce and Ryan out a little bit; however, she also wasn't ashamed to admit that she'd already fallen. Fast. And hard.

"Oh my God," Sarah continued, "it's someone I know, isn't it? Someone from the gym?"

Elle recovered, nodding slowly, smiling a little as she set her glass down.

"Wait. Don't tell me," Sarah said, tapping her finger on her lip. "Let me think for a minute... Jesus! It's Ryan, isn't it?"

Elle gasped. "How did you guess that?"

"Please honey," Sarah replied with a knowing smile. "Nate has even noticed it. You two, the way you stand next to each other at the gym. The way you smile at each other. Your body language when you guys talk. It's like there's no one else around."

"Oh my God," Elle replied, surprised that she was so transparent. "Really? There is? I mean, we do?"

"Don't worry," Sarah laughed, patting Elle on the hand. "It's doubtful anyone else would put two and two together, if that's what you're worried about. Nate and I have just known you both for quite a while. And honestly, nothing makes me happier. Ryan is definitely more your type."

"It's, well, not really a secret. I just need to get my divorce finalized," Elle explained. "I'm worried about Todd's behavior lately. He actually followed me to Ryan's house the other day."

"What?!" Sarah exclaimed.

"Pretty sure he just was trying to goad Ryan into, I don't know, hitting him and starting a fight, maybe," Elle replied, shrugging. "Probably wanting to get him arrested. Anything he can do at this point to hurt me would make him happy."

"What a sleazebag," Sarah replied with a frown. "Oh, sorry, I mean ..."

"No, he's a total fucking sleazebag," Elle replied with a grin, holding up her glass to Sarah's. "Good riddance."

"Good riddance! And to new beginnings," Sarah replied, smiling, clinking her glass against Elle's. "For both of us."

Chapter Twenty-Six

Lisa sighed, stretching. She opened one eye. Sunlight was peeking through the blinds across from Conor's bed. She opened the other eye. The bed was empty beside her. Rolling over, she noticed the sticky note on the mug of coffee sitting on the nightstand.

"Thank God, coffee," Lisa murmured, reaching for the covered mug and the note.

Good morning, beautiful. Wanted to let you sleep. I had some issues in the stables. Jimmy will make you breakfast. Coffee is black. Back soon. XO Conor.

Lisa smiled. She'd teased Conor about being an old man, but damn, he had no trouble keeping up with her last night. After they'd had sex on his couch, they'd barely made it upstairs to his bed, before round two. She stretched again. *If I was a cat, I'd be purring right now.* Damn, that cowboy knew exactly how to make her happy.

She rolled out of bed and found Conor's discarded denim shirt, putting it on over a pair of silk boxers she took from her overnight bag. Breakfast sounded pretty damn good, especially if they were going to work on round three–or was it four? She smiled to herself as she made her way to the kitchen.

"Ma'am," Jimmy said, about ten minutes later, seeming surprised to find Lisa in the kitchen, sitting on one of the counters sipping her coffee, legs dangling over the edge. "Um, good morning."

"Good morning, Jimmy," Lisa replied with a smile. "And it's just Lisa. Lisa is fine. No need for the ma'am stuff."

"Yes ma'am," Jimmy said. "Sorry ... Lisa. Are you hungry? I got biscuits and gravy made up and I could fix up some eggs and hash browns too, if you'd like."

"Biscuits and gravy sounds heavenly," Lisa said, hopping off the counter. "Okay if I just eat in here? That dining room is a bit big for one person."

"I suppose that's okay," Jimmy replied as he piled a plate with freshly made biscuits and topped them with sausage gravy. "It's nothing fancy today, just good ol' ranch cookin'."

"Well, it looks and smells delicious, thank you," Lisa said, sitting down on one of the high stools at the big island counter as Jimmy set the full plate in front of her.

"Boss, um, Mr. Conor, is out in the stables, but he should be in soon. Told him I'd save him a plate, too. Normally, he eats by himself in the dining room. This ol' house sure has been quiet lately. It's nice to see Boss with a lady. I never liked that Chloe. She was trouble." Jimmy stopped his rambling, blushing, even his bald head turning red. "Sorry ma'am–Lisa, I tend to talk too much, though it's usually just to myself and even I don't listen much."

Lisa laughed, liking Jimmy more and more. *But who was Chloe?*

"What's going on in here?" Conor asked, coming into the kitchen and hanging his hat on a rack by the door.

"Oh, we were just talking about you," Lisa replied with a wink at Jimmy.

"Boss–I ..." Jimmy stammered, somehow turning even redder.

"Jimmy," Conor said, "go check on the bunkhouse and get a

grocery list together for Riley. I can get my own breakfast. Thank you."

Lisa hid her smile in her coffee mug as Jimmy hustled out of the kitchen. "What?" she asked Conor, setting her mug on the counter and trying to look innocent.

"You're already causing trouble, aren't you?" Conor accused playfully, narrowing his eyes at Lisa while dishing up some biscuits and gravy onto a plate.

"Hmm, I've never been accused of causing trouble before," Lisa managed to say with a straight face.

Conor looked at her and burst out laughing. He set his plate down and came over to her. "Liar," he said, moving her knees apart on the stool to stand between her legs. "I'd say pants on fire, but you don't seem to be wearing any." Conor ran his hands slowly up her thighs, over her silk boxers, then under her–his–shirt. His lips found hers while his hands were busy pulling her silk boxers off.

Lisa reached down, unbuttoning his Levi's. She broke away from his mouth long enough to ask, "Are we going to–"

"Don't worry. Jimmy definitely won't be back any time soon," Conor replied, assisting her in getting his jeans off, then pushing her against the counter.

Chapter Twenty-Seven

"An ex-con, Elle? Seriously? A fucking ex-con," Todd said, laughing. "Glad to see you've moved up."

"Trust me, Ryan is definitely an upgrade," Elle replied hotly, wondering why she even bothered to respond to Todd's jabs. It was pointless.

"My client has nothing to say to you. We'll review the paperwork and meet back at eleven with your attorney," Brian Scott, Elle's attorney said, leading her by the arm down the court hallway to the conference room. "Don't respond to him, Elle."

Elle nodded, allowing herself to be led away from Todd and blowing out a deep breath. "Sorry. He just knows exactly how to get under my skin."

"That's why you have me," Brian replied, leading her into the conference room and closing the door behind him. "Have a seat. Do you want some coffee?"

Elle nodded, sitting down at the conference table. "Thank you. So what's his latest ridiculous demand?" she asked, taking the cup of coffee Brian set before her.

"You're not going to like it," Brian replied, pulling papers out of his briefcase. "Now he wants the house."

Elle choked on her coffee. "What? He can't be serious," she sputtered, setting her cup down on the conference room table with a thud.

"Yes. Says now he's been through emotional trauma after finding out about your affair with ... um, Ryan?" Brian asked, looking up from the addendum paperwork.

"But it's not true," Elle replied hotly. "I mean, yes, I am seeing Ryan now, but it didn't, we didn't start anything until after I moved out. Correction, was locked out."

"Todd claims he confronted you at Ryan's house," Brian said, reading from the paperwork.

"Again, after we were separated. I never cheated on him. He's the one who has been cheating on me! I can't believe this is happening," Elle said, putting her head in her hands with a groan.

"Don't suppose you have any evidence of that?" Brian asked, setting the paperwork aside.

"No," Elle sighed. "I followed him once because I was suspicious, caught him making out with some woman at the country club."

"Did you confront him?"

"No. Not until later. But he admitted it! He actually told me to mind my own fucking business, if you can believe that," Elle said bitterly. She looked down at her coffee cup. "He actually beat me up that night," she added softly.

"What?" Brian asked. "He hit you?"

Elle nodded. "Yeah, not badly enough to need to go to the hospital, but yeah," she admitted, cold anger building in her chest. She wanted to hurt him back. Somehow.

"Wow," Brian replied, leaning back in his chair. "Damn. I'm sorry. What an asshole."

"Yeah," Elle said, chewing on her lower lip. "I know. What are we going to do? I'm not letting him have my house. Not after that. No way."

"Don't worry," Brian replied fervently. "We're not going to let this jerk win. Besides, you purchased the house before you were married, right? So it falls under protected property. He's grasping at straws, maybe playing ..." He paused. "What's the story with Ryan? Is he actually an ex-con?"

Elle nodded slowly. "Yes, but it was years ago, and it was, well, kind of unintentional," she started. Brian listened while she shared the story of what happened with Ryan and Tate.

"Hmm," Brian said when she was done. "Maybe he thinks he can use Ryan as, I don't know, blackmail? Like, give me the house and I won't haul your ex-con boyfriend into court."

"Shit," Elle said, closing her eyes. She never should have dragged Ryan into her messy life.

"Okay, well for today, I'll meet with Todd's attorney and just let him know there's no way we're ever going to agree to give him the house. Can he afford to go to trial?" Brian asked, putting the files back into his briefcase.

"Who knows?" Elle replied with a shrug. "He's got this new woman, Samantha, bankrolling him, so maybe. But damn, a trial? How long will that take? I just want him out of my life."

"Trust me, his attorney doesn't want to go to trial either. Judges hate this shit. And there's no custody dispute, no kids, no business dispute. A judge is going to just tell us to not waste the court's time and work it out," Brian explained. "Todd's attorney knows he doesn't have a case. It's all a lot of bluffing, hoping you'll get scared and cave. Okay? So, for now, do not have any interaction with Todd. If he contacts you, refer him to me and leave it at that."

Elle nodded. "Okay."

"And maybe don't parade around in public with Ryan, for now," Brian suggested.

Elle blew out a deep breath. "Okay. And thank you. I just want to get on with my life."

RYAN PULLED a pan of enchiladas out of the oven where they'd been reheating.

"I'm sorry I changed dinner plans on you," Elle said.

"It's fine. Lisa dropped these leftovers off earlier, so not a big deal," Ryan reassured her, dishing some up on two dinner plates. "Plenty of food."

"It's just that after meeting with Brian today, well, he thinks maybe you and I should stay low-key, I guess," Elle explained. "As much as I wanted to go out to dinner with you, I guess it might be better to get Todd out of my life before we, well, go public, so to speak."

"Elle," Ryan said quietly. "I understand. If you want me to back off until this is over, I will." It would kill him, but he'd do it for her.

"No," Elle replied quickly. "No, I don't want that. I don't want to waste any more time being alone now that I've found you. And even though Todd and I have only been separated for a little while now, I've actually been alone for a long time."

Ryan reached for her hand, squeezing it gently. "I know. Believe me. I understand."

Elle smiled, picking up her wine glass. "Here's to crazy."

Ryan touched his glass lightly to hers. "Here's to crazy," he agreed, smiling back at her.

Lying in bed later, holding Elle in his arms after making love to her, Ryan closed his eyes, pulling her against him. He worried about Todd, wondering if it would be easier for her if he stepped back. But he admitted to himself, holding her close, that he didn't have the willpower to do that. He'd finally found the woman that he'd been desperately searching for his whole life.

Even when he denied it to himself, refusing to let himself feel anything for years, he'd still been searching. There was no way he was letting Elle go now. He figured Todd was going to drag him into the divorce and use his history against Elle, but Ryan would do his best to not let that happen. He would do everything in his power to protect her.

Chapter Twenty-Eight

"Remember to stay light on your feet, Owen," Ryan instructed. "A moving target is harder to hit." He threw a light jab toward the teen.

Owen ducked quickly back out of Ryan's reach, grinning. "Ha. Missed me," he called gleefully, continuing to dance around the ring.

Ryan followed him while Owen held his gloves up protecting his face. "Okay, try to hit me," he instructed.

Owen came closer, throwing a cross which Ryan easily slapped away with his glove. Again he swung, but Ryan batted his glove away with his right hand, bringing a cross around and getting Owen lightly on the chin.

"Damn," Owen said, dancing back again. "Shit, I didn't even see that coming. How did you do that?"

"You need to learn to feint," Ryan explained. "Throw a big, obvious punch. Your opponent will be looking at that swing, trying to avoid it. Then you throw another punch with your opposite hand immediately and it will catch them off guard." He demonstrated in exaggerated slow motion. "Okay, you try it."

Owen danced around the ring, his gloves up, his eye on Ryan

moving around him. He punched out suddenly with his right hand, which Ryan quickly batted away, but Owen swung immediately with his left and caught Ryan square on the jaw.

"Holy shit, I actually hit you!" Owen exclaimed with a huge grin.

"Nice," Ryan replied with a smile, impressed with how quickly the kid caught on. He was happy to see the progress Owen was making, not just in the ring but in his own life. He was walking taller, talking about the future and working on figuring out goals for his future. Ryan loved seeing the teen's confidence building. "That was a great feint, Owen. Good job."

"Thanks," Owen replied, beaming from ear to ear and holding up a glove to high-five Ryan.

"Okay. That's good for today, I think," Ryan said with a grin. "You win this round."

"Yes!" Owen replied excitedly, pumping his glove in the air. "See you tomorrow." He climbed out of the ring and headed for the locker room, a big smile still on his face.

Ryan climbed out of the ring and walked over to where Logan leaned against the door to his office. Ryan pulled his gloves off, tossing them on the counter. "Owen is making some good progress. He's a pretty quick learner," he said.

"Saw that feint Owen threw," Logan said with a little grin. "Did he actually catch you off guard, or were you feinting yourself?"

Ryan grinned back. "Call it a confidence boost. I saw it, but it was good enough I thought I'd let him have it," he admitted.

"Pretty sure I've never seen that kid smile that big before," Logan said. "Thanks to you, he's come a long way in a relatively short time."

Ryan shrugged. "I can't take the credit. Owen has done the work. One of the first things I asked him was what he wanted, besides learning to fight. He didn't have an answer right away, but at the end of our first sparring session he told me that he wants to be eighteen so he can legally get away from his dad. Fucking breaks my heart."

Logan shook his head sadly. "Unfortunately, it's all too common of a story."

"But before we started this session today, he said he has been thinking about going into the air force," Ryan said. "He said he wants to learn to fly, to be a pilot. So, he's already starting to let go of some anger and think about what his future could look like."

"Hey, that's great," Logan replied. "Just proves my point to keep doing what we're doing. Saving the world, one sad, angry kid at a time."

Chapter Twenty-Nine

Lisa leaned back in her office chair and closed her eyes, remembering the morning she'd spent with Conor yesterday. After having sex on just about every available surface in his kitchen, they'd tried to clean up the mess they'd made before finally giving up and taking a shower as she had somehow got gravy in her hair.

After washing up, they'd both taken a nap. As much as Lisa enjoyed sex with Conor, sleeping in his strong arms with her body fitted against his and waking up to his handsome face was almost as enjoyable. *Fuck,* she thought to herself. *You're in deep already, aren't you?*

Her ringing cell pulled her out of her reverie. "Well, hello. I was just thinking about you," Lisa said, smiling as she answered her phone.

"That's good because I was just thinking about you too," Conor replied.

"Oh really?" Lisa asked. She was glad that he called so soon. She hated all the dating rules bullshit. Waiting a couple of days to call, not texting right back, not appearing too eager. Life's too short to play dumb games.

"I'm going to be in Scottsdale Wednesday. Flying Cari up for an appointment she's got in the morning. Would you like to have lunch with us?" Conor asked.

Meeting a sister. Things were getting serious quick. Lisa smiled again. "Sure, I'd love that," she said.

"Good, you pick a place," Conor said. "See you then, babe."

"Okay. See you soon," Lisa replied, hanging up the phone. Her heart fluttered a little in response to the endearment. *Oh boy. Yep, already in deep.*

"Lisa, this is my sister, Cari. Cari, Lisa," Conor said.

"Nice to meet you, Cari," Lisa said, giving Cari a quick hug. They were having lunch at Francine, her favorite lunch spot in Scottsdale. She turned to Conor. "There's a reservation under Daley."

"I'll go check us in," Conor replied as he headed inside, leaving Cari and Lisa standing by the entrance.

Cari looked at the restaurant's sign and outdoor patio seating. "I've always wanted to try this place out."

"It's one of my favorites. The food is incredible and the service is great," Lisa replied. "Which is good, because I'm starving."

"Me too," Cari said with a grin. "I have a Peloton out at the ranch, and I've done five classes in the last three days. I tend to spend too much time sitting and editing photos and then I get carried away, overdoing the exercise bit. I don't know what I was thinking. I'm legit dying."

"I've been wanting to try spin. My workouts consist of laundry and chasing kids," Lisa replied with a laugh.

"Okay ladies, you ready?" Conor asked, coming toward them. "Our table is ready."

The group got settled at their table. "So, how did you two meet?" Cari asked after their server opened a bottle of wine for her and Lisa, Conor sticking to iced tea, and took their orders. "Conor has been evasive." She narrowed her eyes at her brother.

Lisa was in the middle of taking a sip of wine and almost choked, swallowing quickly and glancing over at Conor, who shrugged.

"Maybe I'll let Lisa explain that one," Conor said, grinning.

Cari raised an eyebrow.

"Um, well, we met at Jack's," Lisa explained. "Which is a little dive bar my brother and I go to often in downtown Scottsdale. Our folks used to be good friends with Jack, the owner. It was actually the first bar I ever went to, even before I was twenty-one. Jack makes his own rules, always has."

"I love a good dive bar. Met a few ex-boyfriends in dive bars," Cari said, smiling wryly.

"Anyway, I'd gone on this terrible Tinder date and, needless to say, it ended early. So I decided to go to Jack's since I already had a babysitter. I was sitting at the bar drinking a beer when someone asked if the seat next to me was taken," Lisa explained with a grin. "I was going to tell him to fuck off, but instead, well, I took one look at Conor and changed my mind."

"Yeah, he thinks he got all the looks in the family, but he's wrong," Cari replied, tossing her long brown hair over her shoulder with a grin.

"Not wrong," Conor shot back at his sister, then gave Lisa a cheeky grin. "And aren't you going to tell her the rest of the story, sweets?"

Lisa kicked him under the table, glaring over her wine glass.

"What's the rest of the story?" Cari asked, taking a sip of her wine.

"Maybe we should save that for another day," Lisa replied, looking down into her wine glass and not making eye contact with Cari.

"Let's just say Lisa really likes my truck," Conor said with a big grin.

Cari's eyes widened. "Conor, you're such an asshole," she said, smacking him on the arm.

Lisa could tell Cari got the picture.

"What?" Conor smirked, taking a drink of his iced tea. "We're all adults here."

Cari rolled her eyes. "Well, no judgment here. I've had a few one-night stands in my day," she admitted with a grin.

Lisa laughed. "Hell yes! I knew I liked you right away."

"Cari!" Conor exclaimed, a look of shock on his face. "What?"

"Hey, two can play that game, little brother," Cari replied with a laugh.

"Jesus, Cari," Conor said, shaking his head.

"Well, I think Conor's punishment should be following us around while we check out the boutiques I saw along this street," Cari suggested to Lisa with a wink.

"What?" Conor asked, shaking his head. "No. Nope. Nooo. Please, no shopping. Anything but that."

"I think that's a great idea," Lisa agreed, clinking her glass against Cari's, already loving her sass. Cari and Conor's playful banter reminded her of herself and Ryan. "Cheers, girl. I think we're going to be great friends."

"Cheers," Cari replied, grinning at Lisa as the outnumbered Conor let out a long sigh.

Chapter Thirty

Ryan pulled his helmet on and climbed onto his motorcycle. He needed to clear his head and the best way to do that was to get out of the city. He decided to ride to Wickenburg Road. He programmed his route into his trail map app and headed out.

Wickenburg Road was one of his favorite places to off-road. Low mountains and narrow desert trails with nice curves. Not much traffic since it was a Wednesday afternoon, and the weather was warm without being too hot. November was one of his favorite months to ride.

Ryan hit the trail, accelerating through the gears he immediately felt better, the tension in his shoulders easing. He still couldn't believe how well Elle had reacted. But he couldn't help being worried. He'd had so much disappointment and heartbreak in his life, he had trouble believing something so good was happening to him.

Could he let himself fall in love with her? Maybe get married again? He wasn't sure he was husband material. And did Elle want to have kids someday? Ryan didn't think he was capable of going down that road again. He didn't think he could handle losing another baby if something happened.

Ryan could be happy just having Elle as his woman, but would she be happy? Maybe she'd be better off with someone who could give her everything she deserved. He didn't have much to offer her. She was used to the finer things in life, though she didn't seem to let it affect her much. Elle seemed happier in jeans and a ball cap than expensive dresses and high heels.

And what would her family think about her dating an ex-con? Elle had told him a little bit about her parents. He knew she was having dinner with her father tonight. She was obviously close with her father, maybe not so much with her mother, who, from what Elle had told him, was difficult. It had just been him and Lisa for so long that he wasn't sure about all these family dynamics coming into play.

Ryan pushed the bike harder, trying to calm the thoughts swirling in his head. There was nothing he could do at the moment, and all this overthinking was making him crazy. He accelerated around some tight corners, forcing himself to turn his brain off. Just feel the bike, the sun, and the wind. Everything else would work itself out. Or it wouldn't.

"I'm sorry your mother isn't here tonight, Elle," Tom said, taking Elle's arm and following the hostess to their table at the club. "She had some crisis come up. Something about missing donations for the annual Scottsdale Emanluel Hospital Thanksgiving charity ball. But she sends her love."

"Oh, it's fine," Elle replied, sitting down and picking up the menu. One dinner a week with her mother was plenty. She could only tolerate Ava in small doses these days. She was insistent on playing matchmaker, usually trying to set her up with someone from the club. Lately she had her sights set on Elise's son. But Elle had bad news. She was officially off the market. At least, she hoped she was. They hadn't really talked about semantics.

Ava was going to hate Ryan. But she hoped her dad and Ryan would get along well, once she explained Ryan's history to her dad. He would probably understand. Hopefully.

"I'm thinking a martini sounds good tonight," Tom suggested. "Crazy day at the office. Would you like one too, honey?"

"Sure," Elle replied, setting her menu down.

"So what did you want to talk to me about? Something about the Nelson project?" Tom asked, referring to Elle's latest project, a huge older home on the Ancala golf course, not far from the restaurant they were in.

Elle shook her head. "No, that's going fine." It was a project she was actually pretty excited about. Christi Nelson was a gem to work with, which made her job so much easier. "We finally got some samples picked out for the kitchen. Going over tomorrow and laying things out and then hopefully getting everything ordered. Christi wanted everything done by Christmas, but I already told her that unfortunately there is no way that is going to happen."

"We've got two teams going on that project but, yes, you are correct, it's not going to be done by Christmas. Thankfully, the Nelsons are flexible. Unlike some of our clients," Tom said, smiling wryly.

Elle nodded in agreement. "Right," she said. Oh, she'd had her share of difficult clients, for sure. Wanting to change colors or fabrics at the very last second, then not understanding why that caused weeks of delays.

"So if it's not work, is it Todd? Is he still fighting you on the divorce paperwork?" Tom asked, frowning.

"Yes, unfortunately, but Brian is working on it. And no, that's actually not what I wanted to talk to you about either," Elle replied, nervously biting her lower lip. How was she going to explain her relationship with Ryan? Fortunately, she got a little reprieve when the server came to take their order.

"All right, what's going on, sweetie?" Tom asked after the server walked off.

"Well, I know this is, um, sudden and probably not great timing," Elle began, fidgeting with her napkin. "But I kind of met someone."

"You met someone?" Tom asked, his eyes widening. "As in you're dating someone?"

"Yes, well, seeing someone," Elle replied, blushing a little. "Ryan Daley. I actually know him from the gym, but we've, um, well, gotten closer over the last few weeks."

"I see," Tom replied with a little smile. "Your mother is going to be so disappointed. She's already planning your wedding to Elise's son."

"Mother needs to just stop. Good grief. Even if I wasn't seeing Ryan, there's no way I was going to go for Todd 2.0." Elle rolled her eyes.

Tom laughed. "Ha, he does actually remind me a little bit of Todd."

"Exactly."

"So, tell me about Ryan Daley," Tom pressed after the server set down their martinis. He took a sip of his drink. "Though, Daley, that name actually sounds familiar. I'm not sure why though."

"You've maybe heard of Daley Charters," Elle suggested, taking a drink of her martini.

"That's it," Tom said, snapping his fingers. "I think I have a couple of clients who use that company. Pretty big company if I remember correctly. This is Ryan's company?" He seemed impressed.

"Well, it was his parents'. They started it something like thirty years ago," Elle explained. "But they were killed in a car accident about six years ago."

"Oh right," Tom replied. "I do remember hearing something about that. They were pretty involved in the community here. Tragic."

Elle nodded. "So Ryan's sister, Lisa, runs it now and he's the airframe and powerplant mechanic. It's actually a much smaller company now. They downsized significantly after their folks died."

"Makes sense. Well, they still have an excellent reputation. First class," Tom said.

"Yes. Mother is going to lose her shit. I'm dating a mechanic," Elle replied wryly, picking up her martini again. "She so had her sights set on a judge or a doctor."

Tom smiled a little. "You're probably right, but it's your life, sweetie. And there's absolutely nothing wrong with being a mechanic. It's a great profession."

Elle nodded, taking another drink.

"Is there something else?" Tom asked, raising an eyebrow. "You look pensive."

"Well, kind of," Elle hesitated, unsure how to tell her dad the next part. "Ryan has had a, well, a hard life, I guess. He landed a full ride to Arizona State and was starting quarterback his junior and senior years for the Sun Devils but then got tackled and blew out his knee and had to have surgery, which basically ended his football career."

Tom nodded. "That also sounds familiar. You know I've never been much of an NFL fan, but I do love college football. I think I actually saw that game. The Sun Devils were on fire that year, I believe because of Ryan. He's tall, big guy, right? Dark hair?"

"Yes," Elle said. She was surprised her dad remembered. "What happened to him after that?" Tom asked.

"Well, he was a little lost for a while and then he met this girl, Candi, and she, um, led him down a bad road, so to speak," Elle said. Their server returned with their food, placing it in front of them.

After the server left, Tom asked, "Drugs, I'm guessing?"

Elle nodded sadly. "Yes. But he's been clean for years now and is back into fitness and being as healthy as possible."

"Well, that's good," Tom replied, digging into his veal and risotto. "You know I would never hold something like that against anyone if they've changed their life for the better. Hell, I've done a few things in my past that I'm not proud of."

Elle raised her eyebrows. She couldn't picture her dad doing anything illegal or immoral. He was the most honorable man she knew, and his integrity was very important to him, especially in how he ran his business.

"Don't look so surprised, sweetie," Tom replied with a grin. "I was once young and dumb."

Elle smiled. She took a bite of her salad, then cleared her throat before continuing. "Well, there's more."

Tom looked up from his plate. "Oh?" he asked.

Elle finished her martini, took a deep breath, and explained the rest—the lost pregnancies, Candi's vicious cycle of addiction, the car accident, the overdose. Tom listened in silence as she talked. Finally, she shared what happened with Tate and why Ryan went to prison.

Tom pushed his empty dinner plate aside and drained his martini. "I think we should get another round of these," he suggested when she finished telling the story.

Elle nodded, wishing she knew what her dad was thinking. She fidgeted with her napkin as Tom signaled the server and ordered two more martinis.

"Elle," Tom finally began, "you're right, it sounds like Ryan has had a difficult life. He definitely got a raw deal with the prison time. And I can't imagine losing two babies. But it also sounds like he's turned his life around and is doing well now. Right?"

"Yes," Elle replied. "He's spent several years working on himself and is very close with his sister, Lisa, and his niece and nephew. And he volunteers at a local boxing gym, working with underprivileged youths. Teaching them how to fight to protect themselves but also channeling boxing into something positive."

"That's good," Tom said, taking Elle's hand, smiling. "Family is the most important thing. And working with kids in the community shows his character. I'd like to meet Ryan. Maybe we could get lunch later this week. Also, perhaps for now, let's not tell your mother anything about Ryan. She's got a lot going on and, honestly, if she has one more meltdown this week, I might lose it myself."

Elle smiled, squeezing her dad's hand. "Please. You are the most patient person I know, especially with Ava. But yes, I'll talk to Ryan. I think lunch is a great idea.

"And thank you, Dad. Thank you for listening. I really like him. It's so different from what I felt with Todd. Looking back, I realize that wasn't love. It was a weird codependence, I guess. We both wanted something from the marriage. Obviously, Todd wanted money, and I wanted to feel loved, taken care of maybe. I think a therapist could have a field day with me," Elle added wryly.

Tom smiled. "Elle, you're not nearly as messed up as you think. We all make mistakes with relationships, learn from them, and then do better the next time around. It sounds like Ryan was very honest with you, and that's the best way to start off a relationship. You know I just want you to be happy, sweetie."

"I am," Elle replied. "I'm mad as hell about Todd, but when I'm with Ryan, nothing else matters. He does make me happy. Happier than I've been in a long time."

"Good. I'm glad. You have seemed happier lately. Now, how about we order some dessert? Since your mom isn't here, I can sneak in some cheesecake," Tom suggested with a wink.

"Absolutely," Elle agreed, relieved at how well the conversation with her dad went. Ava was going to be a whole different story.

Chapter Thirty-One

"I can't believe I let you assholes talk me into going to the gym with you," Lisa gasped, trying to catch her breath as she slowed her treadmill to a walk. She looked over at Elle on the next treadmill, who wasn't even breathing hard. "Why the hell am I running? I don't run. I think I'm going to pass out."

"It's addicting," Elle replied, slowing her treadmill to a walk also. "Trust me. Once you find a rhythm and the endorphins kick in, it gets better. It's kind of a love/hate relationship. Sometimes I do hate running, but when I'm done, I always feel amazing."

"Well, I feel like shit," Lisa replied, wiping sweat off her forehead. "I need a beer. And a couple of tacos. Can we please stop now?"

"What? Quitting so soon, sis?" Ryan joked, coming over to stand in front of them, leaning against Elle's treadmill. "I told you she couldn't hack it," he added with a grin at Elle as Lisa glared at him, still breathing hard.

"You can both kiss my ass," Lisa responded obviously irritatedly, slowing her treadmill to a stop. She liked Elle but was over the gym.

"If we can be done now, I'll buy lunch. Please. Get me out of here. I'm begging."

Ryan looked at Elle, raising an eyebrow. "What do you think? Lisa rarely offers to buy. I think we should take her up on that offer," he suggested.

Elle nodded, bringing her treadmill to a stop. "Actually a beer and a couple of tacos sounds really damn good. I'm in," she agreed.

"Praise Jesus!" Lisa exclaimed happily, hopping off the treadmill with a whoop. "Let's go!"

Chapter Thirty-Two

"Tom, it's very nice to meet you, sir," Ryan said, shaking her father's hand beside their table at the Capital Grille.

"Ryan, nice to meet you too," Tom replied, returning Ryan's handshake before sitting back down and gesturing to the chairs next to him.

"Hi Dad," Elle said, leaning over to give him a quick kiss on the cheek. *So far so good,* she thought. "Thank you for getting a table. They're busy here today."

"No worries, sweetie," Tom replied. "I left the office around noon to run a couple of errands and managed to get them done quickly for a change, so I got here a little early."

"That's always nice," Elle replied, picking up her menu. "Well, it's Friday afternoon and I'm actually done for the day. Shall we order some drinks? The Stoli Doli martini here is incredible."

"Sure, that sounds good to me," Tom agreed. "Ryan?"

"Sure, I'll try it," Ryan replied, glancing up from his menu.

"I might need two of them. Your mother is dragging me to that art show at SMoCA later," Tom said. Turning to Ryan, he elaborated, "If you're not familiar, it's the Scottsdale Museum of Contemporary Art. One of Ava's favorite places to 'be seen.'"

Elle snorted out a laugh. "Dad!" she exclaimed. She was a little surprised at her dad's comment, even though it was accurate.

"What?" Tom asked with a grin. "You know it's true." Elle smiled in agreement.

"So, Elle was telling me about the football injury at Arizona State that derailed your career," Tom said after the server took their drink and food orders. "Crazy enough, I watched that game. I remember the Sun Devils being on fire that year. Pretty sure that's the most exciting office college football pool we ever had."

"Well, thank you. Yeah, I guess at least I went out with a bang," Ryan replied, shrugging.

"Shame that happened. I was really looking forward to seeing you playing in the Rose Bowl. Weren't you guys something like eleven and one?" Tom asked.

"Yes, and the one we lost went into overtime and we lost it by a field goal," Ryan replied. "Sucked. But a pretty good season over-all that year."

The server dropped off their martinis, and Elle smiled as she sipped hers, watching her dad and Ryan continue talking about football. She breathed a mental sigh of relief at how well their first meeting was going.

Chapter Thirty-Three

"Let's see if this helmet will fit you," Ryan said, handing Lisa's old helmet to Elle. "Years ago, Lisa dated this guy, Rafael, who rode a motorcycle, but they broke up and George never had a bike. When she kicked him out, she cleaned out her garage and gave the helmet to me. I figured I'd hang onto it until Cayden or Charlie were old enough to fit in it to ride with me." He helped her fasten the strap under her chin.

"I think it fits," Elle replied, adjusting it on her head.

"It's supposed to be a pretty tight fit, but not so tight that it pinches," Ryan said. "Looks pretty good, I think." He also thought that Elle herself looked pretty damn good. She was wearing a pair of black moto leggings, black boots, and a black tee. Her leather jacket looked designer, but he figured it would be fine. He had no intention of taking any crazy chances with her on the back of his bike. "I can't believe you've never been on a motorcycle."

Elle shrugged. "Nope. My dad was never into motorcycles, and I guess I never dated anyone who had one. Until you. I mean, not to put a label on this," she stammered, visibly flustered. "I guess we haven't really discussed what we are ..." She trailed off, looking up at Ryan uncertainly.

Ryan smiled at her. "Elle, there is definitely no one else in my life. Just you. Which is exactly what I want," he added, putting his forehead against her helmet, looking into her green eyes. "Okay?"

Elle gave him a little smile. "Okay. Good."

Ryan reached for his helmet and put it on, still smiling at how cute she looked.

"And you have two bikes." Elle sounded impressed.

"Yeah, the KTM is more for off-road," Ryan replied, "though it is a dual sport. But I got the BMW for long cruises. It has always been one of the best ways to clear my head. When I got out, the KTM was the first thing I bought. After being locked up, all I wanted was to get on a bike and ride. It was really good therapy for me. Nothing beats the freedom of the open road. The sunshine, the wind, the fresh air. All the things I missed for those years."

Elle nodded. "I get that. I love to get in the Jag and drive fast, music blasting. I always feel better after that."

"Okay, let me get on, and then you can climb on behind me," Ryan said, swinging his leg over the bike and starting the engine, then showing her where to put her feet.

Elle climbed on behind him, placing her feet where he'd shown her and putting her arms around his waist.

"Ready?" Ryan asked, looking over his shoulder.

Elle gave him a thumbs up.

He pulled the bike out of the driveway, heading for the highway. He planned to take her to Cave Creek with a little detour to Bartlett Dam Road, which was only about fourteen miles long with twists and turns down to Bartlett Lake Marina. It was a scenic drive with views of saguaro cacti, blue waters, and mountain peaks of the nearby Tonto National Forest. The route was a total of around eighty miles round trip. A pretty big ride for her first time out, but Ryan knew a great place to stop in Cave Creek for lunch and a little break.

After a few miles on the bike, Ryan felt Elle relax against him. Her arms were still around him but not quite as tight. He hoped she was enjoying herself. Riding was an important part of his life. He wanted this to be something they could share and enjoy together. If she liked it, they'd have to look into getting her some proper gear, though.

After riding down the dam road to the marina to check out the lake and have a pit stop, they continued on to Cave Creek. Ryan took Elle to his favorite place there, the Mountain View Pub, which had incredible views from the open-air patio.

After sharing a pizza and having a beer each, they headed back toward Scottsdale.

On the way back to town, Ryan pulled over into a little dirt lot just off the highway and shut the bike off. He turned to Elle, flipping his visor up. "So what do you think so far, are you having fun?"

Elle held on to Ryan's shoulder as she swung off the bike, unfastening her helmet and pulling it off. "I love it. I admit I was a little nervous at first, but I love how it feels. The corners, the speed, and the best part, holding on to you," she said, smiling up at him as he stepped off the bike and took his helmet off.

"Good," Ryan replied with a relieved smile. "Well, this is the best place I know to watch the sun set behind the mountains."

Elle nodded, looking at the panoramic view before them. "It's beautiful," she breathed out.

"Not as beautiful as you," Ryan replied, the sun setting behind them as he pulled Elle into his arms and kissed her, her lips soft against his. *I'll never get tired of kissing her,* he thought, pulling her even closer against him. His hands moved under her leather jacket around her slim waist as his tongue met with hers, deep and searching. One-night stands with random women had been fine for a while–hell, it had been better than nothing. But this was what he wanted. One woman. His woman. Elle.

"Do you want to fly?" Conor asked, looking over at Lisa sitting in the right seat of his Cherokee. He was having trouble keeping his eyes off her. She looked sexy wearing jeans, boots, and a brown leather jacket over a white tank top.

"Me?" Lisa asked, glancing at Conor, surprise written all over her face. "Fly? Like, fly the plane?"

Conor smiled. "Yes. It's not that hard. You can do it. I'll show you—watch what I do," he instructed, gently moving the yoke to show her. "The yoke controls the airplane's ailerons. Simply put, it allows the pilot to move the airplane left and right. If you push the yoke forward, the plane will pitch downward; if you pull it back, it will climb. The elevator controls climbs and descents, but we'll save that for another lesson. So, gently put your hands on the yoke and just hold it steady."

"Wow," Lisa breathed out, holding onto the yoke, moving it in small increments. "Am I actually flying right now?"

"Yes you are, babe," Conor replied, "and doing it pretty well actually. You're a natural. So this"—he pointed to the ADI—"is the attitude deviation indicator. It shows the airplane's orientation relative to the horizon. So just make sure that you keep that line on those markings. Though honestly, the best advice I ever got was to fly outside the plane. Keep an eye on your instruments but focus mostly on watching your surroundings."

Lisa nodded, focused intently on the horizon.

"Relax your hands, babe." Conor gently reached over and touched her left hand. "And don't forget to breathe," he added with a smile.

Lisa let out a deep breath and smiled quickly at him, looking at the ADI, then back out the windshield. "Got it."

"I'm surprised that you haven't flown before. I mean, you own a charter company. Why did you never learn?" he asked, watching the ADI as she corrected just a little.

"My dad flew. I guess I never felt the need," Lisa replied. "There was always something else to do. After I got my MBA at the W.P. Carey School of Business in Tempe, I started working for my folks. My mom wanted to retire, and I was happy to step in. Then when they died, I had more than I could handle on my hands. Plus George and then the kids. The divorce. It was a lot. I guess I just focused on the business side."

"I get that," Conor said. "The ranch took over my life from basically the time I was old enough to work it. But flying was something I always wanted to do, and my dad encouraged it."

"Wow, this is actually pretty incredible," Lisa said, visibly relaxing. Conor was proud–she was getting the hang of this quickly.

"Everything and nothing," she added with a little smile.

"What?" Conor looked over at her quizzically. "What does that mean?"

"It's kind of my little motto for how I live my life. The everything part is, well, I want to do everything–travel, go on adventures, drink good whisky, drive fast, live dangerously, and take chances. Have great sex," she added, looking over at Conor with a grin, "because life is too short to not live it to the fullest. My parents died way too young, but they also lived great lives full of adventure and love. There was nothing average about them. I want the same thing, for me and for my kids."

Conor thought that described Lisa one hundred percent. "And the nothing part?"

"Well, that's the quiet part. I don't want to say the 'safe' part. I fucking hate that word. Safe. No. No way. Dangerous is the only way to live," Lisa replied, looking over at Conor with a wink. "Kind of like what I'm doing now." She laughed. "But sometimes you need the quiet. Sitting outside with your eyes closed, feeling the sun on your skin and the breeze in your hair. Or watching the sun set, the sky changing colors. Appreciating the peacefulness of hearing the birds sing. I want that balance between everything and nothing."

Conor wondered how he had been so lucky to find this woman. She was everything he never knew he was looking for. Everything and nothing. He agreed.

Chapter Thirty-Four

"Excuse me ... hello?"

Lisa looked up from her computer to find a man standing in front of her desk.

"There was no one in the reception area," he explained, gesturing behind him.

Lisa sat up, pressing the intercom button on her phone.

"Emily!" No response. "Sorry about that. She must be at lunch. Mr. ...?"

"Parker, Todd Parker. I'm interested in getting a quote for a charter," he replied smoothly.

Lisa looked Todd Parker over from head to toe in about three seconds and decided she didn't like him. He was trying too hard to be Mr. Scottsdale Suave and failing miserably. His likely over-priced suit was tailored and his Gucci loafers were casually elegant, but he couldn't quite pull it off. Almost like he was playing dress-up. His smile didn't reach his eyes and he was leering at her like she was something on the menu. Nope. Lisa knew the type only too well. And they usually didn't pay their bill on time either. *Get him a brochure and get rid of him,* she thought.

"What the hell are you doing here?" Ryan asked, appearing in the door of Lisa's office.

"Right. Ryan, is it?" Todd asked, smiling and extending a manicured hand to Ryan.

Ryan crossed his arms over his chest. "I'll ask you one more time, what the hell are you doing here?"

"What's going on?" Lisa asked, standing and coming around her desk, fear growing in the pit of her stomach.

"I think you need to have a talk with your employee, Ms. Daley," Todd replied, putting his hand down. "Though, I suppose when you hire ex-cons, you get what you pay for."

"What the fuck did you just say to me?" Lisa exploded, advancing toward Todd.

"Sis, hold on," Ryan said quickly, getting between Lisa and Todd, holding her by the arms. "Wait."

"We know you don't like to fight, big guy, but it looks like that gene didn't skip your sister. Wildcat there. Are you single?" Todd asked, a small insincere smile on his face.

Lisa suddenly understood. Todd–Elle's ex. Motherfucker. Her blood turned cold, and she narrowed her eyes. "What the hell do you want?"

"What do I want?" Todd repeated, putting on a phony thoughtful face. "I suppose I only want what's rightfully mine. And the sooner I get it, the sooner you all can get on with your little lives. So maybe, if you like not being in prison, Ryan, you can convince my wife–sorry, I mean, your lover–to kindly let me have what I deserve and just sign the damn divorce papers."

"You did not seriously come in here to threaten my brother, did you?" Lisa asked softly.

Todd seemed to sense that quiet Lisa was angry and scary, and started slowly backing out of her office. "Think about what I said. I want a happy ending for everyone," he called over his shoulder as he exited through the main entrance. "Nice to meet you, Ms. Daley."

"I'm gonna fucking kill him," Lisa ground out, clenching her fists to her side, glaring after him as he hightailed it to his black Beemer and squealed out of the parking lot.

Ryan sighed. "Yeah, you get it now."

"What an unbelievably arrogant asshole!" Lisa yelled. "I can't believe the nerve of him, showing up here like that and threatening you. What the hell?!"

"Sis, I'm fine," Ryan said, giving Lisa a hug. "Don't worry about me. I'm not going to take his bait. As much as I'd love to kick his ass, it's not worth it. I'm never going back. Back there."

Lisa returned her brother's hug, which helped bring her blood pressure down a little. "Well, maybe I'll just have to kick his ass then," she suggested.

Ryan chuckled.

"HE *WHAT*?" Elle gasped into her cellphone. "Oh my God. No. Shit." She couldn't believe Todd's audacity. Even so, she was glad Ryan called to tell her what had happened right away.

"It's fine. Lisa scared him and he bolted," Ryan explained.

Elle smiled briefly. Lisa scared her a little, too. She was sort of disappointed she'd missed that.

"So, Lisa wants to have us over for dinner tomorrow. She suggested that we have a little, um, family meeting, I guess. She's concerned about Todd showing up here today making threats," Ryan said.

"Okay, yes. I agree. We all need to talk," Elle replied with a sigh. Wow, really starting this relationship off on the right foot. But better to address this issue than ignore it.

"Elle..." Ryan paused, then asked, "Are you worried ... I mean, do you think Todd would, I don't know, show up at your Airbnb and try and harass you? Because if you don't feel safe at the Airbnb, you can come stay with me."

"I honestly don't know," Elle replied, pondering for a moment. "I don't think he knows where it is, but I'm not absolutely certain of that. And if Todd is feeling like he's losing, he can be unpredictable, obviously."

"Pack a bag then. Come over tonight. I don't want you there alone."

After Elle hung up, she sat at her desk staring at her phone. *This is getting out of hand fast,* she thought in dismay. *Damn Todd.*

"What did Elle say?" Lisa asked, leaning back in her chair as Ryan came back into her office.

"Dinner tomorrow is fine and she's also packing a bag," Ryan explained, stopping near her desk. "She's going to stay with me. I don't trust Todd. I worry he might try to hurt her again."

Lisa nodded. "I agree, though a slime like that would hire out his dirty work."

"Thanks, sis, that makes me feel so much better," Ryan replied dryly.

"Sorry." Lisa shrugged. "I invited Conor, too. I feel like the more people we have on our side, the better."

Ryan nodded. "Are we overreacting?"

Lisa pondered for a moment, then replied, "Remember when everyone said I was overreacting about Tate?"

Ryan nodded again.

"He wanted to kill me. He would have killed me. If you hadn't stopped him," Lisa said, quietly. "And I get the exact same vibes from Todd. He's not going to go away quietly. I think it's better to be prepared."

Chapter Thirty-Five

"I appreciate you driving up here," Lisa said, giving Conor a kiss after he shrugged his denim jacket off and set his hat on the table by her front door.

"It sounded serious," Conor replied, pulling Lisa into his arms and returning her kiss. "You're okay though, right?"

"Yeah, other than I'm mad as hell," Lisa replied, taking his hand and leading him further into her house.

Conor followed her, reminding himself to never make her mad. They entered her kitchen.

"Whisky?" Lisa asked, reaching into her pantry for a bottle.

"Yes, please," Conor replied, watching Lisa pour two fingers of whisky in two glasses. She looked casual-yet-sexy in worn jeans and an old Waylon Jennings concert tee, barefoot, toes painted purple, and her hair in a messy bun. When she'd called yesterday, he'd been more than happy to come back to Scottsdale. *Any excuse,* he thought wryly. She already had him wrapped around her little finger.

"I'll take one of those too, sis." Ryan came into the kitchen holding Elle's hand. "You too, babe?"

Elle nodded. "Yes, please. Hi Lisa," she said, setting her purse on the counter.

Lisa poured two more glasses, made introductions, then gave Elle a hug.

"Kids are at George's tonight," Lisa explained. "I want to keep them as far away from this mess as possible."

"Damn. I'm so sorry for causing all of this fuss," Elle said, sighing.

"Girl, it's not you. It's your asshole ex," Lisa replied with a grin. "And if it makes you feel better, I've got a couple, too."

"Me too," Conor chimed in. "Well, she was more of a bitch than an asshole."

Elle laughed. "Okay, okay, I feel better now, thank you."

LATER, after everyone had had their fill of the pizzas and salads Lisa had ordered, they sat around the dining room table laughing, trading bad ex stories, and drinking more whisky. Elle had been laughing so hard her face hurt. She looked around the table. Ryan and Lisa had great brother/sister sarcastic banter, teasing and joking with each other. Conor was even holding his own, giving as good as he got.

Elle glanced at Ryan sitting next to her. He looked over at her, squeezing her hand under the table. She smiled. *This is how family should be,* she thought, realizing this easy camaraderie was something she'd never had with her parents. Or Todd, for that matter.

"Okay, on a more serious note," Lisa began gravely, looking at Elle. "I think that until you can get your divorce finalized, you need to be hyper-aware of your surroundings. Pay attention to anything that seems unusual. Listen to your gut. If you feel like something is off, it probably is."

"Ryan made me promise not to go back to the Airbnb alone," Elle said. She was glad he'd asked her to stay with him. She honestly never wanted to go back to that depressing place ever again.

"Good. I agree," Lisa responded. She stood to get her handbag off the counter. Reaching in, she pulled out her gun and set it on the table. "Ever since Tate, I carry my 9mm with me everywhere."

"Damn, babe," Conor said appreciatively. "Nice gun."

"Thank you, honey," Lisa replied, turning back to Elle. "I have a .32 backup, if you want to borrow it. Arizona is a constitutional carry state, so you don't need a concealed weapon permit, though I do have mine."

"I don't know," Elle replied, a little uneasy. "I've never shot a gun before. My dad hunts, but I don't have any experience."

"I could take you to the range," Lisa suggested. "It would probably be a good idea to familiarize yourself, anyway. Besides, it's better to have a gun and not need it, than need a gun and not have it."

"I think that's a good idea, too," Ryan said. "I looked into buying a shotgun about a year ago for home protection but decided it wasn't worth the hassle to hire an attorney to get a set-aside after my conviction."

"Okay," Elle agreed, wondering if they were all overreacting. She thought she had known the full extent of Todd's temper, but his behavior lately had been more aggressive than she'd ever seen. Maybe a little protection was a good idea.

Chapter Thirty-Six

"What?" Ryan asked, leaning against the doorframe of Logan's office. "Owen was sleeping here at the gym?"

"Yeah," Logan said. "I came in early to do some paperwork in the office this morning and discovered him sleeping in one of the shower stalls. He said his dad kicked him out two days ago and he spent one night behind the dumpster behind the gym. Last night he must've snuck in before I locked up. Kid was shaking when I found him. Thought I was going to call the cops on him."

"Damn," Ryan said, shaking his head.

"Owen is terrified I'm going to call social services, have him hauled off to foster care or something," Logan explained. "Which I'm not going to do, but that leaves the question of what am I going to do? He can't stay here, obviously."

"No, I agree," Ryan replied.

"He's cleaning the bathrooms now. He volunteered to do even more work around here if I let him stay. He could sleep on the couch in my office for a night or two. I'm not going to just kick him out, but that is not a long-term solution."

Ryan thought for a moment. "I have an idea. Let me make a

phone call and I'll get back to you in a bit," he said, reaching for his cell to call Conor.

A few minutes and a successful phone call later, Ryan stuck his head in the door. "I might have a solution," he said.

Logan looked up from his desk. "What's up?"

"Lisa is seeing this guy, Conor Hayes, who owns a big cattle ranch out near Tucson. He's got about eight hands working the ranch. Conor said in exchange for room and board, Owen could work at the ranch," Ryan explained. "May be a better solution than throwing the kid into the foster care system, especially since he's so close to being eighteen. He could learn some life skills and probably still do online school or something."

Logan nodded thoughtfully. "Yeah, I like it. I'll talk to Owen about it and see what he thinks. Thanks Ryan. This might be a good solution."

"If Owen is agreeable, we could drive him down and introduce him to Conor. Let him see the ranch and everything. Make sure it's a decent fit."

"Good idea," Logan replied. "I'll let you know by this afternoon."

"Okay, sounds good," Ryan said.

Chapter Thirty-Seven

"Just picture Todd's face on the target," Lisa advised, sending the paper target down the lane. "That's what I do. I picture Tate's face. Helps me focus."

Elle picked up Lisa's 9mm, lining up her sight down the lane of the shooting range.

"Just breathe normally, relax, and squeeze the trigger. Don't jerk it," Lisa instructed.

Elle exhaled, squeezing the trigger several times, picturing Todd's sneering mouth and remembering how he had hurt her.

"Damn, girl!" Lisa exclaimed, running the target back. "You're a natural. Look at that grouping. Great job."

"Thanks," Elle replied, feeling more confident. "I think I like shooting. This is kinda fun."

Lisa laughed. "There's definitely something therapeutic about it. I think shooting and hitting the heavy bag that's hanging in the back of the hangar are my two favorite ways to relieve stress. Well, that and sex," she added with a wink.

Elle blushed a little. She and Ryan had apparently been relieving a lot of stress the last few days.

"Okay, let's try the .32. This is a Walther PPK. It's lighter and isn't as good for distance, but up close it will get the job done. Especially if you empty the entire magazine," Lisa explained, handing the gun to Elle.

Elle lifted the lighter gun, focused on the paper target, and fired all ten bullets. *Damn, this feels good,* she thought, feeling more in control of her life than she had in a long time.

"Nice," Lisa said, running the target back. "A few strays, but the Walther takes a little practice."

"I like the feel of it though," Elle said, handing the smaller gun back to Lisa.

Lisa took the gun, showed Elle how to reload, then handed it back to her. "Just so you know, I hated Candi," Lisa admitted. "Maybe I shouldn't speak ill of the dead but I knew she was trouble the first time I saw her with Ryan. He was a different person around her."

Elle looked over at Lisa, surprised.

"And I never really liked Kimberly. She was a stuck-up bitch. Had her and Ryan over for dinner once and Charlie knocked over a glass of milk and some of it ended up in her lap, and she had a full-on meltdown over her ruined silk pants. Good grief," Lisa said, rolling her eyes.

"Wow," Elle replied. "Well, Ryan hasn't told me much about her."

"Good riddance, if you ask me. Ryan is my only family, besides my babies, and I've spent a lot of years looking out for him." Lisa paused. "I think you are good for him. I just want to ... I don't know, say thank you. His past isn't something a lot of women can deal with, obviously, but it's pretty clear how you feel about him and, well, it makes me really fucking happy that you two found each other. He's been alone too long."

Elle set the Walther down, turning to give Lisa a hug. "I know my situation isn't ideal right now, but I want nothing more than to get Todd out of my life so Ryan and I can really be together. I know it's kind of fast, but I've already fallen hard," she admitted.

Lisa smiled. "Good. I'm glad. But as much as I like you, I won't hesitate to kick your ass if you hurt him," she added.

Elle grinned. She didn't doubt that for a minute.

Chapter Thirty-Eight

"Thank you again for everything you've done to help out Owen," Lisa said, curling up in what had quickly become her spot on the couch in the library. She'd driven down to the ranch this time, as Conor had some scheduled maintenance planned for his plane. But she didn't mind. It had given her time to think. She was already falling hard for Conor, but she wasn't sure what she wanted yet. It was complicated, him living at the ranch and her in Scottsdale. It wasn't quite a long-distance relationship, but it was close to it.

And then there were her babies. She'd never dated anyone she had wanted to introduce her kids to. Until now. Which was another thing—was Conor interested in stepping in, being a stepdad? They hadn't talked about it at all. It was a big leap from having fun and great sex to parenting. Did she want to try to pursue something serious?

Conor continued to surprise her. Lisa loved their hot, fast, and noisy sex. But when he took his time, forcing her to slow down while he explored her body from head to toe, driving her to the brink over and over, making her crazy with wanting him ... Well that was pretty damn hot, too. But she wasn't sure she wanted to get married again.

Besides, was that something Conor wanted? He'd never been married before. There were so many hard questions she wasn't sure she wanted to address right now.

"I really haven't done that much," Conor replied, pouring them each a glass of cabernet sauvignon, handing Lisa a glass before sitting down next to her on the couch.

"You've done more than you know," Lisa said, taking a sip of wine. "When Ryan told me about Owen and his story, it broke my heart."

"Hopefully, it will be a good move for him. When Ryan and Logan brought Owen here, he seemed pretty excited. He's definitely got a few things to learn, though, after growing up in the city. But Riley will work with him. He has him all set up in the bunkhouse. We've got a really good group right now. Owen might be about to get more life experience than he's ready for," Conor said with a little laugh. "Though Riley has told them all to behave themselves."

"So, who is Chloe?" Lisa asked, changing the subject abruptly.

"Jimmy has a really big fucking mouth," Conor replied wryly.

"You told me about Maggie, but you never mentioned Chloe," Lisa said. Who could blame her for being curious?

Conor let out a sigh. "Well, yeah. I guess because that relationship was a huge mistake," he admitted.

"Why a huge mistake?" Lisa asked, raising an eyebrow.

"Well, I think I told you that I put the ranch ahead of Maggie for a lot of years before she gave up and left me," Conor began.

Lisa nodded.

"Then I met Chloe and she was incredible, at first. Everything I thought I missed out on with Maggie, I pursued with Chloe. I'd neglected Maggie, for sure, and I definitely went to the other extreme with Chloe. Extravagant trips, shopping sprees, expensive gifts. Where I'd neglected Maggie for the ranch, I neglected the ranch for Chloe. Which caused some financial problems, which I'm actually still working on turning around."

"So, what happened?" Lisa inquired.

"Well, I caught her in the barn with one of my ranch hands," Conor replied, looking down at his glass.

"Oh, damn," Lisa replied, shocked.

"Needless to say, I broke up with her," Conor continued, "and fired the ranch hand."

"Did you beat the shit out of him first?" Lisa asked with a small grin. That's what she would have done if someone had cheated on her.

Conor shook his head. "No, but I wish I had. It would have been more satisfying. But I didn't want a lawsuit or anything to come up. I just wanted them both gone and out of my life."

"And how long ago was this?"

"A little over a year ago. I went on a few dates after that, but my heart just wasn't into pursuing anything beyond that." He glanced over at her, adding, "Until now."

Lisa smiled. "Well, they say everything happens for a reason. Thank you for telling me about her. I admit I was curious, but only because of what Jimmy said. I promise I won't be that crazy person who wants to drag out all of your old laundry. Like how many lovers you have had, etcetera. I don't care. I only care about now."

Conor grinned. "Jimmy needs to learn to keep his trap shut. And maybe I want to know how many old lovers you have out there," he said, raising an eyebrow.

Lisa shook her head. "Confidential information," she replied, leaning in to kiss him, officially ending the conversation.

Chapter Thirty-Nine

Elle looked up from the project she was working on at her desk, hearing her phone vibrate. Brian. *Oh boy,* she thought, picking it up. Hopefully, her attorney had good news.

"I heard back from Todd's attorney," Brian said over the phone without preamble.

Elle sat up straighter at her desk. "What did he say?" she asked nervously.

"Well, interestingly enough, Mr. Monroe is ready to drop Todd as a client," Brian said.

"What? I mean, honestly that's not surprising, but is that good or bad?" Elle asked.

"Well, I've known Ed Monroe for years and he's a first-rate attorney. Also, he doesn't put up with any shit," Brian said. "Ed said that other than his retainer, Todd hasn't paid him for any further work and, well, he basically said the guy is an asshole, which we already know. Said he refuses to listen to his council. Ed told him he doesn't have a snowball's chance in hell of getting the house in the divorce, and apparently Todd lost it. He had some sort of meltdown in Ed's office, yelling at him. Ed said he almost had to call security. So yeah, he's ready to drop him."

"Shit," Elle replied, slumping back in her chair. "So what happens if he drops Todd as a client?"

"Well, unless Todd decides to represent himself, which I see as unlikely, he'll have to find another attorney, who will have to be brought up to speed. So a continuance is distinctly possible. We have the deposition scheduled for next week but, honestly, I was hoping we'd be able to come to an agreement before that, though now it's looking unlikely," Brian said.

Elle closed her eyes, sighing in frustration. Damn Todd.

"I convinced Ed to keep him on as a client until I had a chance to talk to you. I had a thought," Brian said slowly. "I know you want this guy out of your life. I was wondering just how bad."

"What do you mean exactly?" Elle asked, frowning.

"It's just a thought, but Todd seems very financially motivated," Brian paused. "Would you be willing to offer him a cash settlement? Like, a one-time alimony payment. Maybe if he's desperate, it might get him to sign the divorce papers."

"Alimony," Elle repeated, clenching her teeth. "Give him more damn money?"

"Take a day. Think about it," Brian suggested. "Call me tomorrow. Just think about what your peace of mind is worth. I know it's the last thing you want to do, but think about it. It might be your easiest way out. Otherwise, who knows how long Todd could drag this out."

"Okay," Elle replied. "Thanks, Brian."

She ended the call, blowing out a deep breath. It would be so much easier to just shoot Todd. She smiled, thinking about how much she'd love to point the gun currently in her purse at his head. If only.

Chapter Forty

"Thank you for meeting me here," Lisa said, giving Conor a quick kiss on the cheek and taking his hand as they followed the hostess to their table at one of her kids' favorite restaurants. Cayden and Charlie were skipping ahead of them. "I thought this would be a little more casual, having dinner out instead of having you come to the house."

"I totally understand," Conor replied, squeezing Lisa's hand.

"Honestly, you are the first man I've ever dated that I've introduced my kids to," Lisa explained quietly with a shy smile. "The first man I've ever wanted to meet them."

Conor smiled back, then slid into the booth next to her, across from Cayden and Charlie.

"Can I get a banana split?" Cayden asked excitedly, picking up the menu and going straight to the desserts.

"How about dinner first?" Lisa suggested with a little smile, shaking her head. "Then dessert."

Cayden sighed. "Okay, a cheeseburger, I guess."

After the server took their food orders, Lisa relented and let the kids each get a milkshake, knowing she'd regret it later at bedtime.

She turned to Conor. "So, I didn't guess you to be a strawberry-banana milkshake kinda guy."

"What do you mean? They're the best," Conor replied with a wink at Charlie, who had ordered the same thing.

"Yuck, no way," Cayden chimed in. "Chocolate is the best."

"Chocolate is definitely the best," Lisa agreed, grinning conspiratorially at Cayden.

"Do you really have your own plane?" Charlie asked Conor, her eyes big.

"Yes, I do. A Cherokee," Conor replied.

"That's a Piper single engine, right?" Cayden chimed in.

Conor raised his eyebrows. "Yes, that's right. Good job."

"My mom has five planes," Cayden said, putting the emphasis on five.

"I know," Conor smiled. "They're much nicer than mine."

"Would you take me for a ride and let me ride in the cockpit?" Charlie asked. "Mom never lets us ride in the cockpit with the pilots." She stuck out a pouty lip.

"That's because our planes are for business, not for fun," Lisa replied, rolling her eyes. She had figured Conor would be an easy sell with Charlie. Charlie warmed up to most people pretty quickly. She had guessed Cayden would take longer to win over. He was more serious and thoughtful in everything he did, slower to make friends and let people get close. She had a feeling he'd learned that from her.

"Well, if it's okay with your mom, I'd take you guys for a spin," Conor said, looking over at Lisa, who nodded.

"Can I wear a headset, too?" Charlie asked excitedly.

Conor leaned forward, smiling at her enthusiasm. "I could even show you how to fly the plane."

Cayden's eyes got big this time. "Really? I want to be a pilot when I grow up. I have a flight simulator game Uncle Ryan got me. I'm really good. Better than my uncle. I can take off and land without crashing. Uncle Ryan always crashes," he added smugly.

"That's why he fixes planes and doesn't fly them," Lisa said with a grin as the server brought their burgers and milkshakes. They all happily dug into their dinners.

"You've got some smart kids there, babe," Conor said later, holding Lisa in her bed. He had parked his truck down the street a bit and waited while Lisa got the kids to sleep. Then she quietly snuck him into her bedroom.

"I know," Lisa replied with a grin. "Thank you. It's not always been easy, but it's always worth it. I wouldn't change anything. They're my life. And Ryan, of course. And now you," she added softly, leaning in to kiss him as she pulled him closer.

Chapter Forty-One

"Hi honey," Elle said into her cell, leaving Ryan a voicemail. She exited the elevator, heading toward her Jaguar. "Just leaving the office now. I had a long phone conference with a client. I should be at your place in about twenty minutes. Hopefully traffic isn't too bad. See you soon."

Elle got to her car, looking down to put her cell in her purse. As she reached for the driver's door handle, she was pushed up against the side of the car. "What the hell?!" she exclaimed, accidentally dropping her handbag. She tried to turn around, but she was pinned to the car.

"I guess I should have just killed you. You obviously didn't learn anything from the little lesson I tried to teach you. Then I'd have everything plus a tidy little life insurance payout," Todd breathed in her ear, pushing her harder against the car. With one hand holding her right hand tightly behind her back, he reached around to quickly grab her left, pinning both of her hands between their bodies. "Though I guess it's not too late, is it sweetheart?"

"Todd!" Elle exclaimed angrily, trying to wrench free. She

wished she could get the gun that was currently inaccessible in her handbag on the ground. "Stop it. Let me go!"

"Not yet," Todd replied, putting more pressure on her wrists. Then he whispered in her ear, "We need to clear up a few things first."

"I'll scream," Elle threatened, fear forming in the pit of her stomach. She struggled harder, trying to stomp down on his foot with the heel of her pumps, but missing.

"That's not very nice." Todd pushed her harder into the car. "I was being nice. But if you want to play rough, sweetheart, I can play fucking rough. Did you like it when we played rough before? I know I did. It's kind of hard to scream when you can't breathe, isn't it?" he asked softly in her ear. "You know what I want and I'm going to get it one way or another. The easy way apparently didn't appeal to you, so now we're going to do it the hard way. Do you understand? Nod if you understand."

She flashed back to when he'd hit her, panic filling her. Elle nodded, pushing back against him as hard as she could, but she was having trouble getting air into her lungs from the weight of him against her back.

"Good girl," Todd responded, squeezing her hands even harder between them. "You will sign those papers. I'm thinking by tomorrow. Or else I'll just have to make other arrangements. Trust me. You really don't want me to do that. Got it?"

Elle nodded again, still struggling to breathe, tears springing to her eyes. She felt nothing but revulsion as he pressed himself against her.

Todd leaned closer, still whispering in her ear. "Though it does turn me on when you fight me. This is what was missing from our marriage–foreplay."

Elle suddenly threw her head back, hard, catching him right in the nose. It made a satisfying crunch, his grip loosening on her wrists as he yelped. She gasped, trying to take in air as he backed up, clutching his nose.

"Fucking bitch! You broke my nose!" Todd yelled. He whipped Elle back by her hair, grabbed her right hand again, and spun her around to face him.

Elle tried to reach down for her bag, but Todd was too fast.

He pushed her back against the car, both of his hands wrapped around her neck, squeezing as blood ran down his face. "You're going to pay for that," he growled.

Elle choked, frantically grabbing at Todd's hands. She tried to pull them away from her throat, hysteria filling her, unable to breathe.

"It didn't have to be this way," Todd snarled at her, squeezing harder. "Stupid bitch. Why couldn't you just sign the damn papers? I'd have been out of your life. Well, it was your choice. You can die now."

"Hey, what's going on over there?" a voice called across the parking garage.

Elle blinked, trying to clear the fog from her head. People were yelling. Todd dropped his hands and ran as she slid down the side of her car to the ground.

"Is she okay? Someone call 911." Elle heard more voices, but her body felt heavy, blood pounding in her head. Her wrists were on fire. Everything hurt. *It's so dark,* she thought as she closed her eyes, mentally calling Ryan's name.

Chapter Forty-Two

Conor got to the top of the ridge and eased Noche to a walk, bringing the horse around to the edge of the hill. "Whoa, buddy," he said, stopping and looking back down at the ranch. The cattle sale had gone well and brought a much-needed influx of cash. That cash would be good for the future of the ranch.

Thinking about the future brought him back to Lisa. Damn that woman. She was all he could think about lately. How he had felt about Maggie and Chloe was nothing close to what he was feeling right now for Lisa. Laoise. She was fire and passion, setting him on fire like no one ever had. He loved everything about her.

Love. *Hmm, yeah,* he admitted to himself. He had definitely fallen hard for her.

But what would happen next? He knew he wanted her in his life, in his bed, in his home. But did she want that? Would she want to live at the ranch? She had a successful business she was running back in Scottsdale. As much as he wanted her–and Cayden and Charlie too– at the ranch, he wasn't sure that was something Lisa wanted. Difficult questions he had no answers for at the moment.

Chapter Forty-Three

Elle slowly opened her eyes, quickly closing them again with a low moan.

"Elle, honey," Ryan said, gently touching the side of her face. "Elle, can you hear me?"

Elle nodded slowly, then fell back asleep.

"Ryan," Lisa said quietly, putting a hand on his shoulder. "The doctors said she's going to be fine. She just needs to rest."

Ryan stood up from the side of Elle's hospital bed. He and Lisa walked over to the window. "I'm going to fucking kill Todd," he said softly.

"I know you're angry, but–"

"Angry? You think I'm angry?" Ryan choked out fiercely, grabbing Lisa by the arms. "I almost lost her. She almost died tonight. If those people hadn't gotten off the elevator when they did, Elle could be dead. God, if I lost her now … I can't even imagine. She is my life. She's the most important thing in my fucking life."

"I know. God, I know. But she's okay, Ryan. That's the most important thing. Please don't do anything yet. Just let me–" Lisa began.

"Ryan," Elle called softly.

"Honey, I'm right here," Ryan said, coming back over to her side and leaning down to stroke her hair. "You're safe. I'm here, I'm sorry. I am so sorry. I promise you that I will never let him hurt you again." Ryan looked back at Lisa, tears in his eyes.

"My head ... it hurts. It hurts to swallow," Elle whispered.

"I'll get you some water," Ryan said, reaching for the hospital sippy cup on the tray next to her bed. He held it for her. Elle took a few small sips before she leaned back against the pillow, closing her eyes again.

Lisa grabbed her purse off the chair and headed for the door.

"Sis, where are you going?" Ryan asked, frowning and looking over his shoulder at her.

"You stay with Elle," Lisa commanded.

Ryan set the cup down and got up, coming around the side of Elle's bed, eyes narrowing. "Sis. No," he said emphatically.

"You stay with her," Lisa repeated quietly. "There is no fucking way I'm letting you go back to prison."

"What do you think you're going to do?" Ryan asked, shaking his head. "And before you answer, no. That's a terrible idea."

Lisa smiled, putting her hand on his arm. "Don't worry about me. I have a plan."

"Stop. Just wait," Ryan said, running his hands through his hair and letting out a deep breath. "You can't fight all my battles for me, you know."

"*Your* battles?" Lisa replied. "No. Not anymore. This is about family. This is my fight too, little brother. Family takes care of family. And Elle is family now."

Ryan leaned down and put his forehead on Lisa's, reluctantly giving in. "I love you, sis. You better know what you're doing."

"Don't worry about me," Lisa repeated, giving him a quick hug. "I love you, too. Take care of our girl."

Ryan watched, torn, as Lisa left the hospital room. He looked back at Elle, so fragile and small in the hospital bed. He couldn't leave her side. He hoped Lisa knew what she was doing.

Chapter Forty-Four

"I thought you might show up here," Lisa said. She sat in her dark office, the only light coming from the outside flood lights illuminating the office just a bit. She had a glass of bourbon in her hand and her feet up on her desk, leaning back casually in her office chair.

"Wildcat and smart," Todd replied, leaning against the door.

"You forgot mean," Lisa responded, taking a slow sip of her bourbon.

Todd laughed. "You going to pour me one?" he asked, coming into her office.

Lisa reached over for the bottle of Maker's Mark, poured two fingers into a glass and slid it across the desk to Todd.

"Elle was nothing. She is nothing. You, on the other hand, you're dangerous. I recognize it. I respect it. You want to kick my ass, don't you?" Todd asked, picking up the glass and taking a drink as he slipped into the chair across from her. He unbuttoned his jacket then leaned back, slouching in the chair and resting his drink on the arm.

"You don't want to fuck with my family," Lisa said calmly, taking another sip. "You didn't need to attack Elle."

"That wasn't my plan. All I wanted to do was talk, then that bitch broke my nose," Todd said, gently rubbing the bridge of his nose.

Lisa smiled. The bruises under his eyes made her happy. *Good girl, Elle.*

"You almost killed her," she said, narrowing her eyes, no longer smiling.

"Did I?" Todd asked thoughtfully, reaching up to straighten his tie. "Something I should have considered doing earlier. I'm just too nice. One of my faults, I guess."

"Elle is lying in a hospital bed because of you," Lisa said through clenched teeth. She wanted to pull her 9mm out of her desk drawer and shoot him in the face.

"Better than the morgue," Todd grinned cockily, taking another sip of bourbon.

"You are going to leave her alone," Lisa said, putting her feet on the floor and leaning forward in her chair.

"Why? Do you want to play instead, Wildcat?" Todd asked, raising an eyebrow. The fucker had the gall to seem entertained. "You would definitely be more fun."

"You want to play, asshole? Let's go. Let's fucking go," Lisa said calmly, standing up behind her desk, kicking her Louboutin heels off, ready for a fight.

"Now, now," Todd replied easily, wagging a finger at her. "Sit down. I'm more of a lover than a fighter. I could show you, anytime."

Lisa sat back down, taking a deep breath. She glared at Todd and took another sip of her bourbon.

"There has to be a solution to our problem, a way to settle this amicably," Todd said, inspecting his nails as he talked.

Lisa almost choked on her drink. Amicably? Elle was currently lying in a hospital bed. *I'll show you fucking amicable when I bash you over the head with this whisky bottle, asshole,* she thought, forcing herself to breathe calmly.

"Let's play 'Let's Make a Deal,'" Todd suggested. "You and your brother and Elle all want me to just go quietly away, right?"

Lisa nodded slowly.

"Except that's not going to happen," Todd said smoothly. "Unless, well, maybe we could come to some sort of financial agreement."

"How much?" Lisa ground out.

"Right to the point–I like how you think," Todd said, smiling. "I'm thinking a million would set me up somewhere far away from here."

"And you'll sign the divorce papers?" Lisa asked.

"Sure, why not? Ironic, isn't it? Elle could have just signed the papers and I'd already be gone but now it's really going to cost her," Todd said with a shrug, standing, draining his drink and setting the empty glass on Lisa's desk. "I think it's time to move on from Arizona anyway. Too damn hot here. I'll be generous. A week. One week to get the money together."

"How do I contact you?" Lisa asked.

"Don't worry, Wildcat, I'll find you," Todd replied with a wink before leaving her office, slamming the outer door.

"Please, please fucking tell me that you got all of that," Lisa said into her speaker phone, watching Todd drive off in his Beemer.

"We got it, sweets. Every word," Conor replied, opening the door from the hangar. He and Riley came into Lisa's office holding up his phone.

Lisa blew out a deep breath. "Thank God. That fucker actually confessed to attacking Elle. There has to be a way to use that against him."

"I still think you should have just let me shoot him," Riley said, resting the butt of his shotgun on the ground. "Jesus, what an asshole."

"No way," Lisa replied quickly. "First, he has to sign the divorce papers. The original papers. He's not getting Elle's house. Then, if anyone gets to shoot Todd, it's me."

"Damn," Conor said, coming over to Lisa, taking her in his arms, and giving her a kiss. "I'm impressed. I don't know how you managed to keep your cool. I wanted to come through the door and punch that jerk in the face, especially with the way he talked to you."

"I honestly don't know how I did it either," Lisa admitted, holding the whisky bottle up. "I think I need some more of this. Anyone else?"

"Yes, please," Conor replied, dropping down into the chair Todd had vacated. "Riley?"

"Hell yes," Riley said, sitting in the other chair, resting his shotgun against Lisa's desk, and accepting the glass she handed him. "Thank you, ma'am."

"Slainte," Conor said, raising his glass.

"Slainte," Lisa responded.

"Also, remind me to never piss you off," Conor said with a wink, taking a drink.

Chapter Forty-Five

"R yan," Elle said. "I'm fine, really. This is not necessary."

"Just lie back and relax, Elle," Ryan replied, gently pushing her back against the pillows. "You're supposed to be resting. Doctor's orders."

"But I feel better," Elle protested. "Just a little sore."

Ryan sat down gently on the edge of his bed next to Elle, examining the bruises on her neck. He took one of her hands in his, lightly rubbing the bruises around her wrists, a slow burn of anger igniting in his chest. He wanted to find Todd and hurt him the way he'd hurt Elle.

"Ryan," Elle said softly. "I know you're angry, angry at Todd, for what he did to me. But please, promise me–"

"Elle," Ryan interrupted, "I will never let him hurt you again. That's what I will promise you. Do you understand? I will kill him first."

"As much as I would love for him to be dead, I don't want you to go back to prison," Elle pleaded. "Please, promise me that."

Ryan shook his head. "I won't lie to you. I can't promise you that, Elle. I can only promise that I will protect you."

He hesitated, looking down at Elle, his chest aching a little. Sitting next to her hospital bed, he'd finally admitted to himself that he loved her. She'd somehow managed to get through the walls he'd built around his heart, and he'd fallen hard. His resolve to be alone had slipped away. Hell, she'd forgiven and accepted him when no one else did. She'd been able to see the man he hid behind the coldness and anger.

Just tell her how you feel. What if she had died? Would you have regretted not saying anything?

"Elle, I ..." he started, then took a deep breath. "I've had my, well, my emotions on lockdown for so many years. I was so afraid of getting hurt again that I, well, I stopped living life. I was just going through the motions. Not letting myself feel anything. I've been through so much shit. There's a lot of darkness in my past, some things I'm never going to be able to talk to you about. Do you understand?"

Elle nodded.

"I've spent so many years alone. I thought I was going to be alone forever. Then you came into my life. Now that I've found you, there's no way I'm going to lose you," Ryan said firmly.

"Ryan," Elle said quietly, taking his hand, "I'm not going anywhere. You're not going to lose me."

"I love you, Elle," Ryan said quietly. "I've only said those words to two women in my life, but not until now did I truly know what they meant. When your dad called me and told me what happened, I ... I don't know, I felt like I would have died if something had happened to you. I can't explain it better than that. In a surprisingly short time, you have become my whole life, my love."

Elle smiled, tears filling her eyes. "Ryan, I love you, too," she said, reaching up to touch his face. "I understand, I have never felt this way about anyone before, either. I thought I knew what love was, but I was so wrong. I feel like I can't breathe sometimes when we're apart. And I can't wait to see you, kiss you, touch you, just be near you."

Ryan smiled, leaning down to kiss her gently. "I want you to get rid of the Airbnb. You don't need it anymore. You belong here, with me. Okay? We'll figure everything else out later."

"Good, I never want to go back to that depressing house again," she happily agreed.

Ryan kissed her forehead. "Now please rest, okay? Get some sleep," he ordered.

Elle nodded, snuggling down in the blankets. "Okay. I do feel a little tired, I guess," she admitted.

Ryan nodded, brushing her hair away from her face as she closed her eyes. "I love you," he said again. This time it came out easier. She actually loved him back. He felt something hard in his chest let go, but he couldn't quite embrace the lightness yet. He still had to deal with Todd. He wasn't done with the darkness.

"I love you too," Elle repeated softly, her eyes still closed.

Ryan closed the door to his bedroom gently, going out to the kitchen where Lisa sat at the counter, a bottle of bourbon and two glasses in front of her.

"I hope one of those is for me, sis," Ryan said with a tired sigh, sitting down next to her.

"Indeed," Lisa replied, pouring Ryan a glass. "So how's our girl?"

"She's okay. She's better than I am," Ryan replied. He took a drink of the bourbon, feeling it burn as he swallowed. Kind of like the flame currently burning in his gut. He was torn between his love for Elle and his hate toward Todd. He had a sense of lightness when he was with her, but that familiar darkness returned when he thought about Todd. He hadn't felt anger like this in a long damn time.

He had to force himself to stop clenching his jaw. He took another long drink, finishing the bourbon, and pushed the glass toward Lisa. "Refill me, please."

Lisa refilled his glass and topped hers off, too.

"Thanks. I fucking need this," Ryan said darkly, taking another drink.

"Me too. So what the hell do we do? Pay him? Can Elle come up with that kind of money?" Lisa asked, frowning into her glass.

Ryan shook his head. "I don't want to give that asshole a fucking dime. He doesn't deserve it. What he deserves is to die," he replied angrily.

"Todd isn't going to get away with this. He will get what's coming to him. We're going to make sure of that," Lisa promised.

"The cops are worthless, they drove by his–fuck, *her* house and said there was no sign of him. They've got an APB out on his BMW but he's gone, or hiding. Like the coward he is," Ryan said. "Nothing they can do. That bastard almost killed her and there's nothing they can do."

"They'll find him," Lisa said firmly. "Give them time. Once Elle gets a police report filed, they can charge him officially. He can't hide forever."

Ryan had very little faith that the cops were doing anything significant to find Todd. He had a feeling the only way Todd was ever going to be out of their lives was if he was dead. And Ryan actually had no problem with that. It wouldn't be the first time he had killed someone. Or the second.

OCTOBER 2017

"Jesus, what the fuck happened, Ryan?" John asked, looking down at the body lying at the foot of the cell bunk. "Is that Levi? Fuck, is he breathing? Is he alive?" He leaned down and felt for a pulse. He shook his head, looking back up at Ryan, shock written on his features. "What the hell happened?"

Ryan blinked, trying to clear the blood out of his eyes. It flowed from a gash on his forehead from when Levi threw him up against the metal bunk. "He attacked me. He just came in and jumped me. I don't even know why," Ryan replied slowly, leaning weakly against the bunk, trying to catch his breath. He gingerly touched his ribs. At least a couple were broken.

"Where the hell is everyone?" John asked, nervously leaning out of the cell, looking up and down the hall. It was unusually quiet for cell block C.

"John, I just defended myself. Is he really dead? I didn't mean to kill him. I think his head bounced off the end of the bunk," Ryan said, his eyes wild, still unable to take a full breath. "Fuck. This is bad. This is really bad. John, what ... what do I do?"

John looked at Levi. Levi's face was smashed in, covered in blood, bruises everywhere. He turned to Ryan. "Hit me," he said quietly.

"What?" Ryan asked, bewildered. "Why would I hit you?"

"It has to look like I did this. Hurry up, we don't have a lot of time. Fucking hit me, Ryan," John replied quickly, standing in front of Ryan.

"No. John. No. I'm not hitting you. No way," Ryan said, vigorously shaking his head and backing away.

"Yes, you are. Do it now," John said forcefully, grabbing him by the arm. "You get out in two days. They've always hated that you wouldn't join the Brotherhood. It's why they sent Levi to attack you. Payback. They want you in here longer, they're mad that you're getting out early. The only way they want you to leave is in a body bag, and I'm not going to let that happen. I'm here for life. They can't do anything worse to me. Now fucking hit me."

Ryan took as deep a breath as he could, trying to think, his ribs burning, then shook his head again. "I can't. I can't hurt you. You're the only reason I'm even still alive," he argued. John had saved him on more than one occasion.

John slammed his fist into the metal bunk, first the right hand and then the left, over and over.

"Christ, stop! John. No! What are you doing?" Ryan tried to grab John's bleeding hands as they pummeled the metal bunk.

"I'm saving your life, you ungrateful fuck," John replied, gasping in pain. He finally stopped, holding his beaten hands. "I'm not telling

you again. This was self-defense. Levi attacked you, you fought back, but I'm the one who killed him. Not you. I have to have injuries if we're going to pull this off. NOW HIT ME."

Ryan choked back a sob and swung on his friend, closing his eyes. He felt his fist connect with John's face. He felt his friend's nose break, then his jaw, hitting him over and over until they both collapsed on the floor. Both covered in blood, barely able to move. Ryan thought he'd felt aching coldness and blinding anger before, but it was nothing like what he was feeling now. He'd opened the door to hell and walked through it. There was no going back.

Chapter Forty-Six

"Thank you so much for meeting us here, Brian," Tom said, shaking hands with the attorney as he approached the front of the police station where Elle had been waiting with her father. Ryan and Lisa had agreed that Tom should accompany Elle to the police station to file a police report instead of Ryan.

"It's not a problem," Brian replied. "I have to be in court next door in two hours anyway. And this really shouldn't take too long, Elle, how are you doing?"

"I'm okay. I'm more mad than anything. But Todd did scare me. He was like a totally different person," Elle said. She shivered a little, remembering how cold and cruel Todd had been in the parking garage. Worse than when he'd beat her up at the house. He'd been angry and vicious back at the house, but this time he seemed colder, actually trying to kill her.

"I made a call to a detective friend of mine—he's who we're meeting with to file the police report. He'll want a statement and will also probably want to take pictures of the bruising on your neck and wrists," Brian explained as they walked into the police station. "So be prepared for that."

Elle nodded. "I figured as much. That's fine."

"Also, we need to bring up his history, the previous attack," Brian added.

"Wait, what previous attack?" Tom asked, looking from Brian to Elle.

Elle hesitated, biting her lower lip as she glanced at her dad. "This isn't the first time Todd has attacked me," she admitted quietly.

"What?" Tom exclaimed, turning toward Elle with a look of astonishment as they stopped in the lobby. "What do you mean it's not the first time?"

"He beat me up about eight weeks ago. That's why I left him. It wasn't just his cheating," Elle explained. "I know I should have told you. I was, well, embarrassed, I guess. I didn't want to admit that–"

"Elle," Tom interrupted her, pulling her into his arms and hugging her fiercely. "You should have told me, honey."

"I know," Elle replied, hugging her dad back. "I'm sorry. I didn't want you to worry."

"It's what dads do, sweetie. We worry about our little girls," Tom said, pulling away but keeping an arm around her shoulder.

Elle smiled, tears in her eyes, and leaned against him. She was so very glad he was in her corner.

"Okay, we'll add that incident to the police report," Brian said. "It can only help."

"Yeah, I want it all on the record," Elle agreed.

"Then they'll decide whether or not to issue a warrant for Todd's arrest. I'm guessing they will charge him with assault at the very minimum. Not sure if they will try to go after him for attempted murder, though it sounds like that was Todd's intent," Brian continued, glancing at Elle.

Elle nodded, shivering again. So close. Thank God those people had come off the elevator when they had. She was thankful to be staying with Ryan now. She'd canceled the Airbnb that morning. She felt much safer at Ryan's.

"I'm hoping that with the overwhelming physical evidence, the hospital report, and the witnesses from the parking garage corroborating your story, they may push for attempted murder," Brian concluded. "It definitely won't be hard to get a restraining order against him."

"Good," Tom replied. "The sooner we get that monster off the streets and into jail where he belongs, where he can't hurt Elle again, the better."

"As a quick aside, I spoke with Mr. Monroe and he informed me that he has dropped Todd as a client," Brian said.

"So let's see how things play out with the arrest warrant. We might be able to strong-arm Todd into giving up and just signing the papers."

"Okay," Elle replied. "That would be the best-case scenario." She followed Brian and Tom through the lobby of the police station, but she knew in her heart that an arrest warrant wouldn't stop Todd from fighting to get what he thought was rightfully his.

Chapter Forty-Seven

"To family," Lisa said, raising her glass.

"To family," everyone at the table echoed.

Lisa looked around the table, her heart full. They'd decided to do Thanksgiving at the ranch, feeling it was the safest place for everyone. Away from Todd. Lisa wasn't sure who she was more worried about, Elle or Ryan. Ryan had been even quieter than usual. Scowling and brooding, refusing to talk to her about anything other than work. She worried he was planning something.

At least he seemed to be relaxed here at the ranch. Lisa shook her head. Enough worrying. At least for today.

She looked around the table, which was almost full, in the formal dining room. Ryan and Elle, Cayden and Charlie, Sarah and Nate, Riley, Emma, and Cari, with her and Conor completing the group. Lisa had purposely seated Riley and Emma together. She'd really liked him when they first met. Once Conor confirmed Riley was single, her match-making instinct had kicked in. The pair seemed to be hitting it off so far.

Everyone had arrived at the ranch yesterday, all planning to stay through Saturday. Yesterday had been spent getting everything ready for Thanksgiving dinner. Lisa, Elle, Cari, Sarah, and Emma had been busy baking everything from pies to homemade dinner rolls. Cayden and Charlie were in the kitchen, too, making and decorating sugar cookies. And making a huge mess.

The men had decided their talents were better used outside of the kitchen, drinking beer and playing cornhole out on the back patio since the weather was still sunny and warm. Conor had given both Cayden and Charlie riding lessons, patiently showing them how to saddle the horses and brush them down afterward. He was a natural around kids, Lisa discovered. He had a lot of experience with his nieces and nephews.

Conor and Ryan did a huge prime rib and rib steaks today, while Riley and Nate deep-fried a turkey. All of the usual sides filled the long table–mashed potatoes, sweet potatoes, green bean casserole, and buttery carrots. Cari had opened several bottles of wine and filled the adults' glasses. Lisa smiled. Even her babies were behaving, so far.

"So, are you my mom's boyfriend?" Charlie asked Conor, loud enough that the entire table stopped their conversations and stared at her with a mixture of amusement and anticipation on their faces.

Conor stopped his forkful of mashed potatoes halfway to his mouth in surprise. He looked over at Charlie, then set it back on his plate. "Well, Charlie, I think that's something you have to ask your mom."

Lisa heard Ryan snort at the other end of the table and glared at him before she answered her daughter's question. "Well, sweetie..." She paused, glancing over to Conor for a second before replying. She turned her attention back to Charlie. "As a matter of fact, yes, he is my boyfriend." She looked back at Conor again, daring him to disagree with her.

"Good. I like it here." Charlie dug back into her turkey, apparently satisfied with that answer.

Conor grinned, looking at Lisa. "Guess it's official then, honey."

"So, I'm your boyfriend now, am I?" Conor asked later, as he closed the door to his bedroom, leaning against it.

"Yes. You're my man now," Lisa replied, pulling her dress over her head and letting it drop to the floor, standing naked before him. "You don't have a problem with that, do you?"

Conor swallowed. "No ma'am," he replied, unbuttoning his shirt as she reached for him. He'd been hers ever since that first night at Jack's. No denying it.

Chapter Forty-Eight

"I have to say, I am a little disappointed that you didn't join us at the club for Thanksgiving this year," Ava said. "Who were these friends that you celebrated with? And at some cattle ranch." She wrinkled her nose in disapproval.

"My friends Lisa and Conor," Elle explained, glancing at her dad, "and a few friends from the gym and Conor's sister. It was actually really nice."

"Hmmph." Ava let out a little snort of disbelief, picking up her martini glass. "And this whole Todd situation. How are you feeling, darling? You look a little better at least. That man turned out to be such a disappointment. Have the police found him yet?"

"I'm doing okay, and no, no word of him," Elle replied, frowning. She was constantly looking over her shoulder, worried he'd show up again out of the blue. Security had been walking her to her car every day when she left the office. "I did talk to Brian this morning, and he said the DA is going to charge him with attempted murder, not just assault."

"Good," Tom interjected heatedly. "He absolutely should be

charged with attempted murder. It's what he deserves. Let's hope the police find him before I do. I would love to have a little chat with that poor excuse for a man."

"Dad!" Elle exclaimed, surprised that her father would say something like that. He was always the one to find an amicable solution to a problem. She'd never heard him even raise his voice.

"Though I do feel better knowing that Ryan is looking out for you," Tom continued, grimacing as soon as the words were out of his mouth.

"Who?" Ava promptly asked, narrowing her eyes. "Who is Ryan?"

"Sorry, sweetie," Tom said, with a sheepish look to Elle. "I guess I let the cat out of the bag."

"It's fine, Dad," Elle said. She'd known she'd have to let her mother know about Ryan soon. She couldn't wait forever.

"What secrets are you two keeping?" Ava asked harshly.

"Ryan is the man I've been seeing for a while," Elle explained. "I didn't tell you about him right away just because, well, with everything going on with my divorce and Todd ... I wanted to wait a bit before making any big announcements."

"But you have an announcement to make now, apparently?" Ava asked, frowning.

Elle nodded. "Yes. Ryan is my boyfriend," she said, smiling to herself. Those were words she never thought she'd hear herself say.

"And who exactly is this Ryan person? I'm guessing he's not someone from the club," she said with disapproval.

"No, he's not. Ryan Daley. He and his sister own Daley Charters. Lisa runs the company and Ryan is the airframe and powerplant mechanic," Elle explained.

"I'm sorry. I don't think I heard that correctly," Ava said, setting her martini glass down on the table and staring at Elle.

Elle had to hide a little smirk. Ava had her Botox appointment the day before, so her forehead wasn't quite expressing the full extent of the displeasure she was undoubtedly feeling.

"A mechanic? And ... " Ava paused, glancing over at her husband in annoyance. "You obviously knew about this?"

Tom cleared his throat. "Well, yes. Forgive me, darling. I just know how busy the holidays are for you. I figured Elle would tell you about Ryan at some point," he said apologetically.

"Ryan," Ava repeated, annoyance obvious in her tone. "So you've apparently even already met him. So I'm the last to know."

"I'm sorry, my love, but Ryan has been taking really good care of Elle. I personally feel better knowing he's looking out for our daughter," Tom explained.

"And I'd love for you to meet him soon, Mother," Elle said as enthusiastically as she could muster. Actually, the last thing she wanted was Ava in the same room as Ryan. It had disaster written all over it. Ava would pick him apart in thirty seconds.

"Hmmph," Ava said again with a frown. "We'll have to see. I have a busy schedule coming up, but I suppose I could move things around. I'll let you know, darling. I guess I should meet this mystery man for myself, though I must tell you, I'm extremely disappointed that I couldn't introduce you to Elise's son."

Elle mentally rolled her eyes. Her mother immediately moved on to talking about her busy schedule of galas and spa visits.

All things considered, that had gone better than she'd thought it would. Ava hadn't had a complete freak out. Only a minor one.

ELLE SET her wine glass down with a small sigh of happiness, waiting for Ryan to get home. She was curled up on a chaise lounge on the patio. She leaned back in her chair, closing her eyes and thinking about the crazy few months they had been having.

From separating from Todd and being miserable in her Airbnb, to getting involved with Ryan and the back-and-forth of uncertainty and working everything out. Her past. His past. Ryan saying *I love you.* And finally, moving out of her Airbnb and into Ryan's house. Elle sighed. If it wasn't for Todd and the problems he was causing, she would be so happy right now. Damn Todd.

Suddenly, her head was jerked back by a hand tight in her hair, forcing her to look up.

"Miss me?" Todd asked quietly, keeping hold of her hair with one hand and coming around from behind her chair as she tried to sit up. He pushed her back down roughly with his other hand and climbed on top of her.

"Todd, what the hell?" Elle gasped, trying to free her hair with one hand and pushing on Todd's chest above her with the other.

"I don't know why, but all of a sudden, you are sexy as fuck," Todd whispered in her ear as he pressed himself harder against her. He let go of her hair, grabbing her hands and pinning them down at her sides. "I've never been so turned on by you. Maybe because you're fighting me, but damn, Elle, I want you."

"Get off me!" Elle yelled, struggling to get out from underneath him.

"We had some fun, baby. How about once more for old times' sake?" Todd said close to her ear, nibbling on it lightly. "You know you want it."

"No! No, I don't. Stop!" Elle choked out, her heart pounding with fear.

"Don't you remember? You don't get to tell me no ever again," Todd reminded her, danger glinting in his eyes. "I'm still your husband. You're mine to do with as I please. And right now, I want to have sex with my loving wife."

Elle managed to free a hand and raked her nails across his cheek. There was no way she was letting him do that.

Todd managed to grab her hand again, forcing her arms over her head and squeezing her hands tightly together. He leaned down and forced his lips onto hers. He kissed her roughly, pushing his tongue hard into her mouth, then breathed out, "Yes. Elle. Keep fighting me, baby–I've decided I like it. Though I have to say, I'm a little disappointed with the police report you filed. You know we were just having fun."

"I said no! And no, we were not having fun!" Elle yelled, turning her head away from his mouth and struggling with all her might to free her hands, but he was too strong. He was heavy on top of her, crushing the breath out of her. She felt a cold dread.

Todd moved his grip so he was holding both of her hands in one of his. He pushed her tank up with his free hand, running his fingers slowly underneath it, up her stomach to her breast. He rubbed his thumb over her nipple. "You can hurt me as much as you want, but I'm going to hurt you back," he promised darkly.

Elle twisted under him, connecting her knee with his crotch. "Stop!" she yelled, breathing hard, terror gripping her as she struggled, feeling nauseous at his touch.

Todd gasped in pain, then started laughing. "Yes, Elle. Yes. Hurt me. Our best sex ever," he breathed into her ear as he grabbed the strap of her tank top and ripped it. Moving it out of the way, he grabbed her breast again, squeezing painfully hard. He violently crushed her mouth with his.

Elle opened her mouth just enough to bite down hard on his lip. Her stomach churned in disgust at his tongue in her mouth as she tasted his blood. But she couldn't get out from underneath him.

"You're only turning me on," Todd responded, breathing hard and pulling himself away from her mouth just enough to lick the blood off his lip. "If you think that's going to make me stop, it's not– but remember, I get to hurt you back." He reached up and slapped Elle across the face as hard as he could.

Elle gasped, trying to catch her breath, tears springing to her eyes as the pain in her cheek registered in her brain. Panic consumed her. She wasn't strong enough to fight him off. Again.

"See, baby, how much fun this is," Todd said, grabbing her

bruised cheek, squeezing hard. "I don't want to mess up this pretty face, but I will."

They both heard the front door open and close.

Todd leaned down and licked her face, tasting her tears. "Elle, I can't wait to fuck you again. I'll be back soon. Then we can finish this. Don't worry, I won't keep you waiting too long," he promised, pushing himself off the chaise and hurrying for the side gate.

Elle closed her eyes and curled into a ball. She tried to call out for Ryan while trying to catch her breath, gasping furiously at the memory of Todd choking her even after he was gone.

"ELLE, WHERE ARE YOU HONEY?" Ryan called, noticing the open slider. He looked out and saw Elle curled up on the chaise lounge.

"Ryan," Elle said gasping, her breathing ragged.

At the sound of her choked voice, Ryan rushed across the patio. "Elle, are you okay? What's going on? What happened?" he asked, fear clutching his stomach.

"Todd," Elle sobbed, adjusting her tank top over her exposed breast. Ryan noticed her tank was ripped.

"What the hell?!" Ryan exclaimed, taking in her red and swollen lips, her bruised cheek, and her ripped clothes, his heart pounding out of his chest. "No. Fuck. No, tell me he didn't–"

Elle shook her head, tears running down her face. "No, he attacked me, he hit me, but he heard you come in and ran off," she explained.

Ryan sank down in the chair, pulling her into his arms. He was livid that Todd had attacked her again, had come to his home.

"I'm so sorry," he told Elle. "I never thought he'd show up here. I can't believe I let him hurt you again."

"No, Ryan, it's not your fault," Elle replied shakily. "I tried to fight him. The more I hurt him, the more he liked it. He's insane. If you hadn't come home–"

"No," Ryan said emphatically, holding her tightly in his arms. "No, that will never happen. I will never let that happen."

"He said he'd be back," Elle sobbed, clinging to Ryan.

He picked her up and carried her inside to the couch. "Wait here. I'm packing a bag and getting you some clothes to change into and then we're leaving. I'm taking you somewhere that asshole can't find you," he said as calmly as he could. Though he was almost blinded by the rage he felt toward Todd.

Elle nodded as Ryan covered her with a throw blanket and handed her a tissue.

Ryan hurried into the bedroom, grabbing his cell and calling Lisa.

Lisa answered on the first ring and Ryan relayed Todd's break-in quickly. "Are you fucking serious? Todd did what to Elle?!" Lisa exploded. "I cannot believe it. Why is he–wait, hold on one second." After a quiet moment Lisa came back on the line. "Meet us at the airport. Conor is here–he was going to stay the night, but he's going to fly us to the ranch instead. She'll be safe there."

"Okay, that's a really good idea. Yes, we'll meet you guys there. Sis, thank you," Ryan replied, letting out a deep breath. He'd regained some control while he talked to Lisa.

But he added darkly, "I'm done playing games now. You understand, right?"

"Yeah," Lisa agreed. "I understand. No more fucking games."

After hanging up, Ryan went back to where Elle was in the living room.

"We're meeting Lisa and Conor at the airport. He's going to fly you to the ranch. Here, put this on," he said, helping Elle get a new shirt over her head and throwing her torn tank in the garbage.

"Me?" Elle asked, pulling the shirt on. "Don't you mean us?"

"No," Ryan replied firmly. "You, Lisa, and Conor."

"No, Ryan, no," Elle begged. "Why aren't you coming?" "You know why," Ryan said, pulling her into his arms.

"We tried to play by the rules, but he's never going to let you go. All he wants is to hurt you, and I'm not going to let him."

"No, I can't lose you," Elle cried, clinging to him.

"You're not going to lose me," Ryan replied, holding her close. "I promise." The time had come to deal with Todd.

Chapter Forty-Nine

"Thank you for doing this." Elle fastened her seatbelt in Conor's plane. "I am so sorry for causing all this trouble," she added with a deep sigh.

"It's not a problem, sweetie," Conor replied as he did his inside run-up.

"Well, I appreciate it. I did call my dad and let him know what happened and that Ryan thought I'd be safer down at the ranch for a few days, until the cops can track Todd down and arrest him," Elle explained.

"Good," Lisa replied. "He was okay with that?"

"Yes, he agreed it was a good idea, and he's going to cover a project I've been working on for a few days. Hopefully, the cops can find Todd soon and then we won't have to worry anymore," Elle responded, even though she wasn't feeling overly optimistic about that happening.

"We ready?" Conor asked, looking over at Lisa and back at Elle.

Lisa nodded. "Yeah. Ready." As Conor taxied to the end of the runway, Lisa looked over her shoulder to talk to Elle. "I still can't believe that asshole had the nerve to show up at Ryan's house. Wow.

The balls on that jerk. Are you okay?" she asked with concern in her eyes.

"Yeah, I'm more pissed than anything," Elle replied, lightly touching the spot on her cheek where he'd hit her. It was a little red and swollen, a little sore. "I really had no idea Todd would go off the deep end. It's like he's just lost it. I don't even understand."

"He's a sociopath, Elle," Lisa explained. "Just like Tate was. I recognized it the first time Todd showed up at the hangar. Something in the eyes. It's all a game to them."

Looking back, Elle realized Todd's behavior had never been normal. He used his looks and his ability to charm people to get what he wanted, then he walked away, never looking back. She'd never seen him show remorse or concern for anyone. She'd been so blinded by his charisma and ability to appear loving. *He should have been an actor,* Elle thought wryly, watching out the window as they lifted off into the air.

She looked back down at the hangar where Ryan stayed, worried that Todd would show up there. Worried about what Ryan would do to Todd. Not that she gave a shit if he hurt Todd–she secretly hoped he would–but she didn't want Ryan to get arrested because of her. She'd never forgive herself.

Chapter Fifty

"I guess it's time we had a chat," Todd said, strolling into the hangar where Ryan was working on the Beechcraft King 200.

"I really don't have anything to say to you, other than that if you ever touch Elle again, I will kill you," Ryan replied calmly, setting his wrench on top of his toolbox and wiping his hands on a shop towel, looking at Todd's overpriced suit and shiny loafers. *This guy is a joke.* He so badly wanted to pick up his wrench and smash Todd's face in. Instead, he took a deep breath, forcing himself to stay calm. *You have a reason now to stay out of prison. A damn good reason.*

"Well, considering she's still legally my wife, I'm pretty sure I can touch her any time I want to," Todd said smoothly, putting his hands in his pockets and leaning against the King's engine.

Ryan grabbed Todd by his jacket with both hands, shoving him hard against the engine. He leaned close to the other man's face. "I'm not saying it again. You touch her again, you die," he promised.

Todd nodded slowly then turned suddenly, swinging his fist at the side of Ryan's head.

Ryan saw it coming, ducking just enough that it didn't have much of an impact. Instinct kicked in and he smashed his fist into Todd's

Karina Morrell

already broken nose, knowing the pain that would cause. He followed up with a left hook to the liver, causing Todd to double over in pain. Todd recovered quickly, swinging again and managing to get a solid cross to Ryan's left eye.

"Are you surprised the man in the suit can throw a punch?" Todd asked, grinning as he wiped blood from his nose.

"Not really. We already know you like to hurt women," Ryan replied angrily. "Give it your best shot."

Todd feinted with his right, swinging a hard left hook aimed at Ryan's jaw.

Ryan leaned back, narrowly avoiding Todd's hook. But Todd feinted another cross to his head and got Ryan in the gut with a hard blow. Ryan threw another punch at Todd's face, blood flowing from his broken nose, followed up with another hard liver shot.

"Fucking ex-con. We already knew you wouldn't fight fair," Todd managed, trying to catch his breath. "That's okay. I won't play fair next time I'm with Elle. I think she likes it rough. I just keep learning more interesting facts about my bride."

Ryan felt the familiar darkness consuming him. All he felt was rage. This asshole had hurt Elle, and not just once. He was going to make sure Todd hurt too. He flew at Todd, punching him again and again in the face, then getting in an uppercut followed by a few more hits to the same spot in Todd's liver, causing him to double over again, and this time he didn't get back up. Todd collapsed to the floor, gasping for air.

Ryan clenched his bruised fists at his side, fighting the anger, trying to control himself. *You've already fucked up, but you can't kill him. Not here. Not now. Stop.*

"Had enough?" Ryan asked harshly, reaching down and grabbing Todd by the collar, forcing his head up.

"Yes," Todd choked out. He spat out blood and wiped his face with his sleeve, smiling. He managed to sit up, his face a bloody bruised mess, breathing hard. "Thank you."

"What?" Ryan asked, narrowing his eyes, letting go of Todd's collar and rubbing his bruised knuckles. "Thank you for what?"

Todd smiled, trying to wipe more of the blood out of his right eye, which was swollen shut. "That was assault, pal. If you think I'm not going to press charges, you're mistaken. Payback for the arrest warrant Elle slapped me with. Seems fair. And so, with you out of the way, I'll have no trouble getting to Elle."

"You started this," Ryan said, narrowing his eyes. Shit. He'd done exactly what Todd had wanted. He'd let Todd provoke him. Cold terror gripped him at the thought of not being able to protect Elle.

Todd laughed. "Who is going to believe that? Self-defense? Ha. That I would start a fight with a giant fucking ex-con while wearing a custom Gucci suit? Which, by the way, you'll be getting my dry-cleaning bill for."

Ryan glanced down at the wrench lying on top of his toolbox, still breathing hard.

Todd followed his glance. "Right now, it's just assault. But if you pick that up, you're going away for a long time." Ryan glared at Todd, hating that he was right but also thinking it might be worth jail time to get this asshole out of Elle's life. If he was going back, he was going to make it worth his while. He picked the wrench up.

Todd managed to get to his feet and slowly backed away. "Think about her, Ryan. It's not worth it. Think about Elle."

"Get the fuck off this property before I decide that, yeah, it might be," Ryan replied quietly, setting the wrench back down. He closed his eyes briefly, picturing Elle's face.

When he opened his eyes again, Todd had turned. Ryan watched him hurry out of the hangar as quickly as his injuries would let him.

Chapter Fifty-One

"Fuck, Ryan's been arrested," Lisa said, slamming her cell down on the table.

"What?" Elle cried, jumping up from her chair at Conor's dining room table. "No! Why? What happened? Todd?"

Lisa looked at Elle, taking her hand. "Yeah, Todd. Apparently, he showed up at the hangar and, well, he started it, but Ryan beat the shit out of him," she explained.

"No, no, no," Elle repeated with a little choked sob. "This is all my fault. Ryan can't go back to prison because of me."

"Elle, wait. Don't freak out," Lisa said, turning to Conor. "I have to get back to Scottsdale tonight so I can be at the courthouse in the morning to bail Ryan out. Can you fly me up?"

"Of course," Conor replied quickly. "Shit. This sucks. I'm sorry, babe. I'll go grab a bag and then start my preflight. Meet me out at the hangar?"

"Yes, thank you," Lisa replied, then turned to look at Elle. "You know you have to stay here, right?"

"No, Lisa, please. I need to see him," Elle begged, desperately grabbing Lisa's arms. "Don't leave me here alone."

"You're not alone here," Lisa said softly. "There are a lot of people on the ranch. Cari is out of town working on a project, but Riley is here, and Jimmy and the ranch hands are here. You'll be safe here. I know this is hard. But it's what Ryan would want. You're safer here than in Scottsdale right now, honey. Do you understand?"

Elle nodded slowly. Her heart was sinking, but she understood. All she wanted to do was see Ryan and hold him.

"We'll get him out on bail in the morning and fly him down here, okay?" Lisa reassured her. "Just a few hours and he will be here."

Chapter Fifty-Two

"My client is not a flight risk, Your Honor. He has been employed at the same job for over six years and he also does not have a current passport," Brian Scott explained to the court. He'd agreed to represent Ryan at his bail hearing, at Elle's request. But he'd informed Elle and Ryan that he would have to refer them to a defense attorney if Ryan's case ended up going to trial, as that was out of his area of expertise.

"Your Honor, Ryan Daley is one of the owners of Daley Charters. I think that is the very definition of a flight risk," the assistant attorney general rebutted, looking up from the documents in front of him on the council table. "He could be out of the country in fifteen minutes in a Gulfstream G550, which is an ultra-long-range jet, one of the planes currently owned by the charter company. The others include a G200, a Beechcraft King Air 200, and a Citation II, which has a top speed of 403 knots."

"Your Honor, Mr. Daley is not a pilot, he's an airframe and powerplant mechanic. And his one previous conviction was almost nine years ago. He has had no further interaction with the law," Brian argued. "He's had a stable life here in Scottsdale for years. He also has extensive family here."

"One sister isn't exactly extensive family," the other lawyer interrupted wryly.

The judge held up his hand. "Enough. I've made my decision. I'm granting bail for the sole reason that Mr. Daley has had no further interactions with the law after his release, but bail will be set at $30,000 because of the previous felony conviction," the judge declared, banging his gavel on the desk. "Next case."

Ryan let out a long sigh of relief. Now he could get back to Elle.

"Sis, I am so sorry." Ryan got into Lisa's Mercedes after she'd bailed him out. "I totally let that asshole get to me. Honestly, I'm not sure how I kept myself from killing him," he admitted with a deep sigh.

"Don't apologize to me, little brother," Lisa replied, looking over at him before backing out of the parking space. "I'm glad you beat the shit out of him. I just wish I had been there to see it."

"Yeah, well, what I don't understand is how he isn't the one sitting in jail. Brian said Todd turned himself in when he left the hangar yesterday. Apparently, he's got a friend on the force so he was able to push the paperwork through and he's now out on bail so he could file charges against me. Total bullshit," Ryan said, shaking his head. "So, how's Elle? And thank you for making her stay at the ranch. It would have broken her heart to see me at the courthouse. Something I never want her to have to see."

"She's stronger than you think," Lisa said, giving him a quick pointed look as she turned onto the street.

"I know, but I want to keep her as far away from that part of my life as possible. I'm just pissed that I let Todd provoke me and then have me arrested. I've tried so hard to change my life. It just keeps finding me, sucking me back in," Ryan said darkly, frowning out the window as they drove down the highway. "I'm never going to be able to leave that part of my life behind me, am I?"

"Ryan, shut up," Lisa said sternly, glaring at him. "You already have left that part of your life behind you. Christ, you are nowhere near the same broken person you were when Candi died. Why can't you see how far you've come? How much you've changed? For fuck's sake, I can see it. Elle can see it, even though she didn't know you back then. You're the one who needs to let it go."

Ryan blew out a deep breath, running his hands through his hair. "I'm trying, sis. I'm trying."

"Well, try harder. Also, we're going straight to the airport since it's getting late. Conor is going to fly us back to the ranch," Lisa informed Ryan.

Ryan nodded, staring out at the passing scenery as Lisa drove, his face hard. Getting arrested and being back in jail again had brought back some painful memories.

At least Elle was safe down at the ranch.

CONOR MET them at the Daley Charters hangar, his Cherokee chocked out front. "Hey Ryan, how are you doing?" he asked, shaking his hand and clapping him on the shoulder.

Ryan shrugged wearily. "I'm okay, thanks."

"Well, someone needed to beat the shit out of that asshole," Conor replied with a grin. "I'm just sorry I wasn't there to see it."

"Same," Lisa added, giving Conor a quick kiss.

"So, unfortunately, I've got some bad news," Conor said as they walked toward the hangar.

"What's wrong?" Lisa asked, taking his hand.

"There's a storm already blowing in. Winds are expected to get up to sixty miles per hour. It's not safe to fly in those conditions. I'm really sorry," Conor explained, looking at Ryan. "I know you were anxious to get to the ranch to see Elle."

"I talked to Elle after your hearing, while your release was being processed. I'd promised her I'd keep her posted on how the bail hearing went," Lisa said to Ryan. "She's fine at the ranch. Riley and Jimmy are taking good care of her."

"Should be fine to head out in the morning. Storm is actually supposed to pass around 0200 hours," Conor said, checking the weather app on his phone.

"Okay. I'll call Elle and let her know about the change of plans. I would drive down, but honestly, I'm just exhausted. Didn't get much sleep last night. Do you care if I just crash with you tonight, sis?" Ryan asked with a tired sigh. "I really don't want to be alone tonight."

"Of course," Lisa responded, still holding Conor's hand and taking Ryan's arm, leading them back toward her car. "We can order food and I'll check on the kids–they should be fine at George's for another day or two."

Chapter Fifty-Three

"Hey baby, wake up," Todd whispered in Elle's ear. Her arms were held down and he was climbing on top of her.

Elle gasped, quickly coming fully awake. "Todd, what ... ? How did you get in here?" she asked.

"It really wasn't that hard, sweetheart. No alarm system and all kinds of unlocked doors. Guess you all thought I wouldn't find you all the way out here," Todd explained, shaking his head. "It's amazing the things you can find on the internet. Black Diamond Ranch has a beautiful website, complete with the address listed."

"Get off me!" Elle cried, her heart racing and panic consuming her. Conor hadn't been able to fly because of the storm. Conor, Ryan, and Lisa were all still back in Scottsdale. And Riley was at his place and Jimmy was probably asleep in the bunkhouse. She could hear the wind blowing hard outside. A crack of thunder exploded suddenly right outside of her window, lightning immediately flashing into the room.

"We both know your lover isn't here. No one is coming to save you," Todd said, running his tongue over her lips. "Now we're going to finish what we started the other day. It's all I've been thinking about."

Elle twisted under him, managing to knee him in the crotch. "No! Stop!" she yelled.

Todd grunted a little, moving slightly and pressing himself into her harder, smiling. "So we're going to play rough, are we? Good. I was hoping that would be the case. So hot, Elle."

Elle thrust her head forward, aiming for his broken nose.

"Oh no, baby," Todd said, grinning as he narrowly avoided her. "Now, now, and here I thought Lisa was the wildcat. Turns out my sweet Elle has a little fire in her after all." He reached down, pinning both her wrists in one hand as he reached into his pocket. He pulled out a knife and flipped the blade out. "In fact, I brought a little something to tame you with. Though you can feel free to scream. No one will hear you. In fact, I hope you do."

Elle stopped struggling, fear forming in the pit of her stomach.

Todd slowly, lightly ran the blade up her arm. "I thought this might convince you to see things my way. Don't get me wrong, I love it when you fight me, but I'm really fucking tired of you and your ex-con boyfriend breaking my nose."

"Todd, please," Elle said, trembling a little.

"Mmm, please what, baby?" Todd asked, leaning down to lick her ear. "Please what?"

"You don't need that. Please put it away," Elle pleaded softly, trying to stop trembling, her heart racing.

"I just don't trust you, sweetheart," Todd replied, shaking his head and sliding the knife down to her waist, then under her tank top, using the blade to slowly pull her shirt up, skimming up her stomach and leaving a thin red line that didn't quite break the skin.

"Todd, no," Elle begged, tears filling her eyes. She was unable to keep herself from flinching as Todd ran the knife over her stomach. "Please don't do this. I'll sign the divorce papers. You can have the house. I don't care anymore."

"Why thank you, baby, but I think we're way beyond that. I think the word widower rolls off the tongue better than divorcé. And if you're dead, then the charges against me will be dropped. It's a win-win situation. Well, for me anyway," Todd explained with a manic smile.

"I'll drop the charges. I promise. You don't have to do this," Elle begged, breaking out in a cold sweat.

"But first, we have some unfinished business to take care of. One last time, one last memory of you that I will cherish forever," Todd said, bringing the blade back down her stomach to the waistband of her shorts.

"Don't worry, baby, you're going to enjoy this. Don't you remember how you used to enjoy it?" he said, reaching down with his free hand to undo his jeans. "Come on, I know you do."

Elle knew she only had one chance to stop him. As he looked down, trying to get his jeans off, she grabbed for his wrist holding the knife with both hands, smashing her forehead into his broken nose as hard as she could at the same time.

Todd rolled off her with a moan, his weight shifting slightly to her side, grabbing his nose with one hand and simultaneously jabbing the knife toward her with the other. He managed to connect with Elle's side, thrusting the knife then jerking it back as he tried to wipe the blood away from his mouth. "Fuck. Goddamnit. Get back here," he growled.

Elle scrambled out from under Todd, gasping in pain from the gash in her side. She pressed her hand to the wound, feeling blood ooze out. She managed to get her feet on the floor before he yanked her back, grabbing her by her hair.

"Oh no," Todd snarled, pulling her back toward him on the bed. "Come back here. We're done when I fucking say we're done. You will pay for that, baby," he promised harshly as he ran the knife down her cheek. She felt warmth as the knife left a small line of blood in its wake. He roughly pushed her back down on the bed and then reached to yank his jeans down.

Lightning flashed again, illuminating the bed and the nightstand. Elle lunged over, grabbing the big mason jar of water she'd left next to her bed. She turned, bringing it down on Todd's head with all her strength, causing it to shatter. Glass, water, and blood poured down from his forehead. Anger burned in her chest, pushing the fear away. "I said NO, Todd!" she yelled.

Todd reached up, touching his forehead with one hand, looking a little dazed. He rolled off her again, trying to wipe at the blood flowing into his eyes with his sleeve. "Crazy bitch. What did you just do?" he ground out.

Elle saw her opportunity and lunged for the knife, rolling over on the bed on top of him. She felt shards of glass cut into her knees and legs as she twisted. Her hands wrapped around the handle of the knife as she struggled against him with every ounce of strength she had.

Anger coursed through her as she fought him. Feeling a rage she hadn't ever felt before in her life, she let her anger push the fear away and take over. Todd had made her life so miserable for so long. And he had attacked Ryan and got him arrested. She was sick of being his victim. No more. He needed to pay. He'd caused enough destruction in her life. She was taking back control. Adrenaline surged through her as she let out a scream. "Enough!"

Todd managed to turn the knife toward her as they fought, slicing her shoulder as she struggled to yank the knife away. "Elle. Stop!" he yelled, blinking and shaking his head furiously. "I guess the foreplay is over. Guess we'll just go straight to the main event. I'm so fucking done with you."

Blood had run down the handle of the knife, making it slippery. Elle finally managed to yank it out of Todd's hand and, without hesitating, she thrust it in his neck. A huge spurt of blood poured out as she pulled it out and plunged it back in again and again until she couldn't see through his blood covering her, screaming with rage as tears poured down her cheeks.

"No! I'm so fucking done with you!" she cried, the slippery knife finally falling out of her hands and onto the bed. Exhausted, her shoulder aching, her side screaming in pain, she fell off the bed onto the floor, collapsing. She couldn't catch her breath and her heart was pounding so hard in her chest she thought it might explode, filling her head with its hard beat and making it so that she couldn't think. She closed her eyes, sobbing.

Chapter Fifty-Four

"Jesus Christ, Elle! What the fuck happened?" a man exclaimed, rushing into the room. He flipped the light on. Coming further into the room, he checked the body on the bed for a pulse. Finding none, he turned to Elle and leaned down toward her. "Elle, can you hear me? Are you okay?"

She lunged up, sobbing, her hands hitting his chest as she screamed, "No! No! Todd! Stop!"

"Elle, it's Riley," he said forcefully, grabbing her hands, shaking her a little. "Hey, you're okay. Stop. It's Riley. Listen to my voice. You're okay now."

Elle could hardly see through matted hair hanging over her eyes, wet from blood and tears. "Riley?" she asked shakily, her heart still pounding, all her energy spent as she sagged against him.

"I'm here. You're going to be okay. Where are you hurt? Let me see, okay?" Riley asked calmly, brushing her hair away from her face. After assessing her injuries, he spoke again. "I need to get the bleeding to stop. I'm going to grab some towels, okay? Don't move." He laid her gently back down on the floor. As he left the room, Elle heard him yelling over his shoulder, "Jimmy, where you at?"

Jimmy came into the room, huffing from hurrying up the stairs, followed by another ranch hand. "Holy Mary, Mother of God!" he exclaimed, taking in the scene in the bedroom. "I ran out and got Hank. I wasn't sure what the hell was going on up here. Christ, is he dead?"

"Yeah," Riley replied, coming back with a pile of towels. Kneeling down next to Elle, he put pressure on the gash in her side. "We need to get Elle fixed up, and fast. We'll deal with him later. Hold this towel on her shoulder, it's not too bad. Make sure she stays conscious. She's lost a lot of blood from this gash in her side."

Elle tried to sit up, clutching Riley's arm, choking out in a strangled voice. "He's dead?" She took a deep breath, her side aching. "Is he dead? Tell me!" she demanded, her voice getting stronger.

"Yes, Elle," Riley replied firmly. "Yes. He's dead. He can't hurt you anymore. But we have to get your bleeding to stop. Please listen to me. Lie back down."

Jimmy applied pressure to the wound on her shoulder with a towel, bending down on one knee on the floor next to her. "Don't you worry about a thing, little missy. We got you. Riley is going to get you all fixed up, okay?"

Elle nodded, suddenly feeling light-headed and weak. She wanted nothing more than to close her eyes and sleep. Todd was dead. She'd killed him. She kept repeating it in her head. She'd killed him. He's dead. *He can never hurt me again.* Finally. She collapsed against Jimmy, her strength spent, closing her eyes. The effort to hold them open was too great. Her arms were dead weights. She couldn't even feel her legs. All she felt was the burning in her side. It was on fire, making her breathing ragged as she tried to focus on what Jimmy and Riley were saying to her, but the effort was too much.

"ELLE," Riley said, lightly shaking her. "You need to stay awake, sweetie." He turned to Hank. "Apply pressure to her side as I pick her up. Let's move her downstairs to the kitchen. There's too much glass and blood in here to work. Then I need to call Conor and let him know what happened. Find out what to do about this mess."

Riley gently picked Elle up as Hank nodded, applying pressure to Elle's side with the towel as instructed. They headed for the stairs together with Jimmy following.

"Jimmy, get me some salt from the pantry–a lot of it," Riley instructed as they walked into the kitchen. They gently laid Elle down on the counter next to the sink. Turning the water on, Riley took over putting pressure on her wound as blood seeped through another towel. "I'm going to need more clean towels," he said as he assessed the amount of blood.

"I need bandages, too. The first aid kit is in the bunkhouse. Hank, run out and grab it," Riley ordered. He picked up the last clean towel that Jimmy had brought downstairs and turned back to Elle. "I'm sorry, sweetie, this is going to hurt, but I have to clean your cut," he explained, quickly soaking the clean towel with water before tossing the bloody one aside and wiping blood away from Elle's wound, causing her to moan.

Jimmy returned with a blue container of iodized salt. "Is this what you wanted?" he asked, holding it up.

"Yes, an old cowboy trick," Riley replied, taking the salt and opening it. "Elle, listen to me. This is going to burn, but it's going to help stop the bleeding, okay?"

Elle opened her eyes briefly and started to shiver before closing her eyes again.

"Fuck, I think she's going into shock," Riley said in alarm as he applied a generous amount of salt to her wound. Elle cried out as he gently patted it down as fast as he could. "Go get a blanket, we need to warm her up," Riley instructed Jimmy.

Hank returned with the first aid kit, holding it out to Riley. "Got it."

Once the salt had set and the bleeding slowed, Riley wiped off the excess salt, packed the gash with a clean cloth, gently covered it with gauze, and ran an ace bandage around her to hold it in place. He inspected the wound on her shoulder, making short work of cleaning and bandaging it. He cleaned the scratch on her face but didn't bandage it.

"Here," Jimmy said, returning with a wool blanket which Riley wrapped around Elle, rubbing her arms to get the circulation flowing, trying to warm her up.

Riley finally took a deep breath. "Okay. She's got some color back. I think she's stable, but she's definitely going to need to be stitched up. I need to call Boss right now. Keep an eye on her. Hank, run upstairs, Cari's room is the second on the right. We're going to need some tweezers to get the glass out of her hands and legs. Then we'll go from there."

Chapter Fifty-Five

"Lisa, wake up," Conor said softly, shaking her shoulder. Then a little louder, "Lisa."

"What?" Lisa asked, blinking a few times, confused, looking up at Conor standing over her bed, the light from her bathroom glowing behind him. "What's going on?"

"Get up. We've got to get back to the ranch. Right now," Conor said quickly, buttoning his shirt before pulling his boots on. "I'll go get Ryan. We have to go."

"What?" Lisa repeated, startled and still groggy. "Go where? Why? What's going on?"

Conor sat down on the bed next to Lisa and placed his hands on her shoulders as she sat up. "Listen to me carefully. I don't have time to repeat it. Todd is dead. Elle is alive but in rough shape. We need to get back to the ranch right now," he explained calmly but urgently.

"Oh fuck!" Lisa exclaimed, trying to process what Conor was saying. *Todd is dead? How? And Elle? Oh no.*

"Get dressed," Conor instructed, standing up and grabbing his hat. "I'm going to get Ryan up. Elle will be fine. Riley is taking good care of her. We'll figure the rest out, we just need to get down there, okay? Let's go."

Lisa jumped out of bed and grabbed her jeans and a jacket, snagging her boots as she hurried out of her bedroom, trying not to panic.

"CAN YOU FLY IN THIS?" Ryan asked, folding himself into the back seat of Lisa's Mercedes a few minutes later and slamming the door as Lisa sped out of the driveway. "It's still windy as fuck."

Conor checked the weather app on his phone as Lisa drove, shaking his head and frowning. "Honestly, I don't know. But I'm going to do my damnedest. Wind has calmed down a lot, gusts only up to twenty-two miles per hour now. The majority of the storm has passed us moving south."

"What about the Bravo?" Lisa suggested. "That would be safer to fly in this weather, right? Since it's a much faster plane? How long is your runway at the ranch? Can you land it there?"

Conor thought for a minute, doing some calculations in his head. "Yeah, actually. My father initially built the runway with the intention of eventually buying a bigger plane, so yeah, I could land the Bravo there. The Cherokee, being a single-engine aircraft with top speed only being about one hundred forty-five knots, would get buffeted around in the wind dramatically, but the Bravo is built for these conditions. It has a high-speed cruise of just over three hundred twenty knots true depending on altitude and temperature. One small problem though—I haven't had time to finish school for my type."

"What about the Saratoga? That's still a single-engine," Lisa suggested.

"It's been a long time since I've flown a Saratoga," Conor said.

"Yeah," Ryan interjected sharply, "but can you fucking fly it?"

"I can fly it. There are all kinds of legal complications for flying without your type rating. So the Saratoga would definitely be the better option," Conor replied.

Lisa nodded. "I trust you. It's up to you, babe."

"I'd feel safer flying the Saratoga, honestly," Conor replied, "as long as you're sure."

"I'm sure," Lisa said. "We have to get to Elle."

"Okay, that's settled," Conor said. "I'll have to move the Cherokee to get the Saratoga out of the hangar. But I'll try to be as fast as possible. Ryan, you can do the preflight checks, right?"

Ryan nodded. "Yep. I've done it hundreds of times. I'll get started while you play musical planes. And thank you," he added seriously, grabbing Conor's arm firmly. "I'm all kinds of freaked out, worried about Elle, so thank you for doing this. I will owe you forever."

Conor looked at Lisa, then at Ryan. "It's what family does," he replied.

"Okay, there's no one in the tower at this time of night, but I can use the pilot-controlled lighting system with a few clicks of the mic to get the runway lights to come on," Conor explained as he taxied out onto the runway. Lisa watched as he clicked the mic five times, waiting for the lights to illuminate. "Looks like we've got a headwind, which is good. The FMS will help in calculating wind direction and our range. Ready? Belts on and tight?"

Lisa checked her own belt and looked back at her brother.

"We're ready. Let's go," Ryan replied quickly, his face dark and worried.

Conor looked over at Lisa. "Sorry, babe. It's probably going to be a bumpy ride," he said as he stopped at the end of the runway, spooling the engines up as he readied the plane for takeoff. "But it will be fine. Don't worry. I've flown in a lot of windy conditions–though not too many storms–I try to avoid those."

Lisa nodded, tightening her seatbelt nervously. "When are the refreshments being served?" she joked. "I could really go for a drink right about now."

"You wouldn't even have time to finish one," Conor replied. "Remember how fast we got to the ranch in the Cherokee? Well, this will be even faster. The Saratoga is a high-performance plane."

"Have you not seen her drink?" Ryan asked Conor. "Lisa could probably finish two before we land."

Lisa turned and glared at Ryan. "You're hilarious. And also accurate," she agreed, looking out the window as the plane gained speed, tearing down the runway ... V1 ... rotate, and they lifted off easily. Lightning flashed in the hills beyond Phoenix. She said a little prayer that the storm would continue to head southwest, away from the ranch as they gained altitude and speed.

Chapter Fifty-Six

"Where is she?" Ryan demanded, striding into the kitchen where Riley and Jimmy sat drinking coffee.

"She's upstairs in Cari's room. Hank is with her. If there's any change in her condition, he's to let us know," Riley explained, standing as Conor and Lisa followed Ryan into the kitchen.

"I need to see her," Ryan said shortly, turning to head for the stairs.

"Wait," Riley called after Ryan. He paused and looked to Conor. "Boss?"

"Go check on her, then meet us in the dining room," Conor said, looking at Ryan seriously. "We have some decisions to make. And we need to make them fast–understand?"

Ryan nodded. He understood, but first he had to see with his own eyes that Elle was okay. He turned and headed to see her.

When he entered the room, he took Elle's hand carefully and looked down at her sleeping fitfully in Cari's bed. *Jesus,* he thought. His heart felt like it was going to explode out of his chest. Fucking Todd. It was a good thing he was dead–Ryan felt that old, familiar hot rage burning. He was supposed to protect Elle. He'd failed. More than once. She'd had to protect herself. But damn, he was pretty proud of her.

It would more than likely be ruled self-defense, especially since Todd had attacked her before. But Ryan wasn't sure he wanted to take that chance. He knew firsthand how fickle the justice system could be. He never wanted Elle to experience anything close to what he'd been through. He hadn't been able to protect her against Todd, but he was absolutely going to protect her now.

Chapter Fifty-Seven

Lisa went to the pantry and found a bottle of single malt whisky. "Riley, will you help me by grabbing a couple more glasses and taking them into the dining room, please?" she asked. "I think we could all use a little bit of this."

Riley reached for the glasses, turning to Jimmy. "Jimmy, make some more coffee, please. We'll probably need more at some point. We'll come find you after some decisions are made." Lisa and Conor walked into the dining room, Riley following close behind.

"Where is the body?" Conor asked as Lisa poured whisky into four glasses and passed them around, setting one aside for Ryan.

"Still upstairs. We didn't touch anything, just Elle. I carried her down to the kitchen to get her cleaned up. There was blood and glass everywhere," Riley explained, taking a sip. "I still have no fucking idea what happened. Elle was pretty out of it. Then she went into shock, I think. I'm obviously no doctor. But she seems stable now."

"Fuck," Conor replied, taking a drink of his whisky. He was still riding a little wave of adrenaline after flying the Saratoga in the storm. He had prayed many a prayer on that short flight. The windshear warning tone siren had gone off right after takeoff. But he'd been able to apply full engine power and get up to a safe altitude.

"I've been trying to piece it together," Riley continued. "Obviously, Todd broke in and attacked her. Jimmy was down in the kitchen. Luckily, he had a case of insomnia and heard the commotion upstairs and he came out and got me. But by the time I got up there, it was over. Todd had a knife, a good-sized switchblade, and he got Elle pretty bad in the side, maybe three, four inches across. Luckily just a flesh wound, it didn't go very deep, but she lost a fair amount of blood, probably while she was fighting with him.

"She's definitely going to need stitches, but I didn't want to make that call. I just wanted to get the bleeding to stop until you guys could get back down here. He also got her in the shoulder, but not as bad, an inch or two long. She'll definitely need a few stitches there as well.

"I think she must've broke a big glass over his head. There were chunks and bits of glass all over the bed. That must have been how she got the knife away from him. She stabbed him several times in the neck. He bled out pretty quick, I think," Riley finished.

"Damn," Lisa breathed out.

"I wasn't going to take her to the hospital. I didn't feel it was my place to make that call since she was stable. I didn't want to involve the authorities." Riley added, "I did give her some Motrin, but wasn't sure about anything stronger yet. She was pretty out of it already. Hank found some of Cari's tweezers and was able to get most of the glass out of her hands and knees. I'm sure he missed some, but when she wakes up, we can get the smaller pieces out."

"Okay, well, now we need to decide what to do about Todd," Conor began as Ryan walked into the room, frowning darkly.

Ryan sat down at the table, reaching for a glass of whisky. "Well, here's my opinion. As far as Todd is concerned, I say we bury that fucker out in the woods where no one is ever going to find him," he said fiercely, looking around the table. "Elle is not going to go down for this. No fucking way. I won't allow it," he added.

Lisa nodded, looking at Conor, who glanced at Riley. Seemed they were all in agreement.

"Okay. Well, that's been decided," Conor agreed. "No police involvement. We handle this ourselves."

"My first concern is obviously Elle. What sort of medical training does your crew out here have?" Ryan asked. "We obviously can't take her to the hospital. They'll ask too many questions."

"I already talked to Hank. He was a medic in the army. He can get her stitched up. It might not be pretty, but he can do it," Riley volunteered.

"How is she doing right now?" Lisa asked Ryan.

"She was sleeping when I went up, but she was fairly restless," Ryan replied, frowning. "I didn't want to wake her up. Let's get her stitched up and assessed before we try to talk to her about anything that happened. I'm concerned about how she's going to handle this. Hopefully, she will sleep, at least while we deal with Todd. I don't want her involved in any part of that."

"I agree," Lisa replied. "She's been through so much already. She did the hard part. She doesn't need to be involved in the cleanup."

"Okay, then let's take care of Elle. Get her stitched up and Lisa can keep an eye on her," Conor said. "Riley, once Hank is done stitching her up, I want him and Damon to get rid of Todd's Beemer. We saw it parked behind the hangar when we came in. Hank can follow Damon. Try to avoid cameras, but I think Damon should drive Todd's car because of all the hands he looks the most like Todd. Especially if he wears a ballcap.

"I think we should take his car down to Yuma and dump it somewhere where it looks like he fled over the border," Conor suggested. "It will look like he's trying to avoid the warrant out for his arrest. He'd be looking at serious time if convicted of attempted murder."

"Yeah, and someone like Todd wouldn't last two days in prison," Ryan replied grimly.

"And once he's over the border he could have gone anywhere."

Conor turned to Riley. "We'll work on getting the room cleaned up and then you, Ryan, and I will take care of the body."

Riley nodded.

"Okay, we have a plan," Ryan said, draining his whisky and standing up. "Elle first. Let's get this done."

"So, we obviously have no numbing agents of any kind. But Jimmy had a prescription for oxycodone from his hip surgery. I managed to wake Elle up and get a couple pills and a few crackers in her. I tried to explain to her what was happening, but she's still pretty weak and basically went right back out. I dealt with enough trauma in the army to understand. Even though she seems really out of it, that's actually a good thing right now," Hank explained to Ryan and Lisa. "Her body and her mind need to rest and heal.

"Unfortunately, I need to clean the wound and put some iodine on it, and that might be painful enough to wake her up. Ryan, I'm going to do this as quickly as possible. Once the area is clean, I'll start stitching. You're going to have to hold her down. She might not resist, but if she does, it could be a mess. We don't want her to struggle and start bleeding again, especially since she already lost so much blood. That's dangerous territory, as we have no way to give her a transfusion."

"Understood," Ryan replied, sitting carefully on the bed next to Elle with Lisa on her other side, leaving room for Hank to work. He nodded at Hank. "Ready."

Chapter Fifty-Eight

"How is she?" Conor asked as Lisa came into the kitchen.

"Okay," Lisa replied, sitting down at the counter, exhausted, watching him make coffee. "Hank actually did a really good job. Ryan is helping him clean up. The oxycodone should keep her out for a while. Would you pour me one of those, please? I'm going to go back up and stay with her just in case she wakes up. I don't want her to wake up alone."

Conor nodded, pouring coffee in a mug and setting it in front of Lisa. "How are you doing?" he asked, coming around the counter and pulling her up into his arms.

"I'm okay," Lisa replied, hugging him back. She let out a long sigh. She needed his strong arms around her for a minute. Watching Hank stitch up Elle had been difficult. Elle had woken up when Hank doused the wound with alcohol, fighting against them holding her down. She was crying and moaning, but also pretty out of it. Lisa knew Ryan was struggling, but he was holding it together surprisingly well.

"A couple more hurdles to get over and then we can put this nightmare behind us," Conor said, holding her tightly against him.

"I hope so. But do you think the cops are going to go looking for Todd? Like after they find his car? Are they going to question Elle?" Lisa asked worriedly. "Or worse, Ryan?"

Conor shrugged, leaning back to look at her. "There's no point in worrying about it. Let's just focus on getting Elle better and handling the rest."

"Conor," Lisa began, looking up at him, "I'm really sorry we've dragged you into this. I mean, you shouldn't have to be dealing with our problems. This is a huge thing we're asking of you and your men. It could have serious consequences for everyone involved."

"Babe, if you haven't figured it out by now..." Conor paused and cleared his throat. "Then I guess I need to explain something to you. Your problems are my problems now. Do you want to know why?"

Lisa nodded, looking into his eyes, her heart beating faster.

"Because I love you," Conor continued, reaching down to frame her face with his hands. "I think I fell in love with you the night we met. I've never met anyone like you. Ever. When you took off from Jack's that night, I made a vow to myself that I would track you down. I wasn't going to let you get away. I was going to find you, and I was going to marry you. I'm never going to let you go. Do you understand Laoise? I love you."

"I love you, too," Lisa replied with a smile, leaning in to kiss him. "I love you. And yes."

"Yes what?" Conor asked, breaking away from her lips to give her a confused look.

"Yes, I'll marry you," Lisa said with a teasing grin. "About damn time you asked."

Conor leaned down and picked her up, spinning her around as he kissed her. Finally setting her down, he said, "I guess I kind of ruined the surprise. I had–"

Lisa reached up and put her finger over his lips, shaking her head. "No. Don't tell me. Later. Do this properly later. Got it, mister?"

Conor nodded as he leaned down to kiss her again.

Chapter Fifty-Nine

After they reassembled in the kitchen, Riley brought the group up to speed. "Hank and Damon have left. Hank is following Damon in his truck. No ranch logo or any identifying marks on it. He's going to call me when they're heading back. Should take them around four hours or so to get down there."

"Good," Conor replied tiredly, taking a sip of coffee. The sun had risen while they dealt with Todd's body and the bedroom upstairs. Stripping the bed, cleaning up the glass and blood. Scrubbing every surface. They'd decided to just burn the towels and the sheets. Lisa had gotten the rest of the bedding in the wash.

Riley and Ryan had wrapped up the body in an old tarp from the barn and taken it out to the empty horse trailer. It was cool enough outside that the body would be fine for a bit while the group took care of other matters. The overnight rain would actually be helpful–it would make digging a grave that much easier.

"I think everyone needs to get a few hours of sleep," Conor suggested. "It's been a wild night and we still have a few things to finish getting done. Namely, Todd. I don't want any mistakes, so let's get a little rest. Ryan, you and Riley meet me back here at noon. Then we'll head out."

"Sounds good, Boss," Riley agreed, heading back to his place.

"I'll be upstairs with Elle," Ryan replied, rubbing his hands over his eyes, "but I will try and sleep a little. Thank you again, Conor. I said before that I am forever indebted to you, and I mean it."

Conor stood up, nodding and patting Ryan on the shoulder as they headed to the stairs. "Well, I have a favor to ask of you soon."

"Anything," Ryan said firmly, "you got it."

Chapter Sixty

"Ryan," Elle said weakly, opening her eyes slowly and looking around. She didn't recognize the room. Pink wallpaper on the walls and white drapes over the windows. Ryan snored softly next to her, covered by a floral comforter. She blinked a few times, registering the pain in her side and her shoulder.

Suddenly, it all came rushing back. Todd attacking her again. Fighting back. Oh God. She'd killed him. A small cry escaped her lips as she remembered stabbing him over and over.

"Elle, you're awake. Hey. It's okay," Ryan said softly, opening his eyes and turning toward her.

"Oh no," Elle exclaimed weakly as she tried to sit up but gasped in pain, falling back down on the pillows. "What happened? Todd is dead, right? Where am I? Did the police come? Am I going to be arrested?"

"Hey, one question at a time," Ryan replied, smiling at her. "Don't get too wound up, please. Todd got you pretty good in the side but we got you stitched up. We don't want any of those stitches to come out, okay?"

"Okay, but how—?"

"Just listen, please," Ryan said calmly, gently touching her face. "Elle, we've taken care of everything. Me, Lisa, Conor, and Riley with a little help from Jimmy and a couple of ranch hands."

"Taken care of everything?" Elle asked. "What does that mean?"

"It means that Todd is out of our lives forever. He can never hurt you again."

"But I killed him–the police will want to question me," Elle insisted.

"Not if there's no body," Ryan said quietly. "Not if Todd was never here. Not if he never showed up at the ranch."

Elle closed her eyes for a minute trying to process Ryan's words. The pain in her side made it hard to concentrate. How could there be no body? He was dead, there had to be a body.

"There was no way we were going to involve the police, Elle," Ryan explained. "There was no way in hell I was going to take a chance that you would take the fall for this and get sent to prison."

"Oh no," Elle said worriedly, opening her eyes, comprehension dawning. "What did you guys do? You got rid of him? How? Where?"

"Elle, please," Ryan begged, putting his hand on her arm, "please just rest. I will get you some more pain meds. You need to rest and heal, and we can discuss everything later, okay?"

Elle let out a sigh, nodding as Ryan got up. He came around the bed and leaned down to gently kiss her. Then he shook a couple of pills from the bottle on the nightstand and handed them to her with a small glass of water. "Here, try to eat a few saltines, too, we don't want you getting sick from the pain meds."

She swallowed the pills and managed to eat a couple of crackers as Ryan watched her with concerned eyes.

"Now, please try and sleep, okay?" Ryan implored. "Lisa is going to come and sit with you for a while."

"Why Lisa? Where are you going?" Elle asked, taking his hand.

"We have some business to take care of," Ryan replied. "Don't worry though, everything is fine. Your job is just to rest."

Elle wanted to know more—she figured the business they needed to take care of was dealing with Todd's body. But the pain pills made her drowsy and unable to focus enough to argue with him. She closed her eyes with a sigh, giving in to the meds.

"I JUST GAVE Elle some more pain meds," Ryan said, coming into the kitchen where Lisa, Conor, and Riley sat drinking coffee.

"She woke up? How is she?" Lisa asked, her eyes worried.

"She's okay. Sore and a little confused. I didn't tell her much, just the bare minimum. I didn't want her getting upset," Ryan explained. "Hopefully she'll sleep some more now."

"Okay, good," Lisa replied, getting up and giving Conor a quick kiss. "I'm going to go up and sit with her. I don't want her to be alone."

"Thank you, sis," Ryan said, reaching for her hand and squeezing it gently. "Thank you for everything."

"Oh don't worry," Lisa replied with a little smile. "You'll pay later, baby brother."

Ryan smiled back. He didn't doubt that for a second.

"You boys good? You got this?" Lisa asked, pausing at the doorway to the kitchen, looking back at them.

Conor and Riley exchanged a look. Conor said, "Yeah, we got this, sweets. We'll be back soon."

Chapter Sixty-One

Elle opened her eyes to find Lisa curled up in a white fluffy chair next to the bed wrapped in a pink throw blanket and looking at her phone.

"Hey, you're awake," Lisa said, setting her phone down as she got up. She sat down gently on the bed next to Elle. "How do you feel?"

Elle shook her head, tears forming in her eyes. "Lisa, Todd ... he ... I–" she tried to get out, choking back a sob.

"Elle," Lisa said sternly, taking her hand, "I know. I know, sweetie. But you're okay. You're going to be fine. And don't you dare cry one fucking tear for that monster."

"But–" Elle began, unable to stop a tear from rolling down her cheek. She reached up to brush it away.

Lisa shook her head. "No, it's over," she replied. "You did the right thing, sweetie. Don't ever question that. Todd hurt you one too many times and he absolutely got what he deserved."

Elle actually agreed with Lisa. She didn't feel anger or distress, only a quiet relief that he was finally out of her life. But she was worried–they were all taking a big chance handling everything themselves and not getting the authorities involved. She understood, though, why Ryan didn't want the police involved. She knew he was doing this for both of them.

"I know. I'm truly not upset that he's dead. I should feel something for him, I guess. But I don't," Elle admitted quietly. "Only relief."

"Good. Don't waste any more time thinking about it. Lord knows I won't lose any sleep over Todd being dead," Lisa said firmly.

"But I am worried about Ryan. About Conor and you, and Riley," Elle said, frowning. "Won't someone come looking for Todd? Asking questions? What do we do then?"

"We lie," Lisa replied calmly. "They're going to find his car down in Yuma. It will look like he went over the border to escape getting arrested. I seriously doubt they'll expend too much energy searching for him."

Elle nodded. She would absolutely lie. She'd do everything in her power to protect Ryan. To protect everyone. She could very easily be sitting in a jail cell right now if it wasn't for all of them. She would take this secret to her grave.

Chapter Sixty-Two

"Everything go okay?" Lisa asked as Conor, Ryan and Riley came into the kitchen, all looking tired.

"Yeah, no problems. It's done," Conor replied, sitting down at the island counter with Riley.

"Hank and Damon are on their way back too. Everything went according to plan," Riley reported.

"Good," Lisa said, coming over to give Conor a kiss. Then she turned to Ryan and said, "Elle is awake. She's actually feeling hungry, so I'm heating up some soup for her."

"Good," Ryan replied, pouring himself a cup of coffee. "How is she? Have you been able to talk to her?"

Lisa nodded, going to the stove and pouring the soup into a bowl. "Yes. She's okay. She's actually more worried about us having to deal with everything than anything else."

Ryan smiled a little. "Well, that's good I guess."

"Remember me telling you that Elle is stronger than you give her credit for?" Lisa said with a pointed look at Ryan as she placed the soup on a tray with some crackers.

"Yes. I know. She definitely is. If there was any doubt, she proved that last night for sure," Ryan replied, reaching for the tray. "Here, sis, I'll take that up to Elle. I want to check on her anyway."

"Okay, you should try to get some rest, too. You look tired," Lisa said.

"I'll try," Ryan replied, heading out of the kitchen. "Thanks, sis."

After Ryan left, Lisa sat down next to Conor at the island counter. "So Emma is scheduled to fly the Saratoga Thursday. Are you okay with flying it back tomorrow? Then you can get your plane?"

"That should be fine," Conor said, taking her hand.

"I need to talk to Ryan and Elle and find out what they want to do. I'm thinking maybe they'll want to go home, too, if Elle is up to flying," Lisa said. "And the kids have been at George's too long. I miss my babies and I need to spend some time with them."

Conor nodded in agreement.

"If you're all good here, I'm going to head out to the barn. I need to check on some stuff," Riley said, getting up and grabbing his hat off the hook by the kitchen door.

"Thank you, Riley," Lisa said, standing to give him a big hug. "I mean it. Thank you for everything you've done to help us. I won't soon forget it."

"It's what we do, ma'am." Riley hugged her back. "Tell Emma I said hi," he added as he went out the door.

Lisa took Conor's hand once they were alone in the kitchen. "Once we are back in Scottsdale, I want you to spend the night with me," she said. "I want the kids to get used to you being around. Being part of their lives. I'm assuming that's what you want. Because we're kind of a package deal."

"Babe, it is one hundred percent what I want," Conor replied, reaching up to touch Lisa's face. "A family. With you. Our family."

Lisa smiled. "Good answer," she replied, leaning in to kiss him.

Chapter Sixty-Three

"I think Elle is up to traveling back to Scottsdale today," Ryan said when Lisa came into the bedroom to check on them the next morning. "We were just talking about it. I think we need to have a business-as-usual approach right now. Make it look like everything is normal. Just in case the police decide to look into Todd's disappearance and possibly question Elle."

"Okay, I agree," Lisa said, sitting down in the chair next to Elle's bed. "At least it's Friday. You'll have a couple of days to rest. Do you think you will be up to going back to work on Monday?"

"Maybe," Elle replied, sitting up gingerly. "I called my dad to check in this morning. He's got everything handled on a project I was working on. By Monday I think I could be okay to go back to the office. I already feel a little bit better today. Sore for sure, but not as weak. Also, I didn't tell him about anything that happened, just that everything here was fine. I don't want to involve him in any of this."

"I agree," Ryan said. "The fewer people who know about this, the better. But you're obviously injured. What's the story going to be there? Your side injury will be the easiest to hide and your shoulder can be hidden with a sweater or something, but Todd scratched your face pretty good. How are we going to explain that?"

"I fell off a horse," Elle suggested. "That's totally believable because I don't really ride. I think I've ridden a horse twice in my lifetime. And tumbled into a bush?"

Lisa nodded. "That'll work. Actually, that's a really good idea. You could have bruised a rib and your shoulder in the process."

Ryan nodded. "Okay. Sounds like we have a plan. I'll get our things together. We'll be ready when Conor is ready to go, sis."

Lisa leaned over to give Elle a hug. "You have proved how tough you are. We'll all get through the next part, okay? Who knows, maybe it's all over and we can just get on with our lives now."

Chapter Sixty-Four

"Hi honey!" Elle called, coming into the house and setting her purse on the table by the front door. She kicked off her heels and went into the kitchen where Ryan was opening a bottle of wine.

"Hi," Ryan replied with a smile, turning to give her a kiss and pulling her into his arms. "You're home sooner than I expected. I'm glad."

"Me too," Elle said with a tired sigh, leaning into him. "It's been a hard week of pretending everything is normal. I feel totally wiped out."

Ryan leaned back a bit, running his thumb over the big scratch on Elle's face. He was glad it was finally healing. "I'll bet. Well, you can rest now over the weekend. Lisa wants us to come over for dinner tomorrow evening, if you're feeling up to it."

Elle nodded. "Yeah, that sounds nice, actually."

"Okay, I'll let her know. Do you want some wine?" he asked, watching her closely as she sat down gingerly on a bar stool at the island counter. He knew she was still dealing with some residual soreness in her side. But he was more worried about the scars she carried on the inside. It had been a week since they'd flown home.

While Elle appeared to be healing outwardly, she was still jumpy, tired easily, and had been very quiet all week.

Ryan knew she had told everyone about her horse-riding adventure at Conor's ranch. Everyone seemed to buy the story, even Tom.

"Yes, please." Elle leaned her elbows on the counter and rested her head on her hands with a sigh. "I had an interesting conversation today with Brian," she added, watching as Ryan poured wine into two glasses and handed her one.

"Here's to crazy," Ryan said with a little smile, lightly clinking his glass against hers.

"Here's to crazy," Elle replied taking a sip.

"So, what did he have to say?" Ryan asked, taking a sip of his wine to calm his sudden nerves.

"He said his cop friend called him and informed him that Todd's Beemer had been discovered down in Yuma and impounded. No sign of Todd," Elle relayed. "Brian also said that he hadn't heard anything from Todd, no threats or demands. He thinks that maybe the arrest warrant scared him, so he took off for Mexico. Basically, that he gave up and ran."

Ryan breathed out a slow, tentative sigh of relief. "Thank God. So the cops are buying that Todd took off. That was a brilliant move on Conor's part, coming up with that plan. Did Brian say anything else?"

"Not really," Elle said, "just that if any more information comes to light, he would let me know. He said it sounded like the cops were going to leave it as an open case. Todd is officially a fugitive from justice and if he ever shows up again, he'll be arrested."

"Good." Ryan nodded.

"So, you know this whole situation presents a major problem, right?" Elle asked, frowning.

"What's that?"

"I'm still technically married. Todd never signed the divorce papers and obviously he's never going to now," Elle explained, chewing on her lower lip and looking down at her wine glass. "So what does that mean for you and me?"

Ryan came around the island and pulled her off the stool and into his arms. "It doesn't change anything between you and me. Is that what you've been worrying about all week?" he asked softly, tilting her chin up, forcing her to look into his eyes.

Elle nodded. "I can't get a divorce. I'm still legally married to him. No one knows he's dead. Which means I can never get married again. I mean, not that that's even something you want to–"

"Elle," Ryan said, looking into her sad green eyes, his heart touched that she was so upset about this. "Sweetie. I don't give a shit about a divorce decree. As far as I'm concerned, when we put Todd in the ground, you were officially divorced. And I don't know about the legal ramifications of him leaving, but I'm sure there's something ... abandonment, maybe? Where you can petition the court to set aside your marriage? I'm obviously not a lawyer, but at some point in the future we can broach it with Brian and see what advice he gives us, okay? In the meantime, all I care about is that we are together and Todd is out of our lives, forever."

"That's all I care about too," Elle said with a smile.

Chapter Sixty-Five

"Do you want another beer?" Conor asked Ryan as he reached into Lisa's outdoor mini-fridge next to the barbeque where Ryan was grilling steaks.

"Sure, thanks," Ryan said, trading his empty bottle for a fresh one.

"So, remember at the ranch, I mentioned needing to ask you a favor sometime soon?" Conor began.

"Yeah," Ryan replied, turning to give Conor a grave look. "As I said, anything you need, ever, all you have to do is ask."

"Well, it's probably not anything like what you're thinking," Conor said, pausing and glancing through the glass slider to where Lisa was busy in the kitchen making a big salad to go with the steaks. Elle sat at the island counter looking at some drawings Charlie had made for her in a get-well card. He smiled. That little girl already had his heart, just like her mother.

"What's up?" Ryan asked.

"I–well–I know your father has passed away. So I need to ask you ..." Conor said, looking at Ryan and clearing his throat. "I'd like to ask your permission to marry Lisa."

Ryan blinked, looking at Conor. After a moment, he started grinning. "Fuck yes, you have my permission," he replied, grabbing Conor by the shoulder and giving him a hug. "Hell yes, brother. Nothing would make me happier."

Conor hugged him back. "Thank you," he said as he pulled away, looking again through the slider to where Cayden was sitting on the couch with his guitar, practicing the chords Conor had taught him the week before. "I wanted to ask you first, but I'm also going to ask Cayden. I think it's important to include him."

Ryan nodded. "Cayden is a little man now. I think he'd really take something like that to heart. That's a great idea."

"I plan on taking her up in the Cherokee tomorrow. I'm going to propose at sunset. I'm a nervous wreck," he admitted. He'd gone the day before and picked out a ring. He hadn't slept at all last night. Even though she'd already technically said yes, he was anxious about actually proposing. Now he just needed to make it official. His wife. Laoise. The woman he'd been waiting for his whole life.

"This is my mother, Ava Campbell," Elle said a few days later, introducing Ryan to Ava. "Mother, Ryan Daley."

"It's a pleasure to finally meet you, Mrs. Campbell," Ryan said, taking Ava's hand and shaking it lightly. He turned then to Tom and shook his hand. "Nice to see you again, sir."

Ava nodded at Ryan. Tom held her chair for her as she sat down at the table.

"Shall we order a bottle of wine?" Tom suggested, looking around the table and then at Ava. "Darling, what would you like tonight?"

Ava glanced at the wine menu. "I feel like some champagne, just some Veuve Clicquot would be fine," she responded. "The auction for the children's hospital went so well yesterday that I believe a little celebration is appropriate."

"That's wonderful, Mother," Elle said graciously. "You do so much for our community."

Ava shrugged one shoulder lightly. "I only do what I'm called to do," she replied, looking back at Elle. "You should be more involved, darling. I have an open position on the board at the club, if you're interested."

Elle smiled at her mother uncommittedly and said, "I'll think about it." There was no way in hell she would be interested. Granted, she knew her mother and her friends did some amazing things for the community, but they were a smug, snarky bunch and she had no interest in spending time with them.

After they ordered the champagne and their food, Tom turned to Ryan and asked, "Did you see that the Sun Devils are going to be in the Rose Bowl this year?"

Ryan nodded. "Yeah, I did. They've had a great season this year."

"I actually scored a couple of tickets to the game," Tom said. "Do you want to go with me? I would have to drag Ava kicking and screaming to a football game." He smiled at his wife.

"Such a brutal sport," Ava said, frowning.

"Sure, that would be great. I've never gone to a Rose Bowl game," Ryan said. "I wanted to go to the one we played in my senior year, but I was still recovering from surgery."

"Good, sounds like a plan then," Tom replied.

Ava rolled her eyes. "Well, they are having brunch at the club on New Year's Day. Since apparently your father and Ryan will be at a football game, why don't you join me, darling?" she suggested to Elle.

"Sounds good," Elle replied. She'd honestly rather go to the football game with Ryan and her dad. Oh well. She could suffer through brunch with her mother. At least it was guaranteed there would be mimosas and Bloody Marys.

Chapter Sixty-Six

"So, we have an announcement to make," Conor said, standing up at the head of his dining room table on Christmas Eve. He was so incredibly happy looking down the table filled with people he loved. Lisa, Cayden and Charlie, Elle and Ryan, Riley, and his sisters–Cari, Cate with her family, and Claire with her husband. A far cry from the Christmas last year that had been just Cari, Riley, and him; even with Cassidy and Christine at their in-laws for Christmas this year.

The ranch was decorated just like it used to be when he was growing up. Conor lost count, but he thought Lisa and his sisters had put up six different Christmas trees throughout the house. Cayden and Charlie even had their own little tree they'd decorated with popcorn strings and homemade ornaments. Lisa had even made sure Hank, Owen, and the rest of the hands had a tree in the bunkhouse, while talking the ranch hands into helping her put up Christmas lights outside. He didn't think he'd ever seen so many lights on–or in– the house.

Jimmy had officially been kicked out of the kitchen so the women could bake pies, cookies, pastries, and rolls. All of it made Conor happier than he'd ever been.

He looked down at Lisa, taking her hand and pulling her up out of her chair. "There's going to be a wedding at the ranch this spring," he announced to their friends and family, a huge smile on his face.

Lisa held up her left hand, grinning as everyone exclaimed in surprise and happiness, then jumping up to give hugs and congratulations.

Conor had talked to Cayden, asking his permission to marry his mom. Cayden had taken it very seriously. He'd solemnly nodded his approval and threw his arms around Conor for a big hug. Conor's heart had been so happy that day.

And every day since. He and Lisa had several serious conversations about the future. So many big decisions to make.

"I want you to live here, at the ranch, with me," Conor said, sitting down next to Lisa who was curled up in her spot on the couch in the library the week prior. "Honestly, I thought for a while that I wanted to just be done with all of this, the ranch, everything–but I realized it's my legacy. My family's legacy. And I need you here with me. You, Cayden, and Charlie. Is that something you want to do?"

Lisa smiled. "I thought you'd never ask. Obviously, the kids love it here, but I do, too. The first time you had me over for dinner and I walked into the house, it was like coming home. I don't know how to describe it exactly, but I feel so happy here. At peace. Everything and nothing," she said, reaching for his hand.

"Good," Conor replied, letting out a breath he hadn't realized he'd been holding. *Thank God,* he thought happily as he kissed her hand with a smile. There was nothing he wanted more than a family in this house again. His family this time. "What about your house? And the business?" he asked.

"I've actually been thinking about it for a while now. I'll sell the house. If we're going to live here, I don't need it," Lisa explained, "and as far as the business goes, I can run it from here. It won't be that difficult, really. I've hired a great new office manager, as you know, so she can handle the day-to-day stuff. Ryan is always there, too, if there's a problem. And if I do need to go to the office, well, it's not a big deal to drive up there."

"Or fly," Conor added. "Anytime you need me, babe. I'm happy to be your pilot. I know it's a big sacrifice you're making moving down here."

Lisa shook her head. "It's not a sacrifice, honey. It's what I want. This is the life I want. Here," she said, setting her wine glass down and leaning over to kiss him, pulling him down on top of her, "with you. And our family."

Chapter Sixty-Seven

"Wow, what a great game. That was awesome," Ryan said, sitting down in his seat in the Bravo.

"Yeah, it was. Pretty exciting end. I still can't believe they lost. So close," Tom agreed, sitting across from Ryan and buckling his seatbelt.

"You two almost ready?" Emma asked, coming into the main cabin. "We should be able to get clearance in about ten minutes."

"Yes," Ryan replied, "we're ready."

"Thank you again for flying us here for the game," Tom said to Emma. "It's been an awesome day. Talk about first-class service."

"It's what they pay me to do." Emma winked. "There's beer in the little fridge in the back if you want some. I'll let the Hollywood Burbank tower know we're ready," she added, heading into the cockpit.

Ryan hopped up. "Tom? Would you like one, too?" "Sure, sounds good," Tom agreed. "Thanks."

Ryan retrieved two beers from the mini fridge, popping the tops and handing one to Tom before he sat back down. "It's Lagunitas IPA. Never tried it before, but it's what was in there."

"Cheers," Tom said, taking a drink.

"Cheers," Ryan agreed. "Well, thank you again for inviting me to go. I've always wanted to go to the Rose Bowl."

"Of course, and you'll have to thank your sister for the use of the plane," Tom replied, "though I'd still like to contribute to the charter fee."

"Not necessary," Ryan said, shaking his head. "You paid for the tickets. Least I could do is provide transportation. Plus, this is much better than driving all the way here from Scottsdale."

"True, that would have been a long drive," Tom agreed, taking a drink of his beer. "Though now I'm going to have to book a charter and fly Ava somewhere, or she'll never let me live it down."

"Oh," Ryan said with a grin, "just let us know when. We can get you the family discount."

Tom laughed. "Deal."

"Speaking of family," Ryan began, clearing his throat nervously. "There is something I've been wanting to talk to you about."

"Sure," Tom replied, "what's up?"

"Well, it's about Elle," Ryan said. "You know how Todd seems to have disappeared off the face of the earth ..." *Or into the earth, more accurately.*

"Good riddance if you ask me," Tom said, shaking his head and frowning. "Though I wish he would have signed those damned divorce papers before he disappeared."

"That's kind of what I wanted to discuss," Ryan said. "I'd like to ask your permission to marry your daughter. I realize that legally it's not possible yet. But I'd like to have an informal ceremony. I was thinking of having something simple on the beach, just the two of us. I think it's what Elle would want and, who knows, if Todd continues with his disappearing act, maybe we can petition the court to annul the marriage at some point. And then do it legally."

Tom nodded thoughtfully. "I think that's a really nice idea, Ryan."

"I love Elle so much," Ryan said quietly. "I realize it's been a relatively short time that we've been dating, but, well, we've been through a lot the past few months. It's really brought us close, and I think I actually realized right away that she was the woman I was searching for my whole life, even before I admitted it to myself. I know my past isn't, well, isn't something I'm proud of, but I hope you can see—"

"Ryan," Tom interrupted, "there's not even any need to discuss your past. I can see the man that you are now. I see how you treat my daughter. How you love her. It's obvious—even to Ava. And she's a hard sell." Tom grinned.

Ryan smiled back. "Well, thank you, sir," he said, feeling a huge relief. He had worried his past would prevent Elle's parents from accepting him even though he knew no one had told Ava about Candi or his prison time. They had agreed there was no reason to dredge it up again. Time to leave it buried. Where it belonged.

"I've got a plan," Ryan revealed. "Lisa actually helped me with most of it. It's all arranged. Elle's birthday is coming up and I want to surprise her then. Emma will fly us down in the Gulfstream. But I wanted to make sure I had your permission before I gave them to her."

"Ryan," Tom said as he leaned forward in his seat, reaching out his hand, "you have it. Welcome to the family."

Chapter Sixty-Eight

Elle took a sip of her champagne and gazed out over the patio, beyond the pool to where the waves were crashing on the beach. She let out a contented sigh. Ryan had surprised her with a trip to Mexico on her birthday and told her they were leaving in two weeks flying down in the Gulfstream.

He had renewed his passport and planned every detail.

Ryan had rented a beautiful private house, right on the beach north of the marina in Puerto Vallarta, with three bedrooms and its own pool overlooking the ocean. After an incredible dinner at Café des Artistes, they'd come back to the house. Ryan had opened a bottle of champagne and handed her a glass, then disappeared into the house.

As Elle sat watching the sunset behind the bay, she realized that she felt a lightness in her chest. And felt happier than she'd ever been. Her scars from Todd's attack had faded and the scars he'd left on the inside were fading, too. She could finally let everything he'd done, every time he'd hurt her, go.

Elle was grateful to Ryan and Lisa and Conor and everyone who had helped her and been beside her, but she was the one who had finally taken back control of her life. No one had done it for her. She'd done it herself, and she was pretty damn proud of that.

"I have something for you," Ryan said, coming back out of the house and walking toward her.

Elle looked over. Ryan had a big white box with a huge pink bow around it. "What is that? Is that for me?"

Ryan nodded, setting the box down on the table next to Elle. "Yes. This is for you."

"Can I open it?" Elle asked, widening her eyes and looking up at Ryan expectantly.

"Yes, go ahead," Ryan replied. She reached for the box, pulling the bow off and pushing it aside before lifting the lid. "Ryan," Elle breathed out softly, "oh my God. What is this? It is beautiful. A dress?" She looked up at him in surprise, then back down as she gently lifted the white silk dress from the box. It had simple lines with a V-neck and a tapered bodice. It was sleeveless and had a flowing skirt. *A wedding dress?* she thought.

RYAN GOT down on one knee next to Elle's chair, taking her hand and opening her palm. He put a little blue Tiffany box in it, opening it so she could see the diamond solitaire ring nestled in the folds.

"Ryan, what ...?" Elle gasped. "How? What are you ...?"

"Elle," Ryan began, looking up at her, still holding her hand as he looked into her eyes. "I love you. Words I never thought I'd say to another woman as long as I lived. But here I am. You came into my life and saved me when I thought I was beyond saving. Beyond loving. You showed me what real love is, what it means to love unconditionally. Something I've never experienced before in my lifetime. I knew I had been in a dark place for a long time, but you showed me the light. The light that was still in me, that I had hidden in that darkness. You have no idea how much you mean to me.

"I want to spend the rest of my life with you, loving you. Maybe I can't officially marry you, but we can have our own ceremony. In every way that matters, you will be my wife. So, Elle, my love, will you marry me?" Ryan asked softly.

Elle nodded, tears of happiness springing to her eyes. "Yes. Yes!" she said as he took the ring out of the box and put it on her finger. She jumped out of her chair and launched herself into Ryan's arms as he stood up to catch her. "Yes yes yes, a million times yes. I love you so much."

Ryan caught her and spun her around in his arms, holding on to her tightly, elated. He stopped and leaned down to kiss her. He smiled at her words, closing his eyes as he continued to kiss her, the darkness finally fading completely away from his heart. For good.

Chapter Sixty-Nine

One year later.

"Ryan," Elle said softly to Ryan as he stood next to her hospital bed. "I think we should name him Liam Jacob Daley."

Ryan looked down at Elle holding their son, tears of joy filling his eyes. He had been so fearful every single day of Elle's pregnancy. He had barely let himself take a full breath. He'd been so worried, worried that he was never meant to have a child. That they would lose this pregnancy, too. Now, looking down at his son, he still couldn't believe this was real. A son. His son.

"Here, hold him," Elle said, gently handing the baby to him.

Ryan carefully took him, holding the small bundle against his chest with one arm. "Liam Jacob," he repeated, holding one of Liam's tiny hands in his. His heart pounded in his chest, a little terrified, but a lot happy. He finally allowed himself to relax just a little, knowing he had a healthy baby. He also knew with every fiber of his being that he would protect this child with his life.

"Yes," Elle whispered, smiling up at him, her eyes bright with unshed tears. She moved over a little so Ryan could lay down carefully on the bed next to her, their baby sleeping quietly on his chest.

"Thank you," Ryan said, looking at Elle.

"For what?" Elle asked.

"For giving me everything I always wanted. Even when I couldn't admit it to myself, this is what I've always wanted. A family. Our family," Ryan replied with a smile.

They had submitted a petition to the court against Todd for abandonment. Brian was hoping to have the papers filed by the end of the month. Then they could go to the courthouse and get married legally. Ryan knew Lisa was already planning the reception of the century for them once everything was finalized. *Another one,* he thought with a smile. The huge wedding and reception that Lisa and Conor had at the ranch the previous spring had been such a happy day. He was looking forward to having their own celebration. One their son could be a part of, too.

"You've given me that, too," Elle said, smiling and reaching over to hold one of Liam's tiny hands in hers. "We saved ourselves, but we also saved each other."

The End

About the Author

Karina, a fresh voice in literature, emerges with her debut novel, a captivating story inspired by a vivid dream. Based in Lake Havasu City, Arizona, Karina uses her connection to the desert to inspire her writing. Her husband, four daughters and three grand babies have been her biggest support system, encouraging her to chase her dreams and turn her imaginative stories into reality.

In her free time, Karina enjoys working out at the gym, drinking a nice glass of wine, and listening to her favorite music. With her debut novel hitting the shelves, Karina is excited to share the first book in The Everything Series, inviting readers to join her on a journey through the power of words.

Acknowledgments

A huge thank you to my niece, author Starla DeKruyf, for answering literally hundreds of questions regarding the writing process. Her insight was invaluable.

My fabulous editor, Lindsey Hinkel, helped make my words even better, even if she did cut a lot of them.

Thank you to Vanessa Jacobson for being my beta-reader and giving me great suggestions and correcting all of my spelling and punctuation mistakes.

Larry Heller for all of his help with my fight scenes and for allowing me to shoot his KTM for the cover of the book.

Mike Prescher for allowing me to have his Saratoga Piper on the cover of my book—and letting me fly it. And for a great line, that I'm sure he'll recognize.

Jim Polder for correcting all of my mistakes regarding arrest and prison scenes.

Rick Danesi and Tony Castleforte for all their help with the technical flying scenes and aviation knowledge. All mistakes are mine alone.

Josh DeJulio for agreeing to model and grace the cover of my first book.

Kirsten Morrell for the stunning photography and making my vision a reality.

To Kevin Edgley for all of his help editing photos.

To my husband and daughters for their endless support and love.

www.ingramcontent.com/pod-product-compliance
Lightning Source LLC
Chambersburg PA
CBHW070920260626
47162CB00007B/2746